The enemy may be his only hope…

Fallen angel Kasdeya hates all mortals. They're little more than playthings, as far as he's concerned. But when he finds himself facing a thousand-year prison sentence, he has no choice but to call on the one woman who might set him free: the Summoner.

His plan is simple…seduce her for his own purposes, then throw her away. If only she weren't so argumentative, so intelligent. If only she weren't so damned sexy!

I0677682

Books by Alicia Steele

The Summoner

Published by Kensington Publishing Corporation

The Summoner

Alicia Steele

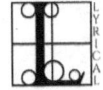

LYRICAL PRESS
Kensington Publishing Corp.
www.kensingtonbooks.com

Lyrical Press books are published by
Kensington Publishing Corp. 119 West 40th Street New York, NY 10018

All Kensington titles, imprints, and distributed lines are available at special
quantity discounts for bulk purchases for sales promotion, premiums, fund-
raising, and educational or institutional use.

Special book excerpts or customized printings can also be created to fit
specific needs. For details, write or phone the office of the Kensington
Special Sales Manager:
Kensington Publishing Corp.
119 West 40th Street
New York, NY 10018
Attn. Special Sales Department. Phone: 1-800-221-2647.

First Electronic Edition: September 2009
eISBN-13: 978-1-61650-076-4
eISBN-10: 1-61650-076-X

First Print Edition: September 2009
ISBN-13: 978-1-61650-906-4
ISBN-10: 1-61650-906-6

Printed in the United States of America

For my ever patient husband. Thanks, babe, for getting up with the kids every weekend so that I could write the nights away.

Chapter 1

Alex sat at her vanity, brushing her long toffee-brown hair. One hundred strokes. Every night. Religiously. It didn't matter that they'd proven it wasn't at all beneficial and that it, in fact, caused breakage. It was a habit, and Alex Brannigan was nothing if not a slave to her habits.

She'd already washed her face and gotten into her favorite nightie, a short white one with *La Nightshirt* in big black text across the front. It was so ancient that the fabric was practically see-through at her shoulders and across the top of her modest, B-cup breasts. And didn't that make her feel older than dirt. She'd dated guys who were younger than her sleep apparel.

"Yep, gettin' old," Alex grumbled, leaning in to examine her "not quite" wrinkles in the mirror. She scrunched up her face and pursed her full lips to see the lines more clearly. Nope, not quite wrinkles. Not yet... but soon. Wannabes, that's what they were. Wannabe wrinkles.

She put down the brush and reached for the new night cream she'd picked up that afternoon. It was guaranteed to make her skin look as dewy and fresh as a sixteen-year-old's. After all, it had elasticin, whatever that was, and vitamin C! Alex snorted. That was probably twenty bucks well wasted. But hell, with her thirtieth birthday only three years away, she was more than willing to part with a little money in an honest search for the fountain of youth.

She was wrestling with the anti-tamper seal that cosmetics manufacturers think is funny to Krazy Glue to the top of their products when the bathroom lights did that dimming thing, the one the lights always seemed to do right before the power cut out completely.

"Shit!" she hissed, real panic tingeing her voice. "God-damned house!"

Alex lived in an historic Queen Anne two-story complete with a turret room, two unnecessary balconies and abundant stained glass windows. It was lovely, a true pleasure to own—when the power and plumbing were actually working.

"Please, please, please!" She leaped up from the low brass stool, but forgot that she had her left ankle hooked through the stool's support bracket. Rather than the mad dash out the door she'd been trying to accomplish, all she managed to do was land face-first on the floor. The lights gave another feeble flicker before the room plunged into darkness.

Alex moaned in terror as the familiar, sibilant voices swelled to life.

"Aaalexxx…"

"Alexaaandraaa…"

"Hear me, Summoner…"

All four walls of the bathroom—from waist height to the ceiling—were covered in mirrors. It was a feature that had almost dissuaded her from buying the place. Honestly, what was the look they were going for, Victoriana meets the Playboy Mansion? The fact that no one should have mirrored anything in a period home wasn't the issue—it was the mirrors themselves. Or rather, what lurked inside them.

But Alex refused to live her life in fear. So she'd gone ahead with the purchase with plans to have the mirrors ripped out at the earliest possible opportunity. It was an opportunity that, unfortunately, hadn't come yet. She wasn't even finished unpacking; this was only her second week in the house.

Alex kicked her foot, shaking off the stool and sending it skittering across the tiles. Taking care to keep her head well below the white wainscoting, she scrambled on hands and knees toward the door. There was no moon out tonight and the room was completely black. On the one hand, she was grateful for that. It meant she couldn't see the owners of those whispering voices beckoning to her from within the glass, the half-formed ghosts that always appeared to her in darkened mirrors. On the other hand, it also meant she misjudged where the exit was by a good foot and a half. Alex, with lowered head, slammed full tilt into the bathroom wall.

"Ahh, there're the lights," she mumbled as she crumpled into an undignified heap. Indeed there were lights now, pretty white and purple ones that danced playfully across her vision.

Alex laid her face against the deliciously cool floor and succumbed to unconsciousness.

* * * *

This dream again?

How fabulous.

Not.

Alex tentatively touched the egg-sized knot gracing her forehead. It hurt! People weren't supposed to feel real pain in dreams. She knew that. But apparently she was an exception. Pain. Pleasure. Hot. Cold. Her subconscious faithfully rendered each sensation.

Her breath misted the already thickly fogged air around her, and she was still clad in just her short nightgown. Alex wrapped her arms around her torso, making a valiant attempt to ignore the chills racking her body, and took stock of her surroundings.

It had been almost ten years since she'd been treated to this particular nightmare. Alas, it looked like nothing much had changed. It was still a never-ending plain of murky darkness, and it still appeared to be full of vague bogeymen whose only motivation, so far as she could tell, was to torment her with their calls while staying just out of sight, hiding in the edge of her peripheral, helped in their shyness by the eternal gray, unrelenting fog.

And yes, it was still a scary, sucky place to find herself.

As if on cue, the voices started up again. The sounds were so much more chilling, so much closer, on this side of the glass.

"The Summoner..."

"She has come..."

"Alex..."

"Alexandr—"

Her name rose on a growling howl, only to abruptly cut off.

Alex whirled in place, trying to catch sight of her tormentors, but the mist was too dense. All she caught were hints of large, misshapen forms sliding inhumanly fast through the fog. Her skin was already goose-pebbled from the cold air but, nonetheless, it tried to tighten even further. Her hair did its best to lift straight off her body, as if it were planning to leave regardless of whether she was fool enough to stay.

From previous experience, Alex knew that trying to find a way out would be futile. There wasn't one. And though she had always awoken after her regulation eight hours, often more tired than when she'd fallen asleep, while she was here time stood still. This was eternity, and she was trapped in it.

She twirled again when unseen hands stroked her back, only to lose her footing and stumble to her knees in the gray mud. Her admirer, as usual, was nowhere to be seen.

"Aaalexxx..."

"Shit!" Tears sprang to her eyes. She hated feeling alone and afraid. In her real life, she was always strong. People admired her for her calm manner, for her level-headedness in the face of any crises, for her guts. She couldn't have run the Seattle chapter of Dovescot, a refuge for battered women, without her share of guts. Many was the time she'd chased a pissed-off Bubba from the front lawn of the sprawling women's shelter with only a rifle and her own unswerving faith in her invincibility. Never mind that she was only five-two and weighed all of a hundred pounds; Alex knew she could take those wife-beaters down, and when they looked into her cold blue eyes, the bastards usually realized that they weren't all that willing to test her resolve on the issue.

Yet here she was, crying in the mud. Well, she'd be damned if she'd give them the pleasure.

Alex had been having this dream since she was a child. Not every year. Not even every second or third year. Not often at all. She could count on one hand the number of times she'd been subjected to this hell, but the infrequency didn't make the experience any less terrifying. The difference now, though, was that she wasn't a child anymore.

"Alexandra…"

"What?" she shrieked. Mud squelched between her fingers as her hands clenched. "What? What the hell do you want?"

"Summoner…"

The whispering was driving her mad, but the voices weren't answering. Again she was touched, on her head this time. Alex refused to acknowledge the phantom hand and, in a moment, it retreated. "Summoner," they'd called her. Over and over.

Well, all right then.

"Come on, already!" she said. "Show yourselves. I… I summon you!"

* * * *

"And it's about bloody time too."

The fingers were back, smoothing over her hair, and this time they didn't disappear.

Crap! That had definitely not been a well thought-out plan.

The tendons in Alex's neck creaked as she turned her head to look up at the speaker. Her breath left her in a gasp. She scrambled out from underneath his palm, any dignity she still possessed quickly lost in her slipping, sliding retreat. "Jesus Christ!"

He smirked and crossed his magnificently muscled arms across his chest. "No, I'm afraid not, pet. I've never even met the man, though he and my brother have a passing acquaintance."

When she finally regained her feet, Alex took stock of the creature standing at ease in front of her. The huge black wings were so distracting that it actually took her a moment to notice he was unclothed. Her gaze followed the sweep of feathers down to the earth in fascination, and it was only on the return journey that Alex realized the alabaster white of his skin was a naked expanse in front of those wings.

Her cheeks flamed and she rushed to bring her gaze to his face. At least, she tried to look up; her stare kept getting snared along the way. She'd never seen a man with elegant feet before! From there, her gaze naturally wandered up his strong, smooth legs. A thatch of black decorated their apex, surrounding his cock, which was half hard but lengthening quickly. The heft of it made her mouth water.

It took some strength of will but she managed, after a second or two, to look away. His pubic curls pointed a graceful arrow to the indent of his navel, lovingly framed by a perfectly formed…eight pack? Was that even possible? Up and up—he was so tall, easily six and a half feet—to his sharply defined pecs and the alluring shadows of his nipples: tiny, perfect dots of mauve peeking cheekily at her above his folded arms.

Her mouth watered again, and she had to swallow the flood of liquid to avoid drooling. The knife edge of his clavicle was swept by shimmering waves of hair the same sultry blue-black as his stunning wings. His throat was long and graceful, his jawline chiseled. Of course. His lips, when she finally got there, were wide, lush and curved up into the most egotistical grin she'd ever seen. Perfect teeth flashed behind them.

At the sight of that mocking smile, Alex's gaze leaped the short distance to his eyes. She hardly noticed the ruler-straight line of his nose or the proud flare of his nostrils. A fan of black lashes, which would probably have looked more appropriate on a cow, outlined his midnight eyes. One thick, black brow winged up.

"Looked your fill yet?" His voice was deeper than the first time he'd spoken.

"Jesus," she whispered again.

"No." His wings unfurled to stir the air behind his shoulders. "Kasdeya."

Chapter 2

"I had thought you would be younger, Summoner." Kasdeya's voice sounded harsh even to his own ears, but he was surprised, and not pleasantly so. The last time he'd spied her through the mists, which was only a few days before, she had seemed a child—something she certainly didn't seem now.

The Summoner was prettily disheveled, with mud in her hair and on her face, but that wasn't what he found so damned distracting. What was causing him problems was the way her clothing had turned clingy and see-through in the wet air. The way her small, dark nipples caught at the transparent fabric as they puckered in the cold. It had been a long time since he'd felt such searing, instant attraction. And he'd never before felt it for a human. How could he? They were less than nothing in the eyes of the Brethren. God's cosmic joke. Kasdeya had spent the aeons since his plummet doing his best to wreak havoc among them, particularly the daughters of Eve. Thus, his reaction to her was inexplicable, and he was disgusted with himself.

It was highly unfortunate that his plan involved seducing the beautiful little nothing. That's what he told himself—how unfortunate it was. If only he could convince his body he meant it. His traitorous prick had leaped to attention under the weight of her stare, eagerly awaiting the unfortunate event.

* * * *

His own perusal was much more perfunctory. A quick flick of his eyes up and down her body. If his gaze lingered anywhere, Alex didn't see it.

Her cheeks, still reddened from the cataloguing of his assets, burned even hotter under his dismissive glance. She looked down at herself, eyes widening in dismay. Her feet, legs and stomach were covered in viscous gray sludge, which also coated the ends of her waist-length hair and was, by the feel of it, drying into a cakey mess on her face. She must have smudged some there when she'd swiped at her tears.

She straightened her shoulders and did her best to mimic his haughty pose. So she didn't exactly look her best. That was no reason to start tossing insults around. "And I thought you'd be more."

Kasdeya's brows shot up at her comment. "More than I am?" His hand swept down his flawless body.

Alex's lips tightened into a thin line. How she wished she could say yes, if only to wipe that smug look off his face. But no, that wasn't what she'd meant, and how could he be expected to be more than perfect anyway?

"No," she said, her voice strained. "I had expected there would be more of you when you finally deigned to show yourselves. There are dozens of voices that call to me."

"Ah." A dismissive shrug lifted his wings. "They won't be bothering us."

"Who's 'they'?"

"Others who have managed to offend." His eyes narrowed. "Others who, most likely, do not deserve to be left in this purgatorial wasteland any more than I do. Prince Shaitan can sometimes be…overzealous in his reprimands."

"Shaitan?" she repeated. "I'm afraid I don't understand."

Kasdeya stepped closer and took her face between his palms. His fingers slid through her hair to cup the back of her skull while his thumbs stroked lightly along her jaw. "Why don't we talk about it further at your home, Alexandra? Once there, I would be more than happy to explain anything you desire."

Alex licked her lips nervously as she looked up into his beautiful face. "Gee, I'd love to go home, Kasdeya…"

His fingers distracted her as they kneaded the small muscles at the base of her neck, though in truth, that was the least of the distractions he represented. She brought her hands up to push him back and uttered a breathy little sigh—quite unlike her—at the feel of his silken white skin under her fingertips. As smooth as a baby's bottom. With the thought, a giggle welled in her chest. She hastened to tamp it down, mortified by the way this creature seemed able to reduce her to a schoolgirl with her first crush. Kasdeya's black eyes twinkled as if he could read her thoughts. The dark aura of danger and eroticism he exuded made it very difficult to concentrate. His magnificent midnight wings moved to enfold her.

"Step off, dark man," she warned. "You're too close."

He leaned in farther until his face was only inches from hers. His hands slipped down her back to her waist. He didn't seem to care if he got covered in mud. "You are the Summoner, woman. If you want to leave this plane, all you have to do is summon your own to you." His breath washed her lips, the scent an odd, euphoric combination of cinnamon and roses. Alex's eyes drifted shut as she inhaled the wonderful perfume.

"Summon my…" She shook her head, trying to clear it, and pushed at his chest more forcefully. This time he let her go. "Wait a minute. Are you telling me that all I've ever had to do to leave was click my ruby slippers together and wish myself home?"

His brow furrowed as he looked down at her feet. "Your feet are bare, Alexandra, so I do not believe slippers to be a necessary part of the ritual. But yes, essentially all you have ever had to do was wish yourself home."

She rubbed at the lump on her forehead in irritation. "Well, fuck-diddly-uk, Flanders, that would have been some useful information to have about twenty years ago."

* * * *

Kasdeya decided to ignore the uk-flanders reference, having no idea what she was talking about. He'd been many years away from the mortal plane and speech idioms had apparently progressed into strange new realms. The twenty-year reference was interesting though. He'd only been calling her to join him for a few weeks, and none of the lesser Brethren would have had the strength required to pull a mortal soul into their realm. The time difference between his plane and hers must be vast. All the more reason to hasten his seduction and convince her to set him free. A handful of days, at best, and she would be dead. And who knew when another Summoner might be born.

He again moved to take her in his arms but Alexandra was having none of it. She quick-stepped to the left. "Just stay back, dark man. I can't think when you're so close."

His smile was sinful and, in a move too fast to follow, his arm whipped out and wrapped around her back, pulling her into his side. "Thinking is not necessary." The fingers of his free hand trailed up the center of her body, from her belly button to her chin, angling her face to his. Alexandra's half-formed words of protest were cut short as he lowered his mouth.

* * * *

His lips were firm and strong, and Kasdeya's taste was as exotic as his scent—an entrancing mix of sugar and smoke, spice and honey. Alex opened her mouth for him before she even knew she intended to. His rough, catlike tongue surged inside, stroking aggressively along her palate and the back of her teeth before retreating. It taunted her with rapid, sexy flicks against her lips, first the top and then the bottom, and darted away mischievously when her own tongue tried to catch it.

With a muffled moan, Alex came up on her toes. Her hands twisted in his sleek mane, tugging his head closer. They were pressed so tight together that his rumble of amusement was felt more than heard as it vibrated through his torso. His lips under hers widened into an arrogant grin that she could picture all too well and, without even stopping to think about it, Alex took the bottom one between her teeth and bit.

Kasdeya sucked in a breath at the feel of her small, pearly teeth in his skin. He pulled back his head to glare down at her.

Alex was as shocked by her audacity as he was. Her own breath caught in her throat at his fierce expression and she instinctively tried to back out of his reach. His hand slid from her waist to her ass, splaying across the curve of it to keep her in place. His other hand moved to seize a handful of hair. He wrenched her head back. "Is this how you would prefer to play, pet?"

"I'm not your pet." She wished her voice didn't sound quite so shaky while she made her brave declaration.

"I beg to differ."

His lips were bruising as they again slanted over her own, his tongue a violent intrusion between her lips. There was nothing gentle or playful about his kiss this time. It was intense, wicked and erotic. Fire licked up her spine to curl lovingly around the pain of his fist in her hair. Her nipples hardened to a stone-firm sharpness that Kasdeya surely felt against his torso. It was the trickle of liquid shivering down her inner thigh though that served to bring her to her senses. Her intense reaction to the winged man—no, let's call a spade a spade here—to the demon, frightened her.

And he must be a demon, she figured, trying to convince her legs to propel her away from him, because God surely wasn't punishing his elite by sentencing them to this wasteland. Anyway, Kasdeya didn't seem to be the angelic type.

When his hand left her hair to test the firmness of her small, high breasts, Alex panicked. There's no place like home, there's no place like home... The vision of her body lying still and cold on the bathroom floor swam before her eyes. *I summon you!* she shrieked desperately in her mind. And, just like that, she was there.

* * * *

Kasdeya cursed as the girl dissolved in his arms. That had certainly not been in the plan. She was supposed to have taken him with her. He had

Alicia Steele

already wasted more time than he would have liked calling her to him, and finally the Summoner had come. Finally she had uttered the words he required to show himself. He had been so damnably close to escaping! What in the nine hells had gone wrong?

Chapter 3

Kasdeya rested his forehead against the glass separating his world from hers. The muscles of his shoulders slowly unknotted as the Summoner woke.

"Oh God," Alexandra groaned, clutching her head and levering herself onto her elbows. The early morning sun poured cheery streamers of light into the bathroom's yellow and pink windows.

"Awake at last, pet? I had begun to worry."

Begun to worry? He'd been half out of his mind with concern, watching anxiously over her motionless body as the hours ticked away. And, despite what he told himself, his concern was more than that of a captive for his freedom. The sight of her slight, still form spread across the sterile white floor had filled him with fear. She'd seemed so delicate. So fragile. So in need of someone strong to take care of her.

Kasdeya gave his head a sharp shake at his turn of thought. She may indeed need taking care of, but that wasn't his job. At any rate, she seemed fine now. He eyed her coltish legs as she gathered them beneath her and stood swaying dizzily from side to side. Yes, she was very fine.

Alexandra cleared her throat several times. "What the hell are you doing in the mirror? It's daylight out."

Kasdeya leaned casually against the barrier that separated their planes. "We have a deeper connection now that you have summoned me once."

Indeed they did, and their timelines seemed to have synced; every minute he'd watched her, so pale and motionless, had passed with the same excruciating slowness in both worlds. A natural side-effect of her power, he assumed. How convenient. He'd be able to monitor her continuously from now on, which would give him ample time to wear her down.

Not to mention that it would have distressed him to see her age past the beauty she currently possessed in just a matter of hours and to weaken and die in a few days. Yes, it would have distressed him greatly. But perhaps "distress" wasn't the right word. The thought of her infinitesimal mortal life and its inevitable end made his heart race with an emotion he was unfamiliar with and so could not name. However, it mattered not. He would never have to witness such an event.

Kasdeya pushed the strange thoughts he was struggling with aside and concentrated on his goal. If Alexandra would just call him into her own plane, he could ravish her to within an inch of her life—not because it would be necessary at that point, having already won his freedom, but because he really wanted to. And then he would be on his merry way. One thousand years on Earth was a much more satisfying prospect than one thousand years in this depressing gray limbo and, with luck, the Prince would never know the difference.

* * * *

His smile was indolent as he traced a figure on the glass—a figure that corresponded to her own body's curves. Alex sucked in a surprised breath at the feathery feel of his spirit hand gliding along the side of her breast.

"Summon me but once more, Alexandra, and I'll make you gasp in earnest."

Alex backed away until the door handle declared its presence to her right hip. She fumbled for the knob behind her. "Oh, I don't think so, dark man. What kind of person would I be if I let loose a demon into the world?" Why wouldn't the damn door open? She glanced down to twist the key that had somehow managed to turn itself in the old-fashioned lock.

"We prefer the name 'Fallen.'"

She finally tugged the door open. "Yeah, well, a thorn by any other name…"

Alex beat a hasty retreat.

Chapter 4

"You look like shit."

"Gee, Rosie, you always know just what to say to make a girl feel special." Alex looked up from the computer screen as Rose strode into the tiny room Alex considered her home away from home. Alex's glance took in Rose's floor-length floral skirt—in the most putrid shade of chartreuse—and the threadbare purple sweater—which clashed outrageously with her friend's curly red hair—and she shook her head in fond amusement. Rose's comment was a little like the pot and the kettle, but it wouldn't do her any good to say so.

She'd tried to get Rose to take some care with her appearance. After all, Rose was really quite attractive and only a few years older than Alex. She'd tried to set her up on dates—to no avail. Rose mothered everyone but was, sadly, a mother to no one. She seemed perfectly happy directing all her maternal instincts into her friends. "Plenty of time for that later," she'd say whenever Alex tried to introduce her to a new beau. "I'm busy enough as it is without having to worry about keeping a man happy too." But Alex saw the wistful shine in Rose's eyes when the children ran through the house and the small, sad smile she'd tried to hide when a toddler had grinned at her from his perch atop Daddy's shoulder while they'd waited in line at the bank, so Alex kept trying to set her friend up, no matter how many times she was rebuffed.

Rose snorted and threaded her way through the disaster Alex called an office to deposit her burden of papers onto an already precariously balanced stack. She turned back to her boss—a title that Rose said held little meaning for her considering the pittance she was paid. But Alex knew that Rose was really here because she believed in the work, and because she had become almost like a big sister to Alex. Rose had been wooed by bigger charities for more money and more prestige. Her organizational skills were renowned in certain circles. But she seemed quite happy at Dovescot.

Right now, however, Rose was wearing an expression of such obvious concern that Alex made an effort to wipe the exhaustion off her face and straightened the sleep-deprived slump of her shoulders. She didn't want to worry her friend, and she knew she was doing just that; Rose's "You look like shit," was just her way of saying so. Alex's effort proved too much. With a tired sigh, she leaned back in her cracked vinyl chair. Her palms came over her closed eyes to massage her aching eyeballs. She'd been staring at the grant request forms for about three hours, occasionally typing in one or two desultory words only to delete them a few seconds later. She was furious with herself that she couldn't seem to pull it together. Her work was important. They needed the grant to keep the doors open for another year.

"Well, you know what, babe?" Alex said. "I feel like shit."

"Spill." Rose skirted her bum up on the edge of Alex's desk, accidentally knocking a ream of paper to the floor. Both women made a grab for the paper, but neither was fast enough.

"Just leave it!" Alex snapped. Instantly, a flush of shame heated her cheeks. "God, I'm sorry. I know I've been Bitch Queen of the Universe lately."

"Yeah, you have." Rose crossed her arms over her ample chest. "So what's bunched your panties?"

Alex eyed her speculatively. How could she tell her stalwart, down-to-earth friend that she was being haunted by a demon? A gorgeous demon that mocked her from every reflective surface she came across, at that. His growling voice spoke to her from the silver sides of her toaster. His beautiful face mirrored hers in the glass of darkened windows. Hell, this morning he'd grinned at her from the newly spotless paint on her car. That'd teach her to clean anything.

It had been going on for a little less than two weeks now. She'd covered every shiny surface in her house that she could. Too bad she couldn't make the rest of the world as safe.

Just then, her laptop went into hibernate mode. Because Alex had never bothered to choose a screen saver, Kasdeya's handsome features immediately formed in the hazy, anti-glared blackness. He pursed a kiss at her. With an impatient curse, Alex slammed the laptop's lid down. If his constant attention during the day wasn't bad enough, he visited her dreams every night. She had no idea if it was really him infiltrating her mind or only her own fevered, erotic imaginings, but she wasn't getting much rest either way.

"Well? C'mon, tell old Rose," her friend prodded.

Alex realized she'd been just sitting there staring into space as she daydreamed about Kasdeya's wings, hands and…other things. "I'm not getting much sleep."

"How come?"

She looked past the redhead out the small dormer window and rubbed her neck in discomfort. She supposed she could tell her friend a bit of the truth, if it'd get her off her back. "I've been having these dreams…"

Rose motioned with her hand in the "let's roll this along" gesture, but Alex didn't elaborate. She could feel her face turning hot.

"Nightmares?" Rose finally asked.

"Um, not exactly."

"Then wh—"

Alex shifted in discomfort. Could this be more embarrassing?

Rose's eyes narrowed. "Ohhh!" She laughed. "That doesn't seem so terrible."

"I'm not getting any sleep."

"Take a sleeping pill."

And spend more time in the dark man's arms? Alex shook her head, even though her nipples hardened instantly at the thought. He was a demon—ultimate evil and all that. In fact, she'd Googled him and, according to more than one website, not only was he a demon, he was an upper echelon demon—some kind of big mucky-muck in Hell's army. In the few sources she'd found, every other demon had a clearly delineated rank and position, but the only definition she'd turned up on Kasdeya was that he'd been one of God's best guys until he'd started messing around in human affairs and been cast down. Now his job title seemed to be "The Fifth Satan." While the website hadn't relayed any more info than that, "The Fifth Satan" just didn't sound very good. No, lusting after him was not cool. An unpardonable sin, for sure.

Apparently thinking that Alex's furious head shaking had been at her pill suggestion, Rose asked, "Why not?"

"I, uhh… I don't really like to use drugs."

Rose gave her another funny look—Alex sure was racking them up—probably because her friend was remembering the joint they'd shared at that artist's loft a few months ago.

"I mean pharmaceuticals," Alex backtracked. "I don't like to take pills or anything like that." She smiled weakly. Lame. Really lame.

"Oh, okay. That makes sense." Rose slipped off the desk and retrieved the papers. "Well, listen. Don't paint me with a hippie paintbrush, all right? But there's this cool little shop I go to sometimes for Wiccans and the like."

Alex's brows shot up into her hairline and it was Rose's turn to look embarrassed. "I'm dabbling, what can I say?" she mumbled. "Anyway, the owner, Melynda, carries a lot of homeopathic remedies. Maybe she can help you out."

Alex felt hope rise for the first time in days. Yes! If a witch couldn't help her, who could? Why hadn't she thought of that? Hers was a supernatural problem. She should have been seeking a supernatural solution. "So you're practicing witchcraft?" she asked Rose.

Rose stood and fussed with the papers, using the act of putting them back as an excuse to tidy Alex's desk. She was always trying to do that, apparently not understanding that Alex actually worked better when surrounded by chaos. "Nah," she said. "I'm more interested in the Goddess-Mother aspect. The energy in all living things and how we relate to it…you know."

Actually, Alex didn't know, but she was damned sure going to find out.

"But Mel's the real deal," Rose continued, oblivious to her friend's coiled tension. "Spells, séances, tarot—she does 'em all."

"Spells." Alex uttered an artificial little laugh that earned her yet another puzzled glance. That had to be a record for strange looks in one day. "Hmph. Still, give me her address and I'll pop over. I could really use some sleep."

"Sure." Rose peeled off a Post-it and scribbled down the address.

"Thanks." Alex snatched at the little yellow piece of paper, standing up so fast that her chair flew backward and careened into the wall.

Rose's mouth was a moue of surprise. "You're going right now?" It was one thirty in the afternoon.

"Yeah, I thought I'd—" Alex's head fell back into her shoulders and her eyes squeezed shut in annoyance. "Oh shit. The grant!"

Rose laughed. "Don't worry about it. I'll do it. You really *must* be tired to have forgotten about our funding for the next twelve months. I don't know why you didn't just ask me in the first place. You hate the bureaucratic crap."

"I do, but I was trying to be responsible."

Rose smirked and shook her head as she slid into Alex's chair, pulling it up to the computer. "Dumb ass," she said affectionately.

"That's Mr. Dumb Ass to you." Alex leaned over and pecked her friend's cheek. "Thanks, babe. I owe ya."

"You always do."

* * * *

The shop was a tiny hole-in-the-wall sandwiched between a kosher deli and a secondhand clothing store. Alex had driven past it twice before she'd finally clued in that the psychedelic lettering reading "Magik" wasn't graffiti after all, but the actual name of the place. Why on earth hadn't Rose jotted down that vital piece of information when she'd given her the address?

Alex circled the block several times looking for a parking spot even remotely close when, like a gift from Heaven, a big blue Buick pulled away from the curb right in front of the deli. "Providence," she muttered, slipping her black bug into the spot.

When she got out of the car, she smoothed her denim mini-skirt and, for reasons known only to her subconscious, fastened the top two buttons of her cream blouse. She inexplicably felt like a job applicant going to her first interview; the same trembling feeling was weakening her knees. But she bolstered her resolve, flicked her shiny hair over her shoulder and marched up to the door. She needed help and this might be where she could find it. 'Nuff said.

Sound was the first sense stroked as she stepped into the dim, cluttered store and the melodious tinkle of moon chimes greeted her entrance. Smell was next. Alex shut her eyes, inhaling the delicious aroma of rare herbs, old books and rich incense. It brought to mind Kasdeya's musky cinnamon scent and her eyes snapped open at the reminder of her reason for being here.

Her pupils had expanded enough for her to see the shadowy interior passably well. Alex made some small sound of delight, moving away from the door to run exploratory fingers over the purple crushed velvet covering the display tables, where she spied a lovely mortar and pestle in black marble shot through with veins of red. She'd always wanted a mortar and pestle, though she had no idea of what she might actually grind up with it. They'd just always looked so exotic, so ceremonial to her.

She picked up a silver Celtic cross that easily filled the span of her palm. Alex traced the intricate curves, lost in the elaborate beauty of the ancient design. When her gaze strayed to a scrying mirror hanging on the wall to her right, Kasdeya was in immediate attendance, grinning at her. Alex started so violently at the unexpected vision that the cross slipped from her hand and landed with a heavy thud on the planked floor. She gasped and hurried to pick up the pendant, searching it anxiously for damage.

"No harm done, I'm sure," said someone with a deep feminine voice from the rear of the shop. "That thing could take a bomb blast and not be hurt." The crystal curtain separating the retail area from the storage was pushed aside by a long, red-taloned hand.

Mesmerized, Alex watched as the woman stepped through the glittering drape. She was so…unusual looking. Tight dark-auburn ringlets framed a heart-shaped face. Her lips were thin but painted such a striking, deep crimson that they almost seemed to precede her, drawing one's eyes to the decadent contrast between them and her pale, white skin. Almond eyes sparkled with amusement at Alex's slack-jawed expression.

But it wasn't her face—as interesting as it was—that had caused Alex's jaw to drop. It was her attire. A thick black choker sporting an enormous green, red-flecked stone was at her throat. A dark emerald-green corset cinched her waist to impossibly small measurements and thrust out her bosom. A matching skirt of plush velour fell in intricate pleats to the floor. It split up the length of her thigh as she moved further into the room. Alex was desperate to know where one could acquire such a gorgeous, erotic outfit.

The woman laughed and angled her head in acknowledgment of the admiration in Alex's eyes. "The name's Melynda, and the answer to your next question is eBay," she said. "I shop at a store called Darker Pleasures on eBay. I'll give you their card. Now what can I do for you today?"

Alex carefully laid the cross down in its nest of purple velvet as she considered her response. How exactly did you ask someone how to get rid of a demon? But first, just in case Rose checked up on her, Alex dutifully inquired about natural remedies for sleeplessness, mentioning her friend's name in case Rose got a discount for referrals. In response, Alex was given a tea with valerian root and catnip, of all things. She stood at the counter as her purchase was rung up, still having come to no logical way to ease the question into normal conversation.

Melynda saved her the trouble. "So," she said, handing over Alex's change before leaning her hip casually against the counter, "wanna cut the crap and tell me what you really came here for?"

Alex tucked her purchase into her purse and then slowly looked back up. Then she figured that if Melynda could be blunt, she could too. "I was wondering if you could give me any information on how to…umm…how to unsummon—"

"Banish," the dark-haired woman interjected.

"Right. Uh, how to *banish* a demon."

Melynda tapped thoughtfully at her lower lip with one two-inch red nail. "What spell did you use to conjure the demon?"

"No spell." Alex hastened to assure. "At least I don't think it was a spell. All I said was 'I summon you.'"

Melynda's dark brows rose in obvious astonishment. "I summon you," she repeated. "That's it? No conjuring circle? No blood? Nothing?"

Alex shrugged. "Nope, nothing else. And now he won't..."

Her words faded as Melynda raised her finger for silence and slid back through the curtain. She returned a moment later bearing a tome as large as her torso. The smell of antique leather and rotting parchment drifted up from the crackling pages as she rifled through the grimoire. "Summon," she muttered. "Summon, summon... 'Summoner.'" She read the passage quickly and then lifted her head to regard Alex with unabashed delight. "Tell me, Miss..."

"Alexandra," Alex said, not entirely sure why she gave the more formal version of her name.

Melynda grinned at her as she carefully closed the book. "Tell me, Alexandra, are you, by chance, a Summoner?"

"I... I don't know."

"Did the demon call you by that name?"

"Yes, he—" This time she was interrupted by Melynda's whoop of glee.

"Holy shit! A Summoner in my shop! There hasn't been a known Summoner for more than two hundred years." Melynda hurried around the counter to pump Alex's hand. "It's an honor," she said, all trace of her previously aloof demeanor erased in her excitement. "Who have you nabbed?" Her gaze flicked around the shop as if expecting the demon to appear at any moment. "And where is he? I was under the impression that a demon summoned that way was connected to the Summoner at all times."

Alex resisted the urge to smack her forehead. So that's why Kasdeya wouldn't leave her alone! "He's not on this plane," she said, cutting her gaze sideways to the other woman, expecting the explanation to shock her.

Melynda just nodded. "So now you can't even put your makeup on without him staring back at you, huh?"

Actually, Alex had forgone makeup lately. It just hadn't seemed worth it. But she nodded anyway at Melynda's observation, astounded at the depth of knowledge the woman had about her situation. She obviously knew way more about this than Alex herself did.

"Well," said Melynda, leaning back with her elbows on the counter. "If it were anyone else, I'd send them home with mullein, marjoram, witch grass—you know, the usual. And, of course, the appropriate sigils. But hell, Alexandra..." She tossed back her head and laughed. "You're the god-damned Summoner. Just pop back into that plane and banish him."

"But how do I do that? Banish him?"

"Same way you summoned him. Say, 'I banish you, insert-name-here.' Who did you say it was?"

Alex hadn't said. But she saw no harm in assuaging Melynda's obvious curiosity. "Kasdeya."

All the blood drained from Melynda's already white skin, lending her the hue of a corpse. "You're joking."

Alex shook her head, puzzled at the woman's response. "No, his name's Kasdeya, or so he told me."

Melynda's hand rose to her throat. "A lesser demon wouldn't dare take his name. Punishment would be swift, to say the least, if Kasdeya found out. Jesus, Alexandra, do you know who he is?"

Alex shook her head again, and the dark-haired woman's eyes took on a wistful, faraway glaze as she caressed the smooth column of her neck. "You've raised a high prince of Hell. Practically *the* Prince of Hell, second only to Satan." She licked her lips and cocked her head slyly, leaning closer to Alex. "Is he beautiful?"

Alex's cheeks blazed at the thought of how beautiful he was. "Yes."

"Mmm-hmm. I thought he would be." Melynda sighed, staring into space a moment longer, and then straightened. "Hold on one more sec." She again disappeared into the back, but this time she was gone nearly ten minutes. Alex thought about just leaving; she had the info she needed. But it wasn't in her nature to be so blatantly rude. And, anyway, she kind of liked Melynda, as odd as she seemed.

"Here," Melynda huffed, finally coming out with an armload of books. "Do some reading on...well, yourself." She grinned again. "It might surprise you to know exactly what you're capable of. Oh, and here's the card for Darker Pleasures. On the back, I wrote down my cell, work and home numbers." She was tossing the books into a plain purple bag.

"How much do I owe—"

Melynda shook her head. "Nothing. Just keep in touch, okay? I'd hate to have to explain to my coven how I let a Summoner slip through my fingers."

Alex said she would stay in contact, although she wasn't sure that she intended to keep her promise. A coven? What exactly was she getting into?

"Listen," Melynda said as Alex turned to leave. "Don't be too hasty about tossing Kasdeya back. Lord knows if you'll ever be able to reach him again. A prince in the palm, you know?" She sniggered at her unintentional innuendo. "I know I'd like one in my palm," she said with wicked smirk.

Alex's cheeks once again flared red, and she silently cursed her fair skin.

Melynda laughed at her obvious discomfort. "Just think about it, Alexandra. That's my advice."

"I will," she said with an embarrassed smile. Not!

* * * *

Alex went to sleep with visions of the gray plane focused firmly in her mind's eye. She figured it shouldn't be too hard to reach. She appeared there briefly every night before summoning herself away. Kasdeya's influence, to be sure.

It seemed that as soon as her lids fell closed, she was there. Alex had worn a demure, white flannel nightgown in preparation for her encounter. Although it was May—much too warm to be wearing flannel—she knew the garment would afford her protection from the cold of the plane, as well as from Kasdeya's knowing gaze.

The fogged air was oddly silent, the whisperers nowhere to be found. Alex shivered from more than just the chill. Somehow, the murky darkness seemed extra creepy without the familiar voices calling to her, as impossible as that might seem.

"Kas—" She cleared her throat and tried again, going for something more audible than a mumble this time. "Kasdeya?" Her voice was still a whisper, despite this being her second attempt at it.

"Alexandra," he whispered back, right beside her ear.

"Christ!" There, that was pretty loud. Good for her. Alex whirled around to find him a hairbreadth away. When she tried to retreat, his arms sneaked around her, holding her in place.

"You know," he growled, lowering his head to nuzzle her neck, "hearing you call another man's name every time we meet is starting to annoy me." To punctuate his words, he took her earlobe into his mouth, tightening his teeth around it.

Alex fought the impulse to bare her neck to him, trying to overcome the ripples of delight spreading out from where his tongue was licking away the sting of the bite. Best to just get it over with. "Kasdeya, I bani—"

* * * *

His pulse jumped in alarm. The chit dared try and banish *him*? He slid his mouth up over her jaw, crushing his lips to hers and effectively stopping the offensive word. It took only a moment for her rigid spine to yield, arching in his arms as he ate at her mouth. His kiss gentled at her surrender and he allowed himself to relax and enjoy the seduction. Alexandra succumbed so sweetly, so completely, murmuring wanton little moans against his lips as his tongue played over hers. And she tasted so damned good. His cock was rock hard, harder than he'd have ever believed possible from one simple kiss.

"Pet," he sighed, running his hands down her back to cup her tight little ass through the ridiculous night attire. "Don't banish me. Not yet. You have no idea of the pleasure I plan to give you." To punctuate his point, he pulled her tighter against him, his rigid length pressing into the flat expanse of her stomach.

Alex opened dazed eyes. "No," she said. "Stop—"

Kasdeya shook his head and let go of her bottom to swing her up in his arms. He willed them away to the niche he had carved for himself in this prison and laid her down on his bed of black silk. "I am not overly fond of those words either."

Chapter 5

Alex was trying to bring the image of her own bed into her mind, desperate to escape this bizarre, deliciously sinful encounter. But Kasdeya, as if knowing her intent, wouldn't give her a chance to concentrate. As soon as he had placed her on the mattress, his smooth naked body settled over hers and his mouth renewed its persuasion.

Her body acknowledged defeat before her mind did. A scrumptious lethargy stole through her limbs as the demon ravished her with his clever tongue and even cleverer hands, making her feel as slothful as a cat basking in the sun.

The sound of her nightgown ripping down the center startled her enough to momentarily clear the sensual haze from her head. Oh, but then he moaned, a heart-wrenching, masculine sound of need as he sat back to look down at her nakedness. Alex's sex throbbed in response, releasing a flood of silky fluid at the blatant lust in his eyes and the sexy sound of his desire.

"Little mortal," he said on a sigh, running reverent hands along her neck and shoulders before drifting lower. Her nipples, already hard and aching, strained into his palms. His long, fine fingers caught at the pebbled nubs as he admired the slight weight of her small curves. "You have the beauty of an angel."

And he would know, right?

She told herself to snap out of it. There was no way she could let this happen. "Kasdeya, I banish…"

Kasdeya rolled his eyes and took one hand away from her body to place it gently over her kiss-swollen lips. "Desist now, Alexandra." His index finger slipped inside her mouth and Alex moved her tongue over it, her mind and body still at odds with each other about what exactly she wanted. Kasdeya's own tongue peeked out to touch the deep indent in his upper lip as she suckled him and another groan was torn from his chest. His finger pressed further into the wet heat.

"You want me, pet," he said, his voice a deep burr. The fingers on her breast constricted, trapping the nipple almost painfully. It was Alex's turn to moan. Kasdeya's mouth curved. "I can see it," he continued. "I can feel it." He pinched her nipple again and Alex's head tossed in pleasure, releasing his finger from between her lips. "And I can smell it." His mouth opened, drawing the cool air over his tongue.

Alex blushed in mortification. She could smell the heat of her feminine arousal too, but none of her other lovers had ever commented on it. How embarrassing.

Kasdeya's grin widened and his thumb stroked the heat of her cheek. "You smell delicious, Alexandra. I find myself eager for a taste." He leaned over to brush her lips with his. "So why not forgo this foolish banishment notion?" he whispered, nibbling at her lower lip.

He leaned up again, straddling her thighs, and stroked his long cock. His other hand slid through the dark waves at his temple. "After all," he said, "should you not sample the wares before deciding to turn down the purchase?" His wings opened and fanned the air behind him, creating a stunning backdrop for his unearthly beauty. Alex's breath came in pants as the breeze they created washed over her body. She couldn't make herself form any kind of coherent reply while her gaze tracked the slow, lazy movement of his palm on his prick.

Kasdeya picked up her right hand from where it rested limply on her stomach and wrapped it around his erection. Her fingers barely fit around his girth.

"Touch me, Summoner," he ordered in a harsh, guttural voice, his hand guiding hers over the glass-like smoothness of his shaft. His eyes fell closed and he thrust into her hand. "Yes," he sighed. "Like that."

Alex gave up the ghost. He was right. She did want him—more than anything she'd ever wanted in her life. He was just as god-damned irresistible as he thought he was. She sat up between his spread legs, holding onto the curved muscle of his hip for leverage, and stroked his cock more forcefully. His piloting fingers fell away and came to rest on the gloss of her hair instead, applying gentle pressure to incline her already bent head toward his cock. She went willingly enough, as eager for the taste of his velvety-soft prick as he was for the heat of her mouth.

Alex swiped her tongue over the plum-sized crown and gave a whimper of excitement as the tang of his pre-come flooded her mouth. The flavor was like nothing she had ever encountered before. Ambrosia. Every decadent dessert and every illicit drug rolled into one heady bouquet. She nudged him back so that she could kneel up, the better to swallow his length and taste more of his delicious essence.

* * * *

Kasdeya didn't bother to choke back his groans as she dipped her lovely, fey face and took him deep into her mouth. Being an exceptionally experienced lover, he knew that the sounds of his enjoyment would be a spur to her own. Regrettably, he wasn't exaggerating the strength of his response. This little slip of a mortal was managing to do what countless Angels in Heaven and even more Fallen in Hell had been unable to accomplish: she was making him lose control.

"Damnation," he hissed as her tongue flicked at the underside of his glans. One of her tiny hands slipped between his legs to cup the weight of his balls, which were tightening in anticipation of an explosive release.

His fingers tensed in her hair. He was torn. What he really wanted to do was thrust deeper down her throat and just give in to the pleasure, but he knew he had to push her away. After all, he was supposed to be seducing her, not the other way around.

"Stop," he said, but his voice was too husky to be understood. He tangled his fists in her slinky locks and wrenched her off him, bringing her lips up to his. The taste of himself on her tongue rocked his control even further. Kasdeya snarled as he devoured her mouth, his own tongue becoming violent, demanding everything she had to give. He ground helplessly against the sleekness of her skin.

When Alexandra brought one slim thigh up around his waist to grant him the access he seemed to be asking for, he cursed and pushed her away. She sprawled back on the ebony silk, a look of confusion on her face. "You've had your taste," he said, trying to will himself back to calm. "Now I will have mine."

The confusion was replaced by a knowing feminine smile, the same look all women wore when they realized they were desired. Alexandra relaxed back into the sheets, her eyes falling half shut as she brought her hands up to cup her breasts. She and Kasdeya moaned in unison when her fingers found the sharp peaks of her cherry nipples, plucking them aggressively. Her thighs fell open, allowing him a glimpse of the hot-pink crease nestled within the lacy golden-brown thatch of her pubic curls. Kasdeya's mouth went dry at the sight and he closed his eyes against it, against the temptation to take what was offered in every way known to man and in some ways not yet known.

At the dropping of his eyelids though, her pungent scent became his body's stimulation of choice. Once again he opened his mouth, letting the delectable odor tantalize his palate.

"Well," she urged. His eyes snapped open to see her thighs spread even further, her hips lifted up to him in enticement. "What are you waiting for?"

Control, he wanted to say. But there was no reason to grant her that truth.

"Patience, pet," he murmured instead, lowering himself over her to lick her fingers, which were still restlessly kneading her small, proud breasts. She moved her hand away immediately, sliding it through his thick mane to the back of his skull, urging him closer. He smiled against her skin and took the pert little jewel of her nipple between his lips.

* * * *

Alex sighed in bliss, arching into his mouth. "Kasdeya," she whispered, rolling the syllables in her mouth like a fine wine.

"My pet," he said, trailing kisses across her chest to taste her other nipple.

"I'm not your—oh, Jesus!"

Kasdeya had bitten her. Not hard enough to bruise, but hard enough to send pain flickering along her nerve endings. Pain that was immediately followed by the warm rush of pleasure.

"I'll stop calling you my pet," he said between long, rough licks, "when you stop calling me by my enemy's name."

"I wasn't…" Her words faded away as his hands ended the descent they'd been making down her body at the apex of her thighs. Her muscles tensed in expectation. He didn't make her wait. With no preamble, his hands dipped lower, pushing her legs hard to the side so that she was splayed like a starfish. His thumbs caressed the creamy, damp creases where soft skin met soft hair, and then they darted inward, spreading her wide.

"Chri—" she exclaimed, but the word strangled in her throat.

Kasdeya gave her breast one final kiss and then tilted his head to regard her with amusement as his mouth followed the trail his hands had blazed. "Did you say something?" he asked, his warm breath stirring the curls of her sex.

Alex shook her head.

"Are you sure, pet?" He was so close now that she felt his lips form the words.

"No, damn you," she gasped, pushing up into his mouth.

With a soft laugh, Kasdeya admitted he may have been mistaken before thrusting his tongue deep inside her slick center.

"Oh Go—" Once again, Alex cut herself off. This was going to be hard. She was an "Oh God" kinda gal when things got going. Rifling through her mind for a safe word—she was vocal, she had to be able to moan something—while Kasdeya lapped at her, was a lesson in wicked distraction. "Fuck," she hissed, both in response to her internal query and in response to the external stimuli of the dark man's thumbs rotating in tandem over her distended clit, first one and then the other. His tongue had set up a strong rhythm, surging again and again into her molten core. It felt much longer and thicker than any tongue had a right to be; Alex was sure she could feel it brushing her cervix each time it delved inside.

"Oh fuck!" she said again, happy with the way the word sounded in her mouth. Her hands tightened on what she, at first, thought were Kasdeya's shoulder blades. But no; they were too high, too downy soft.

She raised her head to see her fingers embedded in the thick midnight feathers of his wings. Just then, his hands slipped around to cup her ass and lift her up to his lips. His thumbs were replaced by the strong suction of his mouth and the lash of that sandpaper tongue. Alex gave up caring where the hell her hands were, just using them to hang on as she was catapulted into the most soul-shattering orgasm of her life.

* * * *

Kasdeya drank from her greedily. When she started to descend from the first plateau of pleasure, he moved up, ever so slightly, and pushed down with his tongue, sliding the small swollen hood over her spasming nub, decreasing the intensity just enough to send her soaring again.

"Fuck!" she cried for about the tenth time in the last minute. He repressed a chuckle. Apparently, his little Summoner became rather monosyllabic when deprived of God's name. He thought about the word "fuck" as she came down from her second climax, shuddering and moaning, her sweat-sheened thighs pressed tight to his ears. Was the word Dutch in origin? Perhaps German. Whichever it was, it certainly seemed to be a versatile word. His Prince had taken to using it rather profusely himself in the last hundred years.

Kasdeya shrugged off the idle thought and again switched positions with his tongue. Her clitoris would be too sensitive now for any direct stimulation, but the rest of her pretty, puffy sex was fair game and so responsive with the fresh engorgement of blood. He readied her for a third climb, tracing the butterfly spread of her inner lips, and then pausing to beat a rapid tattoo on the sensitive spot just inside of her now incredibly tight channel. When he'd first started, she had been nicely firm. Not virginal, but toned, sleek. Now…

"God, please stop," she gasped, trying to tug his head away. "It's too much!"

God again? She'd clearly forgotten herself in her delirium but Kasdeya decided to forgive her, just this once. When he felt her muscles stiffen, almost twanging as the third crest hit, he once again plunged his tongue inside, lengthening it to chafe the entrance to her womb.

Alex screamed as her body arched off the bed, held in place by only his hands. Her sex constricted around the length of his tongue, milking it in time to the swells of ecstasy. He expanded his tongue in opposition to her contractions, rippling it inside of her sensitive flesh.

"No more," she whimpered. "Please, no more."

Kasdeya relented, but only because he could not wait one second longer to bury himself in her tight wet heat. If he had been so inclined, he could have gorged on her for hours, bringing her to climax repeatedly until she was rendered unconscious from the sheer orgasmic pleasure.

"Of course more," he said, moving his body up between her lax legs. "We haven't even come to the best part yet, pet."

* * * *

Alex felt as if she'd already had marathon sex. She was vibrating like a tuning fork, still suffering random, heart-pounding quivers of delight. Hadn't come to the best part yet? She couldn't even open her eyes, couldn't seem to control any part of her body. All she could do was whimper and moan.

"No, wait," she mumbled, summoning the energy to turn her face away from his.

He grinned as he picked at a few wet strands trailing across her mouth, cheeks and forehead, and smoothed them back into the hair at her temple. "My, my, little Summoner, you are full of words I prefer not to hear."

Kasdeya turned her face back to his and laughed when she squeezed her eyes shut tighter, expecting him to lay violent claim to her mouth once more.

Instead, he smoothed his cheek over hers while rocking his body, ever so gently, against her. Chest to chest. Groin to groin. The lightest of glides. His hands whispered over her hair as he brought his wings forward to enclose them in darkness. His breath was heavy in her ear, moistening the blackness with his exhalations and establishing an intimacy that was as undeniable as the pounding of her heart.

When her trembling subsided, he once again brought his mouth over hers. He said nothing, did nothing. Alex slid her hands around his lower back and pulled him closer. The almost intangible friction of his prick against her sex became a solid, pulsing thrust. She gasped. She was so sensitized that she felt the heavy vein on the underside of his cock.

"Little mortal," he said in a hushed, strained voice, "I would never take something not freely offered. But if you do not offer soon, I may well die of wanting."

"Angels can't die," she murmured, lifting her head from the bed to get an equally satisfying increase of friction at the point where their mouths met.

Kasdeya smiled when she licked his lips, seeking entrance, but he didn't open for her. "No, they can't. But I'm not an angel." His hands left her hair to tenderly shape her body, drifting down to the curve of her ass. He lifted her so that his cock butted against her wet heat, seeking entrance of its own.

"Demons can't die either." When she realized he wasn't going to kiss her back, she turned her attention to his jawline, nipping and sucking.

Kasdeya tilted his head for her, almost purring when her tongue found his Adam's apple. "Fallen," he corrected, but his reprimand lacked any strength, coming out as it did on a husky moan.

"Whatever." Her hands clenched on his hips and she lifted her body to take him inside, sighing in pleasure when his cockhead parted her, so magnificently hard against her tender flesh. "Look, I'm offering, okay? Please, Kasdeya."

He lowered his head to plunge his tongue deep into her mouth while pressing his prick farther into her snug sheath. His groans trembled against her teeth.

Alex wrapped her legs around his waist, pulling away from the kiss to arch her back in pleasure. He filled her so completely.

"Please," she panted again when he made no attempt at motion once he'd hilted. The feel of his heavy pulse buried between her legs was almost enough to send her round the loop one more time. Almost. "Please. Hard. Now." She raked her nails up his back. "Move, damn you."

Kasdeya's handsome face contorted in what appeared to be either agony or anger. His wings rose violently behind him, unfolding like a black cape. They slapped the air.

* * * *

"Foolish woman," Kasdeya hissed between clenched teeth, lifting his body away until the only parts of him touching her were his cock and his hands. "Give me a moment." He wanted to last, not to spend in the first second like a stupid human. But, by the nine hells, the feel of her was too much.

"No, now." She raised her head to take one of his small mauve nipples between her teeth and bit down, shaking her head like a predator killing its prey. Her nails scored his flesh once more, from below his wings to the cheeks of his ass, and her sex worked over his length, heedless of his desire to go slow.

Kasdeya tossed his head back, shuddering in ecstasy. Such sweet, sharp teeth she had. "Oh Go—" He snapped his mouth shut on the word, unable to believe what he had almost said. "As you wish!" he roared instead. His hips snapped, delivering sharp, brutal thrusts. He could feel the snarl he wore.

Alexandra whimpered beneath him and her mouth on his nipple gentled to the suckle of a newborn. His cock throbbed in time with the pulling warmth. He lifted his hands to tangle them in her hair, forcing her away. Her womb was starting the flurry of ripples that signaled her release and he wanted to watch her this time.

His Summoner's eyes were squeezed shut and her mouth was half open. His cock pulsed again at the sight. His strokes grew longer, harder. Kasdeya fucked her with the full strength of his thighs behind every thrust.

"Kasdeya!" she cried, sinking her nails deep and bucking beneath him.

"Look at me," he commanded, his voice fraught with the tension of holding his orgasm at bay. Her eyelids fluttered open. "Do not close your eyes, pet, stay with me."

She did. Even as her body convulsed beneath him her gaze stayed trained on his face. Alexandra's mouth opened on a silent scream when he dipped his hand between their bodies to pinch her clit. Her inner muscles grabbed and held, refusing to unclench.

"Perfect," he moaned, following her into oblivion. His hips drove forward with what should have been way too much force for her frail mortal body to handle, but she matched him stroke for stroke. Kasdeya's cock erupted, an endless geyser, one pulse followed swiftly by another and another. Pleasure without reprieve.

It was he that ended up breaking eye contact, laying his head in the hollow where her neck met her shoulder and gasping for air at the sheer magnitude of the orgasm she had called forth. It had never been like this before. Never. "Perfect," he repeated incredulously. He sighed in contentment at the feel of her hands petting his skin while his shudders slowly diminished.

"Yes, it was."

Kasdeya could hear the satisfied smile she wore.

Chapter 6

Alexandra was curled on her side facing Kasdeya, her head cushioned on his arm, so deeply asleep that the feel of his fingers on her skin didn't even make her twitch. This was all to the good, because he could not have made himself stop touching her, even if her much-needed rest *had* been threatened. Hair, temple, eyelids and cheeks, lips and throat, shoulders, breasts, nipples—oh yes, a lot of time was devoted to those sweet gems—ribs, waist, outer thigh, inner thigh—but no further. He didn't trust himself that far.

As the night wore on, Kasdeya explored her beauty again and again. Sometimes with sweeping glides of his palm. Sometimes with only the tip of one finger. Eyes closed. Eyes open. Eyes mostly open. He had to look at her.

On the hundredth—thousandth, who knew?—pass of his hand, his fingers sank into her suddenly ghostly form.

"No!"

But it was already too late. His fist pounded the warm indent where she had lain only one second before. "Damn it!"

* * * *

Alex woke up feeling marvelously languid. She opened puffy lids to see sunlight gilding the unpacked boxes under the stained glass window, making the battered cardboard look oddly beautiful in the multi-hued light. She smiled and stretched, letting her eyes fall closed once more. She felt so lazy and tired, she almost seemed detached from her body. Maybe she'd get up and put on a pot of coffee in just one more—

Her eyes shot open again. Sunlight was slanting across her bedroom floor. Her bedroom faced west. "Shit!" she exclaimed, sitting up quickly. Every muscle screamed in protest at the abrupt movement and the world tilted left. She ignored all that, reaching for the ears of her Mickey Mouse alarm clock to turn it toward her. It was two-thirteen. Oh, crap!

Moving as quickly as her fatigued body would allow, Alex crawled to the edge of the bed. Her legs almost refused to hold her when she attempted to stand. Her pelvis had a strange loose feeling, as if it were no longer as firmly seated as it had been the day previous. The tattered remnants of her nightgown fluttered to the ground at her feet and a splash of liquid followed, coating her inner thighs. Alex had a brief moment of confusion before she realized what it must be. Her entire body flushed with a combination of embarrassment and remembered pleasure.

"God," she mumbled, bending to pick up the torn flannel and wipe off the sticky, sweetly scented mess. "Not only did I *not* banish him, I freakin' screwed him."

She couldn't spare much thought for that right now though. The urgent press of her bladder had become the all consuming focus of her world the moment she'd stood up. Naked, Alex rushed out her bedroom door, jiving past the upstairs bathroom, doing the pee-pee dance down the steep stairs to the two-piece bath in the front hall. The house had two bathrooms—one full and one half—but only the half-bath had had a mirror she could remove completely. Knowing Kasdeya could hear her through the covered mirror had made it impossible for her to use the other bathroom for anything but bathing.

The antique silver mirror that had formerly graced the wall over the half-bath's fluted pedestal sink was now in the hall, covered in a towel. It leaned next to a small, Queen Anne console table that held a tiny lamp, her phone and her answering machine. In her mad rush past, she noticed the machine blinking. The number four flashed repeatedly.

After she'd relieved her dire need, Alex shuffled back to the phone and spent one or two guilt-filled seconds just looking at the answering machine. Four, four, four, four. She pushed the play button.

Rose. "Hey, Alex. It's like nine-forty. Did you have an appointment or something that you forgot to tell me about? Well, I guess I'll see you soon. Bye." *Beeep.*

Rose again. "It's eleven o'clock, Alex. Do you know where your children are?" The sound of Rose sniggering. "'Cause I sure as hell don't know where my boss is." *Beeep.*

An automated machine. "Hellooo. This is a friendly reminder from your local Blockb—"

Alex hit the skip button. Oops. She'd get the movies back today, for sure.

And Rose again. "Hey, hon, me again. So, I rescheduled your three o'clock and sent off the grant request. Your signature's way too easy to

forge. You should work on that. Anyway, something important's obviously come up for you, so don't worry about heading in. Everything's fine here. But I'm getting really worried. If I don't hear from you by the time I leave, I'm gonna swing by. Feel free to head me off at the pass. Call me!"
Beeep.

Alex groaned as another wave of guilt washed over her. Dovescot had a full house right now, not to mention the spring fling picnic they were planning for next week. It was way too busy over there for one person to handle. She picked up the phone to call her friend back.

"Dovescot," said Rose in a chipper voice.

"It's me."

"Oh hey! You're not dead. How cool is that?"

"Ha-ha. Look, I'm so sorry. Give me twenty minutes and I'll—"

"Don't worry about it, Alex. Seriously. Everything's under control here."

Alex looked around at the boxes still cluttering every corner. The day was wasted anyway. "Well, if you're sure…"

Rose laughed. "I'm sure! Get over yourself. We won't fall apart without you for one day. But what happened? I had visions of your car overturned on I-5."

"No, no, nothing like that." Alex ran a fingernail through the layer of dust on the cherry Queen Anne table. She certainly couldn't tell Rose she'd been up making love all night. Not without a real live man to back up her tale. Her gaze lit on her purse by the front door and the plain purple bag beside it. Aha! "That tea Melynda gave me must have really done a number on my sleep-deprived bod," she said, relieved to have a somewhat plausible excuse.

"Oh." Rose managed to sound both appeased and dubious with only that one sound. "Weird. Maybe you'll have to get over your fear of pills after all, huh? Well, why don't you take the rest of the day to unpack? Tomorrow's your day off anyway, so I see absolutely no reason why you can't have that house completely done by Monday morning." She ignored Alex's snort of disbelief. "Yep, the painting, refinishing the floors, unpacking, all of it. Get to work, you lazy girl. You promised me a house party, remember? I've got a year-old box of wine my sister brought over, and I can't wait to unload—" The sound of a child shrieking in the background cut her off. "Shit. Nicky just fell off the swing set again. I'll catch you later, hon. Enjoy your day off."

Alex hung up, feeling guiltier than ever. Nicole was a four-year-old cutie who seemed to have some balance problems, no doubt due to the number of blows her father, Darryl Grier, had rained down on her little blond head the night her mother had finally wised up and left the bastard. The restraining order against Darryl was firmly in place, charges pending. They'd booked a CAT-scan for Nicole, but the earliest appointment they could get was in two weeks. Until then, they'd just have to keep a close eye on her.

Alex sighed and ran her hands through her hair, or tried to anyway. Her fingers got snarled at the base of her skull, where a huge rat's nest had formed thanks to all that slip-sliding she'd been doing between the sheets. With a soft curse, she set about pulling apart the hopelessly knotted clump as she walked into the kitchen. Coffee was definitely in order.

* * * *

Alex poured a capful of lavender bubble bath under the running water in the claw-foot tub. Then she picked up the brush and continued the almost impossible task of unknotting her hair.

"Alexandra?" Kasdeya asked in a deep, sexy voice from behind the sheets she'd hung up over the mirrors.

Startled, Alex dropped the brush in the tub. "Uh, yeah?" she called, fishing through the foam.

"Could you pull back the cloth? I'd like to see you."

Looking like death warmed over? She didn't think so! "Umm, I'd rather not."

"Please, Alexandra. I simply want to see if you are well."

"Why wouldn't I be well?" she asked, moving to where her pink terry robe was hanging on the back of the door.

"Last night, I was a trifle…" Kasdeya trailed off, sounding embarrassed. Alex was surprised. If asked before now, she would have firmly stated her belief that nothing could faze this Prince of Hell. "Please, pet. Indulge me."

That's what got me into trouble the first time, she thought wryly. But, after wrapping the robe around her slight frame, she pulled back the sheet over the sink. "See? I'm fine."

He eyed her critically. "I cannot see anything with that housedress covering you. Remove it."

Alex blushed. It was fine for him to stand there all naked and gorgeous, but she didn't happen to have a perfect body, and the daylight was much too bright for her peace of mind. "No way."

He smirked and leaned against the clear wall separating them. "I have already seen you nude, Summoner. Spectacularly so."

"Yeah, well, nonetheless."

Kasdeya sighed and raised one hand to trace his thumb over the glass. She felt the caress against her lips. "Then tell me, are you bruised? Sore? I can see that I've marked your throat. Where else are you hurt?"

"My throat's not…" Her gaze left his to find her own in the mirror. "Oh." There was indeed a large hickey just under her jaw. She edged the robe's collar away and discovered another in the angle where her shoulder met her neck. Great. It was too warm to wear a turtleneck and she only owned one scarf: a horrid blue floral number that her brother had given her as a gag gift. Just great. At least she'd be able to hide the purple marks on her hips.

"Come back to me, Summoner, and I'll heal you. If I overheard correctly, you've nothing else to do right now."

"Quit eavesdropping on me! Anyway, you obviously *didn't* hear correctly. Otherwise, you'd know that I have an entire house to unpack."

"Then summon me to help you." He flexed one bicep for her, the muscles beautifully delineated. "I am perfectly capable of manual labor."

Alex forced herself to turn away from his gorgeous body and walked back over to twist off the taps. An abundance of lilac-tinted bubbles shivered on the water's surface. "I'll manage, thanks." She sat on the tub's edge and started working through her hair once more. If it got wet when it was this tangled, she may as well cut it off; it would be impossible to set straight again. His phantom touch trailed over her head and she shivered, despite herself.

"I could brush your hair, bathe you…" His voice dropped an octave. "Make you scream in pleasure…again. Your wish is my command, Alexandra. All you have to do is set me free."

She shook her head and twisted to look at him, ignoring the pitter-patter of her heart at his outrageous beauty. "I already told you, dark man, it's not gonna happen. I refuse to let loose a demon on the world."

His hand closed into a fist and he slammed it into the glass. The mirror trembled. "Fallen!"

She didn't bother to reply, just continued to brush her hair.

Kasdeya turned away, striding a few paces from the glass. His wings fluffed and fluttered, like a bird's after it's been dunked in water. "What if I vowed that—for the duration of this thousand-year sentence only—I will not harm, or caused to be harmed, any mortal on Earth?"

"How can I trust your word, Kasdeya? The word of a d—a Fallen?"

He whirled around so swiftly that his hair arced out from his head before settling around his shoulders once more. "What an infernally stupid question," he said. "You're the Summoner. Any pact I make with you is unbreakable. Do you not know this?"

She knew nothing of the sort. Hell, he could be lying right now. Alex finished with her hair and walked toward him to close the gap in the sheets. "I'll think about it."

He glared at her from a few feet away. "Wait!"

She was stretched up on her tiptoes, trying to tug the cloth over a bump where the curtain rod was joined. When she glanced into the mirror again, it was to find him directly on the other side. How had he moved so fast?

"Wait," he said in a gentler tone. His gaze was trained on her breasts. She looked down to discover that her robe had parted. Her left breast was fully exposed. Kasdeya licked the mirror and her nipple hardened. She froze, unable to retreat when his ghostly tongue was playing so deliciously over the hardened peak.

"At least come to me tonight," he said between licks, his voice dark and seductive. "Will you do that?"

"Yes," she was surprised to hear herself say. "I'll come." Then she forced her arm to move, sliding the fabric safely between them.

Chapter 7

Alex straightened and rubbed the aching muscles of her lower back as she looked around in satisfaction. Her furniture was finally all placed and everything looked just as good as she'd known it would.

There was a large seating area in front of the fireplace, consisting of a tan leather sofa and a pair of tapestry wing chairs. At the other end of the room, an intimate conversation-slash-reading area had been set up in front of the stained glass window with two deep club chairs upholstered in hunter green velvet.

Alex had even found the energy to hang a few pictures, despite the fact that she hadn't painted yet—just a few, to make it feel like home. Her favorite Whistler print, *The Falling Rocket*, took up the wall opposite the fireplace, and a set of black-and-white winter forest-scapes framed the arched entrance to the dining room, where her shaker table gleamed.

The eclectic mix of contemporary and traditional—like her natural hide, L-shaped couch paired with a Jacobean twist-leg coffee table—suited Alex to a tee. The furniture looked wonderful sitting atop her antique, autumn-toned Persian rug.

It had been an exhausting but productive day and, surprisingly, Kasdeya had left her alone. She'd even unwrapped and hung her empire mirror over the mantle with nary a glimpse of her beautiful dark man. The mirror showed a perfect reflection of her and the room, nothing more. Surely that was relief she felt, not disappointment.

"Enough for now," Alex said sternly as she reached for the knife to slice open just one more box. "Time for another bath." She could smell herself. It wasn't pleasant. She hit the kitchen to grab a beer before making her way upstairs. Halfway up, she turned around, coming back for the bag of books Melynda had given her that were still sitting at the front door. Alex wanted to find out if Kasdeya had been lying about his inability to break his word to a Summoner. If he had been, it was probably best to find out now.

* * * *

Alex closed the book and rested her head back against the curled edge of the tub. God, she was tired. She hadn't stopped unpacking until around midnight, and had been reading for at least an hour now.

Kasdeya hadn't been lying. Imagine that. Not only had he not lied about giving his word, but she'd found out that with the proper invocation, she could have complete control of his actions if she summoned him into her plane—something about her sphere of influence being absolute here. The thought of having power over such a creature both appalled and intrigued her. Did Kasdeya know what he was asking for? Hard to believe. She couldn't imagine him giving someone else that much control.

"I've been very patient, Alexandra," Kasdeya said from behind the sheets.

Think of the devil and he shall appear.

"Have you?" She unplugged the drain and stood. "Well, I'm sorry, but I'm very tired." Plus, she didn't exactly trust herself to be alone with him again. When Alex was around Kasdeya, her good sense seemed to fly right out the window.

"Is it *your* word that is worth nothing, then?"

Her spine stiffened. "I never gave you my word."

His silence seemed to mock her. She wrapped a white bath towel around her body and stalked over to draw the sheet back. "I didn't! You... Oh..."

Kasdeya had moved the bed to sit directly on the other side of the glass. He was lying on his side with his head propped up on one hand. The other hand was gently pumping his long, slick-looking cock. The darkness of the gray plane had been relieved by thousands of tiny white candles floating at various heights and sitting on nothing at all. The bed appeared to be surrounded by white rosebushes.

"You said you'd come, Alexandra. I took you at your word and left you alone. Was I wrong to do so?"

"I'm tired," she repeated weakly.

"Yes, and sore too, I presume." He sat up and crawled to the glass. "I know I've left bruises on your lovely skin. I apologize. Let me heal them. I promise to restrain my enthusiasm this time."

"You don't look too restrained," she said, her gaze flicking down to his groin. Instantly, a pair of black harem-style pants covered him from waist to ankle.

"We don't have to do anything," he said. "Simply let me ease your aches. Let me talk to you without this damned mirror in the way. Let me hold you." His chin dropped so that he seemed to be addressing his hands. "I'm lonely, pet," he admitted in a subdued voice.

She sighed, aware that he was playing her. But, God, just look at him. "Fine, I'll come. But you have to promise to behave."

He raised his gaze with his head still lowered, looking at her innocently through the soot black of his lashes. "I will behave."

"Promise me."

He let out a disgruntled sigh. "I promise I will behave."

"All right, give me a minute."

With a distinct feeling of unease, Alex went back to her bedroom. She chose a floor-length, sleeveless cotton nightgown and a pair of virginal white panties to match. No more facing Kasdeya without underwear on. Lesson learned. She combed her wet hair and twined it into a long, simple braid. Then she flicked off the bedside lamp, crawled into the center of the mattress and laid down. Ten seconds later, she got back up, grabbed her favorite vanilla perfume from the top of the dresser and dabbed it on her throat, between her breasts and, after a moment's hesitation, on her pubic curls. Best not to examine the motivation there. Then, back to bed, where she lay staring up at the ceiling for what felt like hours.

"Did you change your mind again, pet?" Kasdeya inquired from the bathroom, his tone irritated.

"I can't fall asleep."

There was a beat of silence. "So?"

She sat up in annoyance. "What do you mean, 'so'? How can I get there if I can't fall asleep?"

"Alexandra, I will tell you this one more time. After that, I'll have to assume you're stupid, contrary to all the evidence indicating otherwise."

"You're sure making me want to come spend time with you, smart ass," she muttered.

"I heard that."

"Good!"

Another moment of silence. "Shall we continue this argument face to face, pet? Now, one more time, close your eyes." She lay back down and obeyed. "Picture this plane as you just saw it... Are you doing that?"

"Yes." No. She was picturing him, naked and gorgeous.

"Now simply draw it toward you. Summon—" Kasdeya turned to face her as she appeared lengthwise beside him. "—it." He smiled as he finished the sentence.

She crossed her arms rebelliously over her chest. "I'm not stupid, you jerk."

He threw back his head and laughed, sliding his arms under her knees and shoulders to pull her into his lap. "I know. But you are delightful."

She rested her head against his broad chest, relaxing at once into his arms. Probably not good.

Alex tilted her head up and stopped breathing when she realized how close his face was. Without thinking, she raised her hand to caress his silky, poreless skin. Her fingers traced his sharp cheekbones and the hollow beneath, before skimming over his full bottom lip. How could anything be this beautiful? He darted his head forward and took her thumb between his teeth, holding it captive as his tongue tickled the pad.

"I thought you were going to behave," she whispered.

Kasdeya released her finger. "I *am* behaving. You're still dressed, are you not?" He leaned in to kiss her.

Alex wound one arm around his waist and the other found the back of his neck. Her heart jumped when he groaned and her mouth opened, granting him full access. Kasdeya angled his head to take advantage, thrusting his tongue into her with restrained aggression. His hand slid out from under her thigh to grasp her hip as he fell sideways, bearing them both down to the mattress.

Despite the mind-numbing goodness of his kiss, she noticed him inching her nightgown up her legs. On a surge of willpower, Alex reached down to halt his progress at the middle of her thighs. "Behave, dark man."

He groaned again and broke the kiss. "You're right. I'm sorry. Are you sore?"

"I'm okay."

"No. I said I would help, and help I shall." He traced the edge of the nightgown at her collarbone. "But you'll have to take off this pretty, innocent thing first." He grinned at the pointed look she threw him and moved to the edge of the bed. Once there, he dug around in a rosebush for a few seconds before coming up with a wine carafe filled with amber liquid.

"Oh, that's original," she said. "Get me naked, then get me drunk? Jeez, you'd think a guy who's been around since the beginning of time could do better."

He slid back onto his haunches and tilted the bottle right in front of her face. The liquid inside was much heavier than alcohol, leaving thick legs as it rotated in the carafe. Kasdeya took the stopper from the bottle and lowered it so that she could inhale the fragrance. The rich scent of growing things and exotic lilies wafted out.

"I can," he replied. "Now get that silly nightdress off and roll over."

A massage? What a great idea. Alex sat up and pulled the thin cotton garment over her head. Modesty be damned; she hadn't had a good massage in years.

He snapped the waistband of her panties. "These too."

"Nope," she said cheerfully, stretching out on her stomach.

He grumbled and straddled her thighs. "It won't be as effective."

"I'm sure you'll manage."

She sighed when the warm oil splashed onto her skin. It started tingling immediately, the pleasurable itch sinking deep into her muscles as the smell of a rain forest permeated the air. Kasdeya flicked her braid over her shoulder and leaned down to press a kiss to her bared nape before he began.

His hands were wonderful. Brilliant. Working deep into her sore spots until the muscles felt as loose as jelly. First her back, then her shoulders and arms. Alex growled when he slid the panties down to reveal the full curve of her ass, but immediately his thumbs pressed deep into the hollows below her hips, easing pain she hadn't even been aware of, and she relaxed again. After all, he *was* being extraordinarily well-behaved, though every once in a while she felt his lips against her skin, particularly on the purple marks his fingers and mouth had left.

He pulled her underwear back up and set to work on her thighs and calves. When he finally reached her feet, he spent a long time massaging the arches and heels until her toes curled in pleasure. She couldn't contain her sighs of bliss.

"Roll over, pet."

His voice pulled her out of the light doze she'd entered. Alex contemplated arguing about it, but in the end, she just flipped onto her back.

The front of her legs received the same treatment before he straddled her hips and set to work on her stomach and ribs. She tensed in expectation, but he bypassed her breasts, moving instead to the column of her throat. Alex watched him through slitted eyes, marveling that this sinfully gorgeous man was spending so much time trying to please her. It made her wonder if her refusal to summon him to Earth was, perhaps, a mistake. But then, she wasn't so naive that she didn't realize that was the entire point.

Kasdeya moved his palms up her cheeks and used both thumbs to smooth the frown creases in her forehead. "You're thinking too much."

"I'm waiting for the other shoe to fall."

He cocked his head as his fingers slipped into the loose hair of her braid, kneading her skull. "I'm not sure what you mean."

She caught his wrists and stilled them, looking up seriously into his black eyes. "I'm not summoning you to Earth, if that's what this is supposed to accomplish."

He twisted his hands in her loose grasp, catching her own wrists and lifting them above her head. "No, that is not what I'm after." She arched a brow at him and he smiled. "I'm telling the truth, Summoner."

"Then what do you want?"

He stretched out along her body, nestling himself between her relaxed thighs. She could feel the press of his erection clearly through the thin layers of cotton and silk. "I want you to spend your nights here without trying to banish me."

"I don't—"

He cut her off by placing one long finger against her lips. "If you agree to do that, I will no longer hound you during the daylight hours. Also, other Brethren will not call to you, knowing you've been claimed by me. A fact you may have already noticed."

Yes, she had. It was nice not to be whispered at all the time.

"And," he continued, "I will strive to make each evening spent with me more pleasurable than the last." His smile was decadent. "I can be very creative."

"I'm sure," she mumbled under his finger.

"Think about it," he said, before replacing his finger with his mouth.

When he lifted his head a short time later, Alex was in such a state of arousal that she'd have agreed to anything he asked. Silly man, his timing was all wrong.

"Now, little mortal." He shifted lower so that his lips brushed her collar bone. "I have been very good tonight. I have respected your wishes, and I've healed you." Kasdeya's hands smoothed over her hips. His mouth moved lower, his breath warming the slope of her breast. "Your bruises are gone."

"Are they?" she moaned, arching up to meet him.

"Mmm-hmm." Kasdeya's response vibrated through her nipple as he took it between his lips. He tickled his tongue over the hard peak for a minute. "Could I now ask a favor in return?" His chin rubbed the valley between her breasts.

Shit. He was bartering again, when he knew damned well how distracted she was. "That depends." Alex tried very hard to make her voice sound firm, but it still came out breathy. "What's the favor?"

Kasdeya reached for the bottle of oil where it had rolled into her side. "Will you touch me, pet?" He raised his head to look at her, wearing a foolish, kicked-puppy expression, completely at odds with his normally fierce visage.

She couldn't help but laugh. "Oh, I suppose." Her hand gestured to his wings. "Can you lie on those?"

"Of course." The feathery appendages folded neatly between his shoulder blades and he rolled onto his back, pulling her with him. His pants disappeared.

"No, no." She sat up on his thighs and shook her head. "Put those back." He pouted and she laughed again. "Trust me, pet," she teased.

"Tsk." Black silk once again covered his lower body.

"Good. And how 'bout a shirt too? Black with buttons, perhaps."

His pout turned into a frown. "I think you have somehow managed to miss the point of my request, Alexandra." He jiggled the oil.

Alex plucked it out of his hand and put it back on the bed. "I assure you I haven't." She just wanted the opportunity to tease him, the way he seemed to love teasing her.

A shirt appeared made of voluminous silk—white not black—that was so sheer that she could clearly see every ridge of muscle beneath it. Instead of buttons, it had laces. Alex shook her head. What a contrary, vain creature her dark man was. Still, he was cooperating, in his own way. And he did look stunning in his choice of attire.

He tucked his hands behind his head. "Now what?"

"Keep your hands right there, for a start. No touching me back. If I feel your hands on me, I stop."

Kasdeya narrowed his eyes and growled, deep in his chest. Alex folded her arms across her own chest and quirked a brow. "Or I could just not start at all. That's always an option."

"Start."

She leaned over and grabbed the end of her braid to tickle his nose with it. "You're such a sweet talker." He bit at the tail and she used it to lightly slap his cheek. "Be nice."

"You first."

Alex smiled and lowered her voice to a husky murmur. "All right." She straightened back up and pulled the elastic out of the braid, running her fingers through her hair until it flowed in loose, toffee-colored waves over her shoulders.

Kasdeya sighed. "Beautiful."

"Thank you." She reached down and turned his jaw far to the side, baring the strong column of his throat. "Second rule." Alex bent to place her mouth just over his ear. "No talking."

Any response that might have provoked was forestalled when her tongue slithered inside the alabaster shell of his ear. Kasdeya's breath left him on a small sigh of pleasure and she felt his body relax beneath her.

As she played, her fingers slid gently through his dark hair. Suddenly, she closed her hands, balling them into fists and pulling his head back. Her teeth closed on the lobe of his ear.

"Al—" He stopped himself and she smiled, using her handhold to turn his face back toward her.

"Oops," she said with a smirk. "Almost."

His eyes glittered. Alex chuckled and kissed him, using every trick she knew, sucking and biting until his rumbles of pleasure were continuous. She pulled back incrementally. He followed until his head was completely raised, his neck taut with tension at the unnatural position. When Kasdeya realized what she was up to, he let it fall with a stifled curse.

Alex laughed again. Fun! Her mouth left his to trail down his neck. She paused at his Adam's apple, giving it special attention, not having forgotten his response from the night before. He responded just as nicely this time, baring his throat and purring in contentment. When her lips met the collar of his shirt, her hands left his hair and, with excruciating slowness, she slid the first cross of laces out of their holes. Her kisses graced the newly bared flesh. The second cross was undone—and so on.

The muscles of Kasdeya's stomach were jumping at every touch of her lips by the time she reached his navel. When she darted her tongue inside, his hands flew from behind his head to hang over her hair for a second before falling down to his sides.

Alex changed tactics, pulling the edges of his shirt together and biting him through it on her return journey up his body. When she reached his nipple, she licked the cloth, soaking the fine material until it was translucent. Then she blew on it. The nub drew even tighter and a tiny moan was pulled from Kasdeya's mouth. With a wicked grin, she nipped at his skin while reaching a hand between his legs to cup and squeeze his balls through the silk of his pants.

Kasdeya gasped and twisted beneath her, bringing his thighs together to trap her hand. Alex gave him another hard squeeze and turned her head to attack his other nipple with hard, deep bites. Then her mouth abruptly gentled as she nudged the shirt back with her cheek and feathered soft kisses over his reddened skin. Her fingers moved up to his shaft, petting it with slow, soothing strokes.

Her dark man's breath was coming quick and tortured, ratcheting in her ears in time to the lazy caresses of her hand. "What was it you wanted again?" she teased, lifting her head to look at him while her hand continued its petting.

Kasdeya's hips rocked to the sensual rhythm she had established. His eyes were closed and his bottom lip was caught sexily between his teeth. "You," he breathed.

"Hmm, yes, that was it. I like the shirt, keep it, but you can lose the pants now."

No sooner had the words left her mouth, her will was done. She reached for the carafe to pour a generous splash in her palm. Her next stroke was oiled, skin against skin, a slinky-smooth glide up his cock.

He thrust hungrily into her hand. "More."

"Okay." She slithered down his body, still pumping his length. "But don't come," she said, her lips against his glans. His cock jumped at the contact.

Kasdeya raised his head to frown at her. "Alexandra!"

"Kasdeya!" Alex ran her tongue from the flared head of his shaft to its thick base. Now he tasted like oily grass, as well as his signature sweetness. "And no more talking!" she reprimanded with a laugh, turning her head to sink her teeth into his upper thigh.

Kasdeya's strangled groan was her reward.

Still chuckling, she bit him again, higher. Then her mouth was directly over his scrotum. Kasdeya's muscles tensed. Alex quickened her strokes on his cock while swirling her tongue over his balls, and his body shook.

"Alexandra, please!"

She ignored him, licking down his perineum, then back up, to take one of the large, fleshy orbs in her mouth and roll it against the ridges of her palate.

"Damn it, woman! I can't—"

She let go and sat up. "Sure you can." Kasdeya watched her, his mouth set into a thin line. She smiled mischievously. "Can't you?"

He grimaced and gave a curt nod. "Yes, I suppose I can. But not for very much longer."

"No." She let her eyes wander down to his angry cock. "Not for very much longer."

"Your mouth, little one...please."

She cocked her head and considered. "No."

Kasdeya spat an oath at her.

"Oh, hush." She smacked his stomach. "That's not nice. Anyway, I want to try something."

He came up on his elbows to glare at her more effectively. "What?"

Alex grinned and moved off his body to sit between his calves. She slipped her underwear off and tossed it aside before spreading her thighs to hook her legs over his. Kasdeya looked down the length of his body, right into the center of hers. He licked his lips and started to sit up as well.

"No. Stay there."

"Alexandra, you're driving me mad."

"I know."

She used her left hand to spread her sex wide. The fingers of her right circled her clit.

Kasdeya moaned and reached for his own cock.

"No," she warned. "Don't you dare."

He actually hissed at her like an animal, but his hands obediently fisted in the sheets.

She smiled. Her hand shifted lower, dipping into her wet warmth before coming back to swirl over her clit again. She reached her left hand back to brace herself and raised her hips toward him. Her strokes became faster, harder. Kasdeya panted, his legs quivering under hers. She could see large liquid drops rolling from the slit in his cockhead to sheen his length.

Alex was incredibly turned on. She was going to come soon. Maybe too soon, but she couldn't help that. Her inner muscles were already starting to flutter.

Her dark man's eyes were riveted on her—where her hand was working her body. His pupils were huge. Alex's clit throbbed. "Kasdeya," she whispered.

His eyes flew up to hers, his expression tortured. He mouthed the word "please."

"Yes. Yes, now." Her voice rose. "Come now!" she cried, convulsing in pleasure.

And he did. Without a single touch, on command, he came. Hard, splashing jets of semen arced across his torso, coating him up to his chin in pearlescent liquid. Her name was almost unrecognizable in the harsh howl that was ripped from his throat.

Alex fell back, breathing heavily, her legs intimately entwined with his. For a few seconds, the only sounds to be heard were their harsh pants and the soft sputter of candle wax. Kasdeya broke the silence first.

"I could kill you for that."

"Liar." She lightly kicked his hip. "It was great and you know it."

He grumbled and sat up, using the edge of the sheet to wipe himself off. "No. I wanted your body...your mouth."

Alex shifted from between his legs, rolling onto her side to admire his gorgeousness as he tried to clean up the mess he'd made. "I've disappointed you?"

His hands fell still. "No," he said, looking at her gravely.

She frowned. "Then...?"

He sighed and stretched out beside her. "It's..." He sighed again and pulled her closer, burying his nose in her hair. "It bothers me that you were able do that. To make me lose control. I have never—"

"Good," she interrupted. "Then we're even."

He didn't say anything for a while, seeming content to just cuddle her, stroking his hands lazily up and down her skin. "Do I make you feel out of control too, pet?" he finally asked.

Alex had been dozing, wrapped up in his warmth and the serene feeling of strength he seemed to exude. As a result, she didn't think to censor her reply. "You make me feel too much, dark man," she murmured, snuggling closer. "Entirely too much, I think."

Kasdeya's heart sped up under her ear, lulling her back to sleep.

Chapter 8

Alex still wasn't getting much rest. But instead of telling her how shitty she looked, her friends were all raving about how fabulously toned she was, how sparkly her eyes were, how bright her smile. Yes, marathon sex every night was darn good for the body. She looked sleek and trim like a well-kept racehorse, despite the purple bags under her eyes.

The lack of shut-eye was sure messing with her mind though. Her concentration was nil. Poor Rose was picking up a lot of slack and starting to get bitchy about it. But Rose wasn't bitching about the work; she was bitching because Alex was "holding out on her." Alex sucked at lying, so when she tried to deny that there was a guy in her life, Rose would get a pissy look on her face and tell her to "shut the hell up" and that it was "obvious" she was in love, so if it was "a huge fucking secret, then just say that!" And what *could* Alex say? She *was* lying. She *was* in love. She was in love with a god-damned—literally—demon.

How had she let that happen?

One second her mind would be cheerfully chiming, "Going to Hell, going to Hell. In a hand basket!" But the next second she wouldn't care. After all, just look at the basket she got to ride.

Hell! Hell! Hell!

"Oh, shut up," Alex mumbled, turning her attention to the papers in front of her. Arguing with herself had become a much too common occurrence.

At least some progress had been made today. She could see the wood of her desk. That was good. The tables were loaded into the truck for the picnic tomorrow. A sundae machine had been found, after much angst and emailing. And the carousel was *promised* for tomorrow morning. She'd never dealt with this rental company before, but had heard good things, so she was just keeping her fingers crossed. The clowns were booked, balloons blown and the hot dogs and hamburgers were in the freezer, packed into rented coolers, all ready for their trip to the harbor-front park. They were good to go.

Alex glanced at her watch. Eight forty-five. Time to run home to her dark man.

She got up from her chair and stretched, wondering whether the outfits she'd ordered from Darker Pleasures would be waiting for her when she got home. She'd splurged on a black leather corset and two skirts—one long and one micro short—as well as a few other odds 'n' ends. Her splurge had cost a lot and the rush shipping hadn't helped. Oh, but Kasdeya would—

Her pleasant thoughts were interrupted by the unpleasant sound of people shouting from the front of the house. Suddenly, she heard little Nicole shriek, "Daddy, no!"

Fuck.

Alex rushed around her desk so fast that she took the edge in her thigh hard enough to send her spinning into the wall. How did he find them, and how the hell did he get in? She threw open the closet door and fumbled down her rifle case.

"Mommy!" The child's voice was panicked and shrill.

Shit! Why couldn't she get the lock open? Alex took a deep breath and slowed her fingers down. Thirty-two-left, fifteen-right, six-left. "Thank Christ," she muttered, checking to make sure the gun was loaded before running down the back stairs.

"I jus' wan' my daughter," she heard Darryl Grier slur from the front hall. "You bitches jus' get outta my way, and I won' hurtcha."

"Now, Darryl…" said Rose, who must've been located between him and the door. "You know you can't take her. The police will be after you in five minutes. You're blowing your chances for visitation—"

"Fuck tha'! I don' need no one tellin' me if I kin see my own daughter. 'M takin' her. Get the fuck outta my way!"

Alex eased the kitchen door open. Down the long hallway, which extended the length of the house, she saw Darryl. He had one arm wrapped around Nicole's throat. The little girl was on tiptoe, scrabbling at her father's forearm to try to get air. Rose and Sandy, a volunteer at the house, barred Darryl's escape.

Alex slipped out and made her way toward him. She had the advantage; she knew every squeaky board in the place. Rose's gaze flicked to her but she quickly looked away, not wanting Darryl to realize someone was behind him, Alex assumed. A few of the women and children gathered also turned their attention to her. Alex held one finger in front of her mouth, but she knew Darryl would soon notice that their focus wasn't on him anymore, so she rushed the last six feet.

"Wha—" Darryl started to turn around and Alex flipped the rifle in her hands, raising the butt to smash it into his skull before he could complete the maneuver.

Unlike in all those stupid TV shows, he didn't immediately crumple to the ground. He did, however, let go of his daughter.

"Run, honey," Alex told the girl, reversing her grip again to level the barrel at Darryl's topless, sunken chest.

Instead of running, Nicole threw herself in front of her father. "Don't you hurt my daddy!" she screeched, spreading her small, pudgy arms wide in an attempt to shield his worthless body.

Darryl sneered at Alex and petted the top of Nicole's head, as if she was a much-loved hound dog. "Don' worry, baby. She ain't got the balls."

Alex shoved him hard in the chest with the gun and he, in his inebriated state, floundered backward at the abrupt shift in balance, arms wind milling until he landed hard against the front door. Sandy and Rose had stepped neatly out of the way.

Alex grabbed the back of the little girl's nightgown as she once again tried to go to her father. "Where's your Mommy, Nicole?"

"M... Mommy?" Nicole's head turned and Alex followed her gaze to see Jen, Nicole's mother, lying sprawled on the bottom three steps of the main staircase. She had blood sheeting the right side of her face and appeared to be unconscious.

Darryl made a sudden lunge. Alex shoved the little girl behind her back and stood her ground, letting him get within a foot before cocking the rifle's hammer. The sound was quite distinctive, and well-known to him if the flare of alarm in his eyes was anything to go by.

"Sandy, take Nicole to the kitchen for a Popsicle, would you?"

"Uh, sure, Alex." The blond twenty-two-year-old was pale, but she willingly sidled past Darryl and scooped Nicole up in her arms.

"Daddy! I want my Daddy..." Nicole's cries faded as the kitchen door swung closed.

"Rose, you've called—"

"I'm on it." Rose already had her cellphone tucked tight to her ear. "Yes, hi, I need an ambulance and the police to..."

Alex focused her attention on Darryl, who was looking more sober by the second. "The police respond quickly when we call, Mr. Grier. Do you really want to be around when they get here?"

Darryl shifted on his feet, as if contemplating another attack. Alex raised the gun to her shoulder, lining his forehead up in the sight. "I'll be back," he muttered as he scuttled out the door.

* * * *

Four hours later, Alex was trying to find the front door lock with her house key. The porch light was out for some reason, despite that she'd just changed the bulb, and the task of fitting the key in the lock was proving annoyingly difficult. She was bone weary. Giving a statement, seeing Jen to the hospital and getting Nicole settled down had drained her already low resources, and she was reluctantly thinking that Kasdeya was going to have to spend the night alone. She had to be up in five hours to get ready for the picnic.

Hopefully, Darryl would be behind bars by then. The cops had assured her he would be, but they hadn't caught up with him yet. There was an APB out on him though, and his house was being watched. It was just a matter of time.

Regardless, they'd *all* be more careful in the future. Darryl Grier wouldn't be getting in Dovescot again. Sandy, with tears streaming down her face, had admitted that she'd propped the front door open to carry in groceries and then forgotten about it. She'd offered to resign, but Alex had declined. The girl was good with the children, and she really was sorry.

When the key finally slipped home, Alex sighed in relief. As the door swung inward, the little lamp she always left on in the hall illuminated the edge of a box on the front porch. It was tucked in beside the door next to her wicker rocker. Yay! She stooped to pick it up. Tonight might be out, but tomorrow he would be in for—

Just as she bent over, there was a rush of wind and the deafening *thwock* of something hitting the doorjamb at the height where her head had been. Her self-defense lessons proved their worth; without even stopping to think about it, Alex ducked her head against her knees and rolled through the front door, coming to a sideways stop on her hall rug. A man stood framed in the doorway, his face so twisted in anger that it took a second for her to realize it was Darryl Grier. He had a wooden baseball bat grasped tight in his right hand.

"No one takes my family, bitch!"

Alex swiveled—rug and all—and, with all her strength, kicked the door closed as he was stepping through. There was another *thwock* of wood against flesh, followed by a grunt of pain. She sincerely hoped it was his head that had taken the brunt of the blow, but she wasn't sticking around to find out. Scrambling to her feet, Alex raced toward the stairs and the nine-mil she kept in her night table drawer.

The front door slammed back against the wall. "Fuckin' whore!" he bellowed.

She put on a burst of speed and had just made it to the turn, six stairs up, when his hand closed around her ankle.

"Gotcha!"

Alex screamed, more out of anger than fear, as he dragged her backward. When she twisted in his grip, her right shoulder came down hard on the next step. This time, her scream was one of agony.

"Fuck you!" she screeched, lashing out with her sneakered foot. She only grazed his arm, but his attention shifted to swat at her shoe, and her next kick landed with satisfying solidity against his temple. Darryl slipped down, shaking his head.

Rather than turn and run, Alex bumped down a stair to follow him and took another shot at his jaw. That was enough to snap his head back, unbalancing him. He tumbled to the bottom.

Then she ran.

Each step sent a jolt of pain through her shoulder, but Alex ignored it. She could hear Darryl only steps behind her and knew she'd never have time to get to her gun. When she hit the top riser, Alex raced into the bathroom, which was the only door with a lock. She turned the key just in time.

Darryl didn't even try the knob. He just beat on the door with his bat.

"What is happening?" Kasdeya shouted from behind the sheets. He'd been shouting for a while now, but she'd been too distracted to answer.

"I'm having some technical difficulty," she called, looking around for anything she could use as a weapon. The hair dryer? Alex snorted. Sure, she could always blow dry him to death! Brush, towels... Fuck! Why are bathrooms so ill equipped for impromptu battles?

Darryl had concentrated his rage on the doorknob. Any second now...

"Summon me!" Kasdeya ordered.

Alex didn't answer. Her gaze flicked over the toilet then flicked back. She'd once seen a movie in which serious damage had been inflicted with a toilet-tank lid by a girl not any bigger than her. Here's hoping that was more realistic than having someone fall unconscious when hit in the head with a rifle butt. When she tried to pry the ceramic slab off, her shoulder screamed in protest. Alex screamed as well, and Kasdeya's voice became frantic.

"What's happened? Damn you, woman, summon—"

The door finally gave. Darryl inched it open, apparently leery of having her fly at him.

Alex rifled through the various spells she'd been reading. She only had seconds, so she'd have to forgo the usual, drawn-out rituals and get right to the heart of the matter.

"Kasdeya," she whispered. "Bow to my will and heed my call. Slave to my whim, I summon you."

Darryl finally found the courage to enter the room. A triumphant grin split his face when he saw the way she was cradling her arm, her body hunched in pain.

"Well, lookee who's not so—"

The disorienting sound of birds taking flight filled the bathroom. There was a whirling flash of white followed by midnight black, and suddenly Kasdeya stood in front of her, wings extended to brush against the walls. His face was a mask of fury. He took in her damaged state and opened his mouth—no doubt to demand an explanation—but Alex just jerked her chin toward Darryl, who was directly behind her dark man. Now that Kasdeya had arrived, her body was succumbing to shock and her teeth were chattering too badly to say anything.

Kasdeya half turned to glance over his shoulder. Alex's heart paused at the snarl of rage that twisted his lips when he saw Darryl standing there. Darryl must have found the sight frightening as well, since the sharp scent of urine immediately followed his glimpse of the fallen angel's face. He let out a mouse-like squeak and ran.

* * * *

Kasdeya spared a second to turn back to Alex. He was torn between taking her in his arms and kissing away the pain, or hunting down and killing the worm who had dared to hurt her. "Are you…"

She sat down on the toilet seat and nodded, waving him on.

Good enough. The worm won. Kasdeya disappeared in another kaleidoscope of sound and color to coalesce in front of the man as he was half-running, half-falling down the stairs. He didn't say a word as he reached out and wrapped his fist around the worm's throat, lifting him high in the air to strangle him. The man's face turned a satisfying shade of puce as blood vessels burst in his eyes, giving him the crazed, frightened stare of a wounded bull. The fallen angel grinned. "Touching my woman was a mistake, don't you agree?"

The man's hands scrabbled at Kasdeya's. More pungent urine scent sullied the air.

"Don't kill him," Alexandra called in a hoarse whisper from the top of the stairs.

It was unfortunate that she felt that way because the man *was* going to die.

"What the...?" Kasdeya looked at his hand in shock as it loosened in response to her command. He turned to her. "What have you done, Summoner?" His voice shook with anger.

Kasdeya kept enough pressure on the worm's throat to render him unconscious before letting him go. The man tumbled down the stairs. There was a sharp, brittle crack of bone against wood as his skull hit the bottom step. He came to rest looking like a broken puppet, his neck bent at an angle it was never meant to achieve. But technically Kasdeya hadn't killed him. He'd just dropped him.

Alexandra gasped and brushed past, hurrying to the worm's side. Her fingers found his wrist and she grimaced. Next, her hand moved to his neck. She sat on her haunches for a few seconds, feeling frantically for a pulse. When she couldn't find one, she hissed an oath and stood, once again cradling her injured arm.

"I told you not to kill him," she said. "I thought..." Her brows drew down.

"You thought to bind me?" he asked, walking slowly down the stairs. She looked so miserable, skin pale, eyes wide with shock. Kasdeya's anger drained away, replaced by a more tender emotion. "Why?" he whispered, halting in front of her. "Why did you do that, little one?" His fingers brushed her cheek.

Alexandra sighed and swayed toward him. He wrapped his arms around her holding her close, safe.

"I just..." She shrugged, and then winced. Kasdeya placed his palm on her shoulder, directing her dislocation to reset and her torn muscle to heal. Hopefully such a small use of power wouldn't be noticed. He'd set up a guard as soon as he was able. "You just what?"

Her eyes shifted away from his. "Look at who you are," she said. "At *what* you are. I had to try to contain you, don't you see?"

His hand left her shoulder to tilt her chin up. "I already gave you my word, Alexandra. Was that not enough?"

She frowned, tossing her head in the direction of the dead man. "That's what your word seems to be worth." Resentment had crept into her tone.

It was Kasdeya's turn to frown. "That's not fair. He was—"

"Not to harm, or cause to be harmed," she quoted. Alexandra stepped away from him to cross the hall and shut the front door. She slid the deadbolt into place. "Anyway, the binding obviously didn't take. Now I'll have to send you back." She turned to face him, her full lips drawn down in disappointment. "I'd really hoped it would," she said. "Then you could have stayed."

Kasdeya blinked. Alexandra didn't know it had worked?

Good. If she didn't know, then she wouldn't try to control him. But how could he get her to let him remain on Earth without telling her that he was, indeed, well and truly bound?

She crossed her arms, scowling down at the worm's body. "Before I banish you though, could you handle this for me?"

He crossed his own arms. "And what would be my motivation to do that, pet?"

His little Summoner glared at him through the curtain of her long honey-brown hair. Kasdeya ignored the impulse to grab her and kiss her senseless, to make her smile and moan for him again. He was fighting for his freedom here. He had to remain focused.

"Well, gee," Alexandra said. "I don't suppose 'it would be the right thing to do' carries much weight with you. I didn't kill him after all, but if he's found here…"

"I'd be happy to 'handle it' for you, Alexandra. However, I refuse to be sent away like a servant after the dirty work has been done."

She whirled away. "I can't let you stay, Kasdeya. You're a demon. You could—"

Kasdeya leaped over the dead man's body to grab her arms and tug her back around. "If you call me a demon one more time, woman," he growled, "you'll get to see exactly how demonic I can be."

"Oh, for fuck's sake," she snapped, tears welling in her eyes. "Can't you do me this one god-damned favor?"

"Yes, I can…if you let me stay on Earth. You have my word that I won't harm anyone." He gazed seriously down at her, raising a hand to smooth away the water on her face. "Unless they attempt to harm you," he added. "Then I'll do what I have to." He tugged her close to whisper in her ear. "Trust me."

"If I let you stay, you won't just leave?" she asked just as softly, revealing more about what was in her heart than she probably realized.

Kasdeya's chest tightened. He should do exactly that. "I cannot," he said. "I have to stay close to the one who summoned me." He wasn't lying, he just wasn't being entirely forthcoming. Alexandra *could* grant his freedom at any time. That had been the plan after all: to convince her to summon then release him. If he stayed, the risk was…

It didn't matter. She was worth the risk. Kasdeya pressed a kiss to her temple. "Trust me, little one," he said again.

After a second, Alexandra nodded. The corpse disappeared.

* * * *

Alex was furious with herself. She'd just watched Kasdeya ruthlessly kill a man. She should *want* to banish him back to that prison. That thought only made her miserable though. Now that he was here, in her home, she wanted him to stay. She wanted Kasdeya in her life for more than just a few hours a night. She wanted him there all the time, every damn minute. And him cuddling her, being so soothing, coaxing, breathtaking—being his own magnificent self—wasn't any help at all.

Damn it.

"Well," she said in a voice that was as cool as she could manage as she stepped away from his too welcome embrace, "I'll get some sheets and make up the guest bed for you."

She needed to give herself some space to think this through. One night apart wouldn't kill either of them.

Kasdeya scooped her up in his arms. "I don't think so."

"Put me down." She smacked ineffectively at his naked, sculpted chest.

"First, I'm going to bathe you," he said as he ascended the stairs. "*Then* I will put you down in our bed."

"Our... In our bed?" Alex's voice rose in indignation. "It's my—"

His lips cut her off. As usual, his kiss quickly made her forget everything but how much she loved him and how damned much she wanted him. Her hands crept around his neck.

"Shut up," Kasdeya whispered when he lifted his mouth away from hers.

"Okay," she said with a sigh, snuggling closer to lay her head against his heart. His laughter rumbled under her ear, making her smile. Maybe she didn't need to think it through. She loved him, that's all there was to it. The fact that he was a dem—was Fallen... Well, that was a problem for another time.

Chapter 9

"Mpph. Die, Mickey Mouse!" Alex grumbled, tugging her pillow over her head to dull the shrill alarm. Her hand reached out blindly to slap at the top of her night table. She found a warm male body instead.

"I can't seem to turn it off," Kasdeya said, sounding both annoyed and amused.

Alex's eyes snapped open. He was beside her, in her bed. Her stomach fluttered at the thought. Last night, true to his word, Kasdeya had bathed her, healed a huge bruise on her leg that she didn't even remember getting and tucked her in, wrapping his large body around hers. When she'd tried to make things more intimate, he'd refused, saying she was too tired and that, after such a shock, her body needed "rest." That was how he'd probably finished that sentence. Alex couldn't be sure; she'd passed out before she'd heard the word.

"Smack his nose," she instructed, peeking out from under the pillow.

Kasdeya gave the clock a hard slap. The ringing stopped at once. "Ah, yes. Very satisfying." He set the clock back on the night table and rolled to face her, tickling her nose where it poked out from under the goose down. "Come out and play, little rabbit."

Alex sighed and tucked the pillow back under her head. "I'd like to spend all day in bed with you, dark man, but I have to go."

His hand crept under the sheet, sliding down her ribs and across her stomach to end up between her thighs. He gave her mons a squeeze. "Are you sure?"

"Hmm." She turned more fully toward him and hooked a thigh over his hip. "I suppose a quickie might be doable."

His palm had stayed between her legs. One finger crooked to test her opening and Alex moaned, pushing against it. "A quickie?" he asked.

She reached down to stroke his cock. "A really fast fuck."

"Ah, no," Kasdeya said. "I don't do 'fast fucks.'"

Alex gaped at him. "You're a tease!"

"Am I?" Another finger entered her.

"Yes, I think you are," she said with a dreamy smile as he twisted his fingers inside her. Kasdeya leaned in to kiss her but she turned her face away. "Morning breath."

Her mouth flooded with the taste of spearmint and a third finger breached her as his tongue did the same. His other hand joined the first between her thighs to roll her clit between his thumb and forefinger.

Alex moaned and opened her mouth wider for him. Her palm glided over his erection, so hard, so smooth. She closed her fingers, as well as she could, around him. This was *hers.*

Kasdeya gasped her name and his hands between her legs became rough. Her clit was a throbbing ache, caught between cruel fingers. Alex shuddered as the climax she'd been leisurely climbing toward suddenly broke over her without warning.

God, she loved him. "Love..." she gasped into his mouth, clutching him close, "...you."

* * * *

Kasdeya's pulse leaped at her declaration and he pulled his head back. Alexandra's eyes were closed, her mouth slack and slick from his kiss. He realized that she didn't even know what she'd just said. His prick, already like marble, thickened even more as an intense surge of emotion flushed through his body.

The Summoner's hands left his groin to splay across his chest, nails sinking deep. "Kasdeya," she moaned, her head thrashing from side to side.

"Little angel," he growled back, yanking his fingers away to thrust his cock deep into her greedy body.

She screamed when he surged into her. Her hips bucked and her sex clamped tight around him as a second orgasm rocketed through her. In only two strokes, Kasdeya followed. His teeth sank into her collarbone at the same moment his seed flooded her womb. Alexandra whimpered at the pain, but her inner walls tightened around him further and, rather than push him away, his wonderful woman rolled onto her back, pulling him on top of her, and bit his throat just as hard.

The hot hurt was exquisite. Kasdeya couldn't stop groaning, couldn't stop pumping, couldn't stop coming. She was so damned perfect. Shaitan help him, he thought he might actually love her too.

* * * *

Kasdeya's wings were fully extended, taking up almost fourteen feet of space. He fanned their overheated bodies while trying to come to grips with the way this woman made him feel. How in the nine hells could he be in love with a human? How could he be in love at all? To his knowledge, genuine affection was all Angels and Fallen had ever been capable of. He wished he wasn't in hiding because he'd dearly like to ask his Prince if this had ever happened before.

Maybe it was just lust. True, he'd never been this strongly in "lust" before, and lust didn't actually describe what he was experiencing, but—

"I thought you didn't do quickies." Alexandra's tone was husky and intimate as her hands stroked through his hair.

His cock, only half-hard now, gave an excited little jerk, like a dog that hears its master's voice. Kasdeya frowned. No, this was way beyond lust. Dangerous infatuation, maybe?

He raised his head from where it was resting on her breasts to look her in the eye. "I decided to make an exception for you, pet."

"Oh-ho!" Alexandra laughed and shifted her legs wider apart to rub her very wet center against his belly. "And you, of course, gained nothing from the experience."

Kasdeya's lips twitched.

"In fact," she continued, "I'm swimming in so much 'nothing' that not only am I going to have to take a shower—which I don't have time for—but you're going to have to change the sheets while I'm gone."

He lifted himself off her body and looked down. Yes, Alexandra was overflowing with his…infatuation. "Get in the shower then, little one," he said. "I'll change the linens."

She sat up, pouting. "Why don't you change them when I'm gone? I wanted to take a shower with you."

Alexandra seemed to have forgotten that she wasn't going *anywhere* without him. Rather than remind her of that fact, Kasdeya slid to the edge of the bed. After all, he wasn't entirely sure of the spell's range. Maybe she didn't have to take him along if her destination was close. Besides, knowing Alexandra, she'd waste more time arguing about it than it would take to discover the truth for herself.

He strode out the bedroom door in search of clean linens. "If I get in the shower with you, you know you'll never get out of here."

He had to chuckle at her reluctant grumble of agreement.

* * * *

"So, if you're feeling really industrious, there's the floor stripper in the basement," Alexandra said as she twisted her hair up into a bun.

Kasdeya nodded from where he was lounging naked on the stairs. "I'm sure I'll find something to amuse myself. Go. You're late as it is."

She glanced at her watch and her eyes flared with alarm. "God, yeah, I'm so late." She tucked a yellow shirt with a smiley face into her snug, faded blue trousers and then grabbed her satchel from the hall table. "Listen, about Darryl…"

"Who?"

"The… The fellow from last night, he—"

"Is handled."

"But where is he? What did you—"

"I'll explain later." Kasdeya stood. "Go," he said again, taking her face between his palms to plant a kiss on her forehead.

"Okay." She tilted her mouth up to his and wasted a few more precious seconds. Kasdeya didn't complain. She pulled away with a moan. "I've really got to go."

"Who's stopping you?"

Alexandra grinned. "I'll see you tonight."

Probably sooner than that. But Kasdeya just nodded again and shooed her out the door.

When she'd left, he picked up some of the fliers that had dropped through the mail slot that morning. He chose one to leaf through. It was from an establishment called Wal-Mart, which seemed to have many examples of clothing similar to what Alexandra chose to wear. The rest of the papers he tossed onto a box in the corner.

* * * *

It started as an itch behind her eyes. Alex rubbed her forehead and wondered if she was getting a summer cold. No time for that, though. She ignored it.

A few blocks further and the itch had turned into a pounding headache. She steered with one hand while the other shielded her eyes against the glare of the morning sun. When she drove past a pharmacy, Alex U-turned, planning to buy the largest bottle of Advil they had and eat half of it. She really couldn't afford to be sick today.

As soon as she was facing in the opposite direction, the pain began to ease. Good. She had no time to stop, anyway. Alex about-faced again. But right before the ramp onto the interstate, she pulled over, feeling so sick she could barely see, let alone drive. The sudden, thunderous racket of hundreds of birds had her retching. Then the pain disappeared.

She suddenly heard Kasdeya's deep voice from the seat beside her. "You know, you keep assuring me you're not stupid."

She turned her head and gasped. He was wingless. And clothed. What the hell?

"But actions speak louder than words, Alexandra." His black eyes twinkled. "And the fact that you kept going when the pain was enough to bring *me* to my knees indicates that you are not the brightest star in the heavens."

"Where are your wings?"

He twisted in his seat, showing her his shoulder blades. Behind the straps of the blank tank top he was wearing was the most beautiful tattoo Alex had ever seen.

"Take your shirt off," she said softly, awestruck. She unbuckled her seat belt to face him better and ran a finger over the double arch of the image.

"Aren't you late, pet?"

She lightly smacked his ribs. "Just take it off. I'm already so late, what could possibly be the difference?"

As he lifted the shirt over his head—an acrobatic maneuver, to say the least, in her bug's cramped front seat, and she figured he must have dropped a few inches of height to be able to maneuver at all—she smacked him again, not so lightly. "Am I to understand that you knew the pain I was going to be experiencing and happily sent me off anyway?"

"*We* were going to be experiencing," he corrected, his words muffled in cotton. "When I said I was on my knees, it wasn't an exaggeration. And no, I wasn't sure what the range of the summoning spell was—or the effects of separation."

"You must have had an idea though…" She trailed off as she skimmed her palms over the gorgeous wings inked on his skin. They started just under the fall of his glossy black hair, flaring out to cover both scapula and then narrowing to hug his rib cage. Each feather was perfectly delineated, every plume highlighted in electric blue, shading down to deepest ebony. She tried to pull his waistband out to see the bottom of the image, but his jeans were too tight.

"I didn't, Alexandra, or I would never have let you go." He twisted his upper body to look her in the eye. "Believe me."

Alex sighed, still stroking his back. "I do. I'm sorry. I should never have thought you would…" She shrugged. "I'm sorry."

"I forgive you."

When he leaned in for a kiss, she ducked away. "None of that now. Once we start, it's too hard to stop."

His expression wry, Kasdeya nodded his agreement.

Her fingers traced his waistband. "Can I see the rest before we go?"

"You won't kiss me but you want to see me naked?" Kasdeya snorted. "I think not, woman." He turned away again, presenting her with his back straight on. The tattoo flickered and moved, the wings curling tight together and then unfolding once more.

"Oh!" Alex cried, snatching her hand back. She laughed at the start he had given her. "Very impressive, dark man."

"Always," he said, getting re-dressed.

Alex shook her head and started the car. "Modest too."

"I'll pass as a mortal then?" Kasdeya asked, copying her movement as she buckled her seatbelt. He grinned when the little car picked up speed, opening his window to feel the wind in his hair.

She glanced over, trying to see him impartially. He was wearing jeans as faded as hers, the black tank-top and running shoes—no socks, she noticed. He looked just as casual as could be. But human? No. For one thing, his skin was still alabaster white and his face was far more perfect than any man's had a right to be. "Can you darken your skin a little?"

"Yes. Tell me when you'd like me to stop."

She kept sneaking glances at him as she maneuvered through traffic. When he had reached a uniform caramel brown, she stopped him.

"Anything else?" he asked.

Alex thought about telling him to make his appearance less ideal, but she just couldn't make herself utter the words. If he weren't as beautiful as a god, he wouldn't be her Kasdeya. "Mmm, I can't think of—oh, wait. Pores."

"Pores?"

"Yeah." She gestured to her face. "You know, skin pores. All humans have them."

"Ah." He ducked his head close to hers. "Better?"

She risked a full glance at his face, one that lasted much too long while driving at sixty-plus miles an hour. He looked amazing in bronze, although she couldn't see the pores he'd supposedly created. The blare of a horn drew her attention back to the road, where it belonged, and Alex swerved back into her own lane. "Yes, you look fine," she said in a husky voice.

Kasdeya leaned even closer, swirling his tongue into her ear. His hand crept up her inner thigh. "Just fine?"

A full body shudder twitched Alex's hands on the steering wheel. "Stop it. You're going to get us killed."

"I would never let you die, pet," he said, but he sat back again. His hand remained on her leg, however, gliding up and down, up and down.

She racked her brain for something to take her mind off the caress. "Darryl!" she blurted. "Tell me what you did with Darryl." Alex really felt she should be feeling some guilt there, but she wasn't. The guy was an asshole and, in the long run, Nicole and Jen were better off without him. She wanted to make sure that he really was gone though, and not waiting to be discovered in a dumpster somewhere.

"Mexico." Kasdeya gazed out the window in obvious disinterest at the conversation. "There's a deep trench off the coast full of carnivorous squid. Their suckers are lined with razor sharp teeth." He gave her thigh a pinch and laughed at her yelp. "He's gone, Summoner. Do not concern yourself with it further."

Alex nodded, satisfied. Good riddance. She studied her dark man's profile for a second. "You know, a hoop earring would look fabulous on you."

He threw her an arrogant smile. "Do you think so?"

Chapter 10

The picnic was in full swing with the entire house present, as well as their families and friends. There were more than a hundred people, twice as many as they had planned on. Alex was going to have to do an emergency food run soon. Unfortunately, that would mean leaving the sundae machine unattended. Since it was a nice, sunny day and ice cream was so popular, that was something she was loathe to do.

Rose was still shooting her dirty looks whenever she got the chance, which wasn't very often. One of the clowns had bailed and Rose had bravely stepped in to take his place. Her already wild, long red hair was teased out into a monstrous afro and, to make matters worse, she'd fallen over her size-thirteen purple sneakers at least twice.

Truth be told, Alex thought her friend was more pissed at being presented to Kasdeya—"Kas" was how he'd actually introduced himself—dressed in a shiny silver "fat" suit than at Alex for finally turning up with her mystery man.

Kasdeya had smoothly explained that it was his fault Alex hadn't told anyone about him, and had made up some bullshit story about how he'd "had new relationships jinxed too many times" and now insisted on keeping them secret until he was "sure they would last."

Alex had stood behind Rose giving him a "Huh? Are you serious?" look over the redhead's shoulder. But Rose had seemed to go for it hook, line and sinker, and had patted her dark man's shoulder in a very untypical—for Rose anyway—flirty gesture, saying, "I completely understand, Kas." Alex had turned her "Huh?" look on her friend, but Rose hadn't noticed, being too busy batting her ridiculously long, ridiculously purple eyelashes at Kasdeya.

Alex was in the middle of putting sprinkles on a cone for another young Dovescot guest when she looked across the grass aisle to where Kasdeya was working the carousel and saw Sandy hiking up his shirt. A horde of sycophantic women had surrounded him all morning. Even women that professed to hate *all* men had sidled close to Kasdeya for a look and a grope. He'd had so many admirers that Alex had only been able to make out his head and shoulders above the milling crowd. Until now.

Now, she could see entirely too clearly how Sandy's pale blond head was bent close to Kasdeya's back; how her much-too-large breasts in that much-too-tight tee were much too close to her dark man's body. Christ, why hadn't she ever noticed that Sandy was built like a brick shithouse?

Then the little hussy's hands feathered across his broad shoulders and down his ribs to the top of his jeans, which were also much too tight. Was loose clothing passé all of a sudden?

"Tam." Alex reached out to pluck at the jersey of a sullen fourteen-year-old boy as he sidled past. "Take over here, would ya?"

Tam sneered. "Aw, come on, Alex."

Alex gestured to his half-eaten cone. "You can eat it. You can serve it."

She was sick up to here with Tam, who, though his mother had arrived at Dovescot with three broken ribs, insisted that his parents' problems were her fault. He was very resentful at being uprooted from his home, and counseling didn't seem to be improving his attitude much.

"Buck up, kid." Alex untied her apron and tossed it in his general direction. Tam grabbed for it with his right hand, dropping his cone in the process. "There, see," she said. "You can be your own first customer."

With a grumble, the teenager threw the apron over the cart's handle and set about making himself another cone, one at least three times the size of his previous. Alex rolled her eyes and left him to it, beginning her stalk across the thirty feet of trampled ground that separated her from the cute couple. Grass was so unsatisfying to stomp on.

"You aren't seriously going to leave him there, are you?" Rose asked from behind her.

"No, I'm gonna go tear her bouncy little head off." Alex watched through narrowed eyes as Sandy proceeded to lift her pink tee all the way up to the bottom of her bodacious ta-tas to reveal a tattoo of her own. A vine and rose pattern wreathed around her oh-so-cute belly-button.

Rose grabbed Alex's arm. "I meant him," she said, jerking her thumb at Tam, who was lounging against the cart and completely ignoring the two children in front of him trying to order ice cream. Rose's gaze drifted over Alex's shoulder. "Though I can understand why you wouldn't want to leave *him* alone, either. Who knew Sandy was such a playa?"

Alex whipped back around to see Sandy baring her right breast to Kasdeya. What the fuck? All right, so her nipple was still covered, barely, but the rest of the full globe was just hangin' there. Kasdeya had bent over the girl for a closer look at what was, apparently, another tattoo. It had better be another tattoo!

"God damn it." Alex swiped a hand through her hair and half-tore out her bun in the process. With an impatient curse, she ripped it the rest of the way down, letting the pins fall to the ground. "Tam!" she snapped.

He looked up with another sneer. The kid was a real Elvis.

"I made it!" Alex heard a feminine, humor-filled voice behind her. "Didn't know if I was going to. I must have pissed off someone important, 'cause my karma's been screwed all week."

Alex swiveled to greet the new arrival. Melynda was decked out in a black denim mini and a low-cut red top. She was gesturing with a clove cigarette, waving it around in front of her perfectly made-up face and her perfectly tousled auburn hair as she told her tale of woe.

"First, there's a fire in the back of the store," Melynda said. "Nothing serious, thank the powers that be, but still." She took a deep drag of her cig before saying, "Then my ex-mother-in-law pops by for a 'chat.' Seems hubby-be-gone is wanting a reunion." A disgusted roll of dark-lined eyes. "As if. And then today, didn't my entire transmission just hit the friggin' ground." One more drag and she tossed the butt down to stomp it under the three-inch heel of her knee-high leather boots. "But I made it, ladies." She flourished her arm and bowed. "Where do you need me?"

Rose laughed at Melynda's theatrics. "Glad you could make it, hon. We could sure use the help." She nodded toward the ice-cream cart and the sulking boy standing in front of it. "Why don't you start by teaching yon adolescent some manners? Alex needs to go rescue her boyfriend from the evil clutches of that blond bombshell over there, so she has to bail on the cone making."

Melynda's gaze followed Rose's across the way. She whistled long and low. "I usually say let men fend for themselves. Sink or swim, baby. But if any man was worth rescuing, it would be that one." She grinned wickedly at Alex. "I'll expect an introduction later though."

Alex's answering smile was weak. Great! Another hottie to parade in front of him. Only this one didn't have a cheerleader's sweet, virginal look going for her. Oh no. Melynda looked like sex on wheels. "Of course I'll introduce you," she said with a resigned sigh.

"So ice cream, huh?" Melynda looked gleeful. "Is it okay to do the 'one for you, two for me' thing?"

"Absolutely!" said Rose. "I'm supposed to be carrying around a basket of bonbons." She held up her hands and wriggled her fingers. "Do you see any bonbons? I figure if I get to look fat, I get to eat fat."

"Good deal," Melynda said. "And a teenager to slap around? Who could ask for anything more?"

Tam was close enough to hear their conversation. Alex saw his eyes widen before he whirled around and started making ice-cream cones as if his life depended on it. She laughed. "If anyone can whip him into shape, I'm sure you can, Melynda. Thanks for coming to help out, I really appreciate it."

Melynda shook her head. "Are you kidding? Hot dogs *and* ice cream on a sunny afternoon? I wouldn't have missed it." She winked at them and then made a big show of strutting over to Tam. Her sneer beat his hands down. "Don't you dare forget those sprinkles, boy."

Alex and Rose shared a grin as they walked away together. "I asked Mel if she'd mind helping out today," Rose said. "Hope that was okay."

"You know it was. We need all the help we can get."

Rose nodded. "That's what I figured, and she seemed really interested in coming when I told her about it." She cocked her head and cast Alex an odd glance. "She said she wanted to talk to you again anyway. She didn't say about what though."

Alex studied the ground and shrugged. "Beats me."

Rose stopped walking. When Alex looked back up, she saw Rose frowning at her again. "Uh huh. Well, I guess I'd better get back to work," her friend said, about-facing.

Alex sighed. This was starting to really suck. She'd never fought with Rose before and it killed her that she couldn't be truthful with her best friend now.

Then Sandy's breathy giggle pulled her thoughts back to Kasdeya.

She hurried over to disengage her dark man from Sandy's delicate clutches, using the excuse that he needed to lug the ice she was getting on the supply run. The young blonde was left in charge of the carousel, and she didn't look happy about it, a fact which lightened Alex's spirits considerably.

* * * *

"That's the last of it," Kasdeya said as he dumped the final bag of ice into one of the plastic coolers.

Alex was leaning against the edge of a picnic table and rolling a can of Pepsi around on her forehead. It was only spring, but it felt like midsummer.

Kasdeya grabbed a handful of ice chips as he straightened back up. "Are you hot, pet?" he asked.

She eyed him warily and started to edge away. "I'm *fine,* pet. Thanks."

His errant smile was all the warning she had before he lunged. Alex squealed when he scooped her up with one arm, holding her tight around the waist as he shoved ice down the back of her top. Her legs flailed uselessly. "You're so gonna regret that!" she said, reaching behind her to slap at his head.

He was laughing so hard he sounded like he was choking, and her frantic struggles seemed to only be making him laugh harder. Suddenly, a soft female chuckle wove around his louder guffaws. It wasn't Alex's.

"I came to tell you we're out of ice cream," said Melynda. Alex and Kasdeya turned their heads in unison. Melynda was sitting less than two feet away on one of the pop coolers, but they'd been too wrapped up in their game to notice her approach. "I'll take that introduction now, Alexandra."

Alex smacked Kasdeya's arm where it was still snug around her waist, holding her suspended above the ground. She slid down his body and he sniggered again when ice fell out the bottom of her shirt.

She shot him a dirty look. "There are more ice cream packets in the back of Rose's van, Melynda," she said, turning her attention to the dark-haired woman. "And this jerk here is Kasd—"

"Kas," Kasdeya said smoothly, stepping around Alex to present himself to Melynda.

Melynda's mouth fell open. She looked like a modern, sexy version of Munch's *The Scream.* Kasdeya slanted Alex a confused glance. Alex started to shrug her own puzzlement when Melynda slipped off the cooler to one knee. "Prince Kasdeya," she said, bowing her head. "I am most honored."

Kasdeya's breath hissed through his teeth with his sharp inhale of shock. This time, the glance he directed at Alex was full of anger.

"Mortal, you will address me as *Kas* from this moment forward," he said, turning his attention back to Melynda. "Is that understood?"

"Yes, Prince Ka... Er, Kas." Melynda still hadn't risen.

"By the nine hells, woman, get up." He leaned over to grip her arms and yank her to her feet. "You're causing a scene." He turned to Alex. "Who else did you tell about me?" he asked.

Alex frowned. "Just her."

His hands still held Melynda's biceps and his fingers tightened cruelly on her fair skin. "And you?" he asked with a curl to his lip. "How many have you told, witch?"

"M-My coven, my Prince... No one else. I'm so—"

"Damnation," he hissed, shoving her away. Melynda tripped over the cooler and fell against the picnic table before landing back on her knees. Kasdeya rounded on Alex with a pointed finger. "What were you thinking, telling her about me?" His voice grew louder with every syllable. If they hadn't been creating a scene before, they certainly were now.

"I was thinking I needed a little help," she said. "I didn't know anything about you."

"You could have asked!" he roared. "Now—"

"Now," she said, deadly quiet, "you're scaring the children. Lower your voice, dark man. If you have a problem, you can take it up with me later. But there's absolutely no reason for you to lose your mind and assault my friends in the middle of a family picnic. I think you owe Melynda an apology."

He looked at the people around them—folks spread out on a blanket not twenty feet away, a group of kids playing Frisbee just behind them—and, too late, realized that they'd all frozen in shock at the sight of him yelling and tossing a woman around. The sound of a little girl crying as she buried her face in her mother's skirts was loud in the surprised silence. Her mother hushed her and turned her body to shield the child from his view.

Kasdeya swore and ran his hands through his hair. "I apologize, witch," he finally said. He turned his attention to Alex. "If you could hurry up and finish here, Alexandra, I need to get back to the house."

"First off, her name's Melynda, not witch. And second, I have hours here yet. So why don't you go cool off and then take over at the carousel again. Anything you need to do at home is going have to wait until this evening."

Kasdeya's jaw clenched and his eyes locked combatively with hers. Alex glared right back. The tension stretched out like taffy in the hot, afternoon sun.

"Look, I'm sorry, didn't mean to cause a problem," Melynda said tentatively.

Kasdeya broke their staring contest to answer her. "I realize that... *Melynda*." His eyes flicked to Alex again and he graced her with a tight-lipped smile before looking back at the witch. "Nonetheless, a problem *has* been caused." He bowed to her. "It's been a pleasure, I'm sure," he said, his voice dripping sarcasm. With a final, hot glare at Alex, he strode away.

"He certainly is beautiful," Melynda said, after he'd disappeared from sight.

Yep. Too bad he was acting like a raving asshole. "I'm sorry," Alex said. "I don't know what's the matter with him."

Melynda cast her eyes down, looking guilty, and reached into her pocket for her pack of cigarettes. "I think I do." She lit one up. "Please tell the Prince I apologize for—"

"*You* certainly don't have anything to—"

"I do. I should have known better than to talk about him. Demons are secretive for a reason. It was just so exciting, I had to tell someone, ya know?" She rubbed the bridge of her nose. "Anyway, tell him if there's anything I can do..."

"What reason?"

"...You can give me a—Pardon?"

"You said, 'Demons are secretive for a reason.' What reason?"

"Well, so the Powers don't come after them, of course."

"The Powers?"

"Yes. The Powers. God's warrior angels defending humanity from evil's influence. Led by Uriel, otherwise known as"—she made the double-quotations gesture with her hands—"the Lord's cleansing fire, the scourge of demonkind, et cetera."

Alex could only imagine the expression she wore. This was all news to her.

"You mean you don't..." Melynda looked at her askance. "Alexandra, hasn't he told you anything?"

Alex took a seat at the picnic table and gestured for Melynda to sit as well. "No, he hasn't. But you can."

* * * *

The ride home was accomplished in strained silence.

Kasdeya leaned his head against the window and considered how best to apologize. He'd had a damned good reason to be angry though. The witch should have known better! Unfortunately, there was no way to explain that to Alexandra without also explaining the danger he'd put her in just by being in her life and her bed.

He stroked his hand over his mouth. By the nine hells, he should have left by now. Should have stuck with the bloody plan.

Kasdeya glanced over at her. The Summoner was exquisite, even with her brows drawn down and her mouth thinned in anger. Look at her. She was so lovely. So innocent. How *could* he leave?

But if anything happened to her it would be entirely on his head.

He sighed and turned back to the scenery speeding by. Nothing was going to happen. He would reinforce the guard. They'd both be more careful. Nothing was going to happen.

Anyway, he still had time. If it came to it, he *would* leave, draw Uriel away and ensure her safety.

He stole another lingering glance at her profile.

But not yet.

He couldn't possibly leave her just yet.

* * * *

Alex watched in disbelief as Kasdeya walked into the house and immediately headed up the stairs. "I need some time alone," he said.

She tripped over a box in her mad rush to follow him and demand some answers. "Shit. God damn it!" she cursed, leaning one-handed against the wall to massage her sore ankle. Kasdeya rounded the bend in the stairs, not even slowing. She could only see him from the chest down now. Her anger spiked dramatically. "Stop right there, dark man!"

He did so at once and she he saw his hands curl into fists at his side. To say she was astonished would have been an understatement. She had shouted the command with absolutely no expectation of being heeded; she'd just yelled the first thing that came into her head, more for the pure satisfaction of yelling at him than anything else.

She straightened, waiting to see what he was going to do next. He did nothing. How...odd...

A wonderful thought flitted through her head. "Now turn around and come back down," she said.

Like an automaton, he moved to obey. His face was thunderous when stopped on the bottom step. "You beckoned?" he growled when she didn't say anything else.

Alex cocked her head and studied him. "You *are* bound, aren't you?"

His eyes flickered in what might have been alarm before a condescending expression settled over his features. "You saw how well your binding worked last night, Alexandra."

Yes. He'd killed Darryl, even though she'd ordered him not to. But still...

"Kasdeya, are you bound or not?"

"I don't see—"

She held up her hand. "It's a simple question. Yes or no.'"

He ground his teeth.

"Answer."

"Yes!" he spat. "Yes, I'm bound. There, are you happy?"

Alex put on her most sultry smile and walked forward to press her body against his. "Happy doesn't even begin to cover it."

Kasdeya's stiff posture loosened enough for him to wind his arms around her. "How happy?" he whispered. "Show me."

She tightened a fist in his hair and snapped a vicious bite at his throat. "Happy enough that I won't kill you for lying to me, though you deserve it."

His body went taut again. Kasdeya brought his head forward to give her a puzzled look. "I've never lied to you, Summoner."

"No?" she asked, pulling his hair harder. "A lie of omission is still a lie, is it not?"

He reached behind his neck and trapped her hand, bringing it down to his chest. "What are you talking about?"

"I'm talking about the Powers." She didn't miss the apprehension that clouded his eyes. "Want to tell me about them?"

"Who..." Realization dawned. "The witch."

"The witch," she repeated. "Why didn't *you* tell me?"

Kasdeya scowled and stepped away from her. "It wasn't supposed to become a problem," he said, walking into the living room. He sat on the sofa and patted the cushion next to him. "I was doing nothing to draw attention to myself. The house is guarded."

When she'd joined him, Kasdeya slipped his arm around her and sat back. Alex curled into his side, taking a deep breath of his cinnamon-and-rose scent. "The house is guarded?"

"Yes. The Powers shouldn't be able to sense me here. In fact, I was going to strengthen the guard when you so imperiously ordered me back down just now."

If he was waiting for an apology, he'd better not hold his breath. "So we're safe? You're safe?"

He hugged her closer. "I don't know, little one. I think we're all right, but..."

"But?"

Kasdeya looked unsure. Kasdeya never looked unsure. Alex's stomach bottomed out.

"But if they come..." He grimaced and looked away.

"What?" she asked, sitting up straight in alarm.

He took a deep breath. "If they come, are you willing to run with me?"

"What?" she asked again. "What do you mean run? I have a life here, dark man. People who depend on me. I can't just—"

"I know," he said in a low voice. He dropped his eyes to the floor, frowning. "I know you do. But if the Powers come, you might not be safe. I'll try to lead them away, but I—"

"And how exactly would you accomplish that?" she interrupted. "I thought we had to stay together." She wasn't exactly anxious for a repeat of the intense pain separation seemed to cause.

"Yes, well, you'd have to grant me the freedom to leave, of course. Then—"

"I can do that?" she asked, astonished.

He had the grace to look embarrassed, as well he might. "I was going to tell you, pet, I swear. I just didn't want you to…" He shook his head, looking unhappy. "It just seemed easier not to mention the option."

More sins of omission. Could this get any more messed up? She was in love with a demon who'd given no indication that he felt the same way, and now she might have to choose between him and the entire rest of her life. Melynda wasn't the only one with fucked karma, it would seem.

Alex's head hurt. Her heart hurt. There had to be a way to make this work. Hold on a minute… "Couldn't I just banish you back to the gray plane? Then I could summon—"

"No. Not an option. The Prince would surely notice me popping in and out of his little prison. I'm lucky I got away with it the first time."

"Well, then, I could visit…"

"No!" Kasdeya pushed his fingers against his temples. "I have no idea if our timelines would stay synced once you banished me. And if they didn't, you could be eighty or dead before I discovered the error. Not to mention the fact that I don't *want* to go back there."

"Our timelines are different?"

"The first time I saw you, less than a month ago, you looked about six years old," Kasdeya said.

Seven. The first time she'd had the dream she'd been seven years old. Alex's shoulders sagged in defeat. "Oh." Fuck.

* * * *

Alexandra sat beside him looking utterly dejected—eyes sad, little hands between little knees. It had been much too soon to ask her to commit to him. What was he thinking? "Nevermind, pet," Kasdeya murmured, drawing her into his arms once more. "Let's just enjoy the time we have without thinking too hard about tomorrow." He would strengthen the guard and it would be fine. It would have to be. He pressed a kiss to the top of her head. "All right?"

Alex sighed into his chest. "All right."

Chapter 11

Alex wandered the house like a pent-up housecat. Kasdeya had said it would only take an hour to strengthen his guard, but he'd been up on the roof for more than two. What was he doing up there?

Time crawled as she turned their conversation over and over in her mind, and Alex became more restless by the second. So many secrets. Why hadn't he trusted her with the truth in the first place? At least then she would have been prepared, would have realized the choice she might be forced to make before she'd completely lost her heart. God damn him!

The third time she walked through the front hall for no particular reason, Alex's eyes fell on the box she'd tripped over earlier. The box that had saved her life when Darryl had attacked her. The box she'd ordered from a nifty little e-store called Darker Pleasures.

The Summoner smiled—a calculating, crafty smile that would probably have given her dark man pause, if he'd been there to witness it.

* * * *

"Kasdeya…"

Alexandra's sultry-sweet voice surrounded him.

Kasdeya shook off the fugue state he had fallen into as he wove, unraveled and then rewove his defensive spell. It was as strong as he could make it, as strong a conjuration as he'd ever performed. If this was all that was standing between being with her and being without, it deserved his very best effort.

"Bow to my will…"

He squinted as he listened to the words whispered through the ether. "Bow to my will?" That wasn't part of a traditional summoning.

"Heed my call…"

This was the same way she'd summoned him before, he realized. He'd just been too panicked then to pay proper attention.

"Slave to my whim…"

"Clever wench." His cock twitched hard between his thighs. No wonder he was helpless to do anything but obey her. This little spell was almost diabolical in its simple yet effective wordage.

"I summon you."

He experienced a moment of massive disorientation. A moment where he thought he must have fallen asleep up on the roof and was now having the hottest dream he'd ever had.

They were in Alexandra's sweet, pretty, feminine bedroom with its big brass bed, its cabbage rose sheets and its old-fashioned quilt in mint greens and pale pinks. There was her curvy cherry dresser. There was that ridiculously small pink chair. But where was his sweet little Summoner? Because though the woman standing over him was certainly pretty— in a heart-stopping, drop-dead gorgeous kind of way—and certainly feminine—that corset left no doubt as to her sexy, feminine appeal—she was, in no way, sweet.

Good job he'd appeared on his knees because, at the sight of her, he would have surely landed there anyway.

Kasdeya drank her in. His gaze climbed from the shiny pointed tips of her very high, very sexy boots, following the gleaming expanse of black vinyl to the top of her creamy thighs. Once there, a mere inch of skin beckoned before a loosely pleated velvet skirt began. Such a lovely, short skirt. If she were to bend over just the smallest amount...

Another hard twitch for his happy cock.

His wide eyes traveled higher to the black leather corset that cinched so dramatically in at her tiny waist before widening again to thrust her perfect breasts up in front of her. A thin black choker graced her throat and large black hoops graced her ears.

Her makeup had been applied with great care. Deep burgundy glossed her luscious lips and smoky plum outlined her eyes, making them seem very large and almost arcticly blue. Her honey-brown hair was loose around her shoulders. It shimmered in the golden haze of dozens of candles she'd lit around the room.

His woman arched one brow and crossed her arms over her chest, causing her breasts to plump up even more. One cherry nipple peeked cheekily at him above the black leather. Kasdeya groaned.

"Looked your fill yet, pet?" Alexandra asked, deadpan.

He couldn't help but laugh. She must have been saving that. "Come here, wench," he said, standing to take her in his arms.

"You will remain on your knees, Prince Kasdeya."

He dropped back down as if his tendons had been cut.

"I've decided that I'm still annoyed," Alex said. Kasdeya's eyes fixated on her delectable ass as she turned and wiggled over to the bed. Once there, she spent a moment fishing around inside a box sitting on the mattress.

"Annoyed about?" he asked.

"Annoyed about being kept in the dark, about being treated like a child that was too naive to know the truth."

"Alexandra," he said, trying to think of a way to say that even though he had realized he might be putting her in danger, he hadn't wanted her to know, hadn't wanted her to worry. And to say, most especially, that he hadn't wanted her to understand that she could ask him to leave at any time. He was trying to think of a way to say that without coming off as the biggest, most selfish ass in the universe. It wasn't easy.

She turned back around with a smirk on her face and a pair of handcuffs in her hand, and Kasdeya promptly lost his train of thought. "You know those can't hold me," he said. It was true. Nothing made by mortals could hold him. So why was his heart climbing his throat and his prick nudging his bellybutton at the sight of them?

Alexandra just smiled. She dangled the manacles on one finger. The metal caught and refracted the candlelight so that it danced into the corners of the room.

The index finger of her other hand beckoned him closer.

Kasdeya again tried to stand.

"No, no. On your knees, if you please."

With an amused roll of his eye, Kasdeya crawled. It was a unique experience. One he enjoyed, despite himself. When he reached her feet, he lifted his wrists up to her of his own volition. "I can break them," he said in a "pass the butter" tone.

The click of steel sounded very final and, somehow, very sexy.

"Don't," she said, just as offhandedly.

He stared at her in burgeoning comprehension. If Kasdeya had been up on twentieth-century slang, he'd have realized that the word he was looking for was *D'oh!*

* * * *

Alex turned back to the box and the last thing in it. When she had put away her long velvet skirt, she'd been surprised to find something hard wrapped up inside it. Apparently, Darker Pleasures had a free giveaway if you spent more than three hundred dollars. And, sadly, she'd spent well more than that.

Alex caressed the smooth, curved handle before picking the paddle up and testing its heft. It was heavy for its size, made of solid teak. Kasdeya's brows shot up when she faced him with it.

"Oh, please." Laughter vibrated in his words. "Do you have any idea at all of how to use that?"

"None." Alex took a few swipes at the air. "But how hard can it be?" She walked around behind him and used her toe to push his legs further apart. "Lose the clothes, dark man," she ordered, bending to run a hand over his hip and back.

Suddenly, it was his tanned, naked skin under her fingers. Kasdeya leaned forward to rest his elbows on the edge of the bed and craned his head around to look at her. "This should be interesting," he said. "Go ahead then, pet. Take all that nasty anger out on my hide."

He was laughing at her. That wasn't how this was supposed to go. With annoyance, but no finesse, she brought the wood down against his skin. A dull, anti-climactic *whup* sounded.

Kasdeya laid his head against the mattress and sniggered.

Shit.

Another blow, this one with her full strength behind it, landed on his left cheek. The sound of wood against skin was louder this time, and Kasdeya gave a satisfying hiss of pain, but Alex was pretty sure it wasn't supposed to hurt *her* as well. Her shoulder was half-numb from the shock that had traveled back through the wood and up into her arm.

"Use your wrist, not your whole damn body," he snapped. "If I were human, you'd have hurt me—and not in a good way."

"What do you mean, 'use my wrist'?" she asked in frustration. Kasdeya was getting pissed. She was embarrassed. This was *so* not the way she'd imagined this going.

Her dark man sat back on his heels and shook his head fondly at her, spiking Alex's embarrassment up another notch. "Come on, pet. This isn't you."

"Just tell me how to use the stupid thing."

He held up his hands. "You'll have to take these off."

Alex frowned and Kasdeya rolled his eyes. "You can put them back on, if you like, but I can't show you like this."

"I said tell me, not show me."

* * * *

"It's not something that can be told, Alexandra. Besides, if you want to learn how to make others enjoy pain, you have to first learn to enjoy it yourself."

"Nevermind then." She threw the paddle on the bed.

Kasdeya let his hands fall to his lap. "Coward."

Alexandra glared at him. Her color was high, her pupils dilated. She looked so incredibly beautiful in that outfit, trussed up like the devil's own strumpet, that he thought he might die of lust. He held her fierce gaze, hoping with every fiber of his being that she would take the bait.

When she'd brought out the paddle, he'd felt a rush of craven excitement at the thought that he'd be on the receiving end for once. But the poor woman really had no idea. Now he was excited anew at the prospect of turning the tables. She was the one in charge though, and if she wasn't willing to trust him…

"Okay, fine," she said. "Fine."

Alexandra reached for the handcuff keys on the night table and Kasdeya smiled. This might not be *her*, but it was *him* all over the place. If his little Summoner wanted to play with pain, he was more than willing to accommodate her.

He held out his hands again, grinning from ear to ear.

She looked petulant as she unlocked him. "You're just pleased as punch, aren't you?"

He laughed and stood. "I am, but you'll be pleased too, pet. I promise." He slid his arms around her waist and rubbed her nose with his. "You can use the paddle on me later."

"Yeah?" She tilted her head up to look him in the eye. "You spank mine and I'll spank yours?"

Kasdeya smiled and rocked his painfully hard cock against the velvet of her skirt. "Exactly." He stole a kiss before the games began. Then he sat down on the bed and patted his thigh. "Right here, if you please."

Alexandra frowned. "You're not going to hurt me, are you?"

He laughed again. "Of course I'm going to hurt you. What did you think paddles were for, pet?"

She scowled and looked away, chafing her hands nervously.

"Alexandra," he said, tugging her into the vee of his thighs. "You have all the power. If you tell me to stop, I have no choice but to obey."

"I know, but…"

Kasdeya's hands slipped under her skirt and he groaned at the feel of her bare bum filling his palms. "Let me do this, little one," he encouraged. He squeezed her ass cheeks hard enough to redden them and Alexandra gasped. "You *will* scream, but it will be in pleasure, not pain." He looked up at her with heavy-lidded, lust-filled eyes. "Let me."

* * * *

Alex had declined the handcuffs, not wanting to relinquish that much control. Thus, her hands were white-knuckled in the bed sheets as she fought the instinct to reach back and protect her exposed behind. Kasdeya had flipped up her skirt in preparation, but he wasn't doing anything except petting her cheeks, tracing them in soothing, circular motions. The suspense was killing her.

"Get on with it, dark man," she said, turning her head to look at him.

"Patience, pet," he answered, never stopping his gentle caresses. "Anticipation is half the fun." Another swirl of skin against skin. "And you're so damned lovely," he murmured, almost too low for her to hear.

"Kas—"

With a "tsk" of annoyance, Kasdeya raised one hand and brought it down sharply on the skin he'd just been stroking.

"Oww," she yelped, twisting away from the sting.

"Such a baby." Kasdeya gave her another smack. "I've hardly touched you."

"Sto—"

He slipped his palm over her mouth. "Don't say it, pet. Give me a chance." He gave her one more love-tap then dropped his hand between her legs.

Alex could feel how wet she was. So could he. "Mmm," he purred, smoothing the creamy arousal up over her clit. "Very nice."

His hand left her face and he twisted his torso to deliver a staccato volley of slaps to her ass, all the while pinching and rubbing the hard knot of pleasure he'd drawn.

"Oh God," she gasped, burying her face in the mattress.

A vicious blow followed her words. "You know better."

Alex whimpered at the pain—it freakin' *hurt*—but, when combined with the feel of his hand between her legs, it also felt incredibly *good*. Every time he lifted his hand, the heat in her bottom swelled, rushing to her clit. She spread her legs a little wider, raised her ass a little higher, with each successive slap.

Suddenly Kasdeya stopped, withdrawing from between her thighs and letting both hands fall quiescent on her back. Alex's erratic breathing was the only sound to be heard for almost a full minute.

"Up with you, pet," he eventually said. His voice was very rough. "I can't do this properly in this position."

Alex turned her head to see Kasdeya holding the paddle. She scrabbled off his lap. "Look, I get it, dark man. Pain and pleasure. I get it. You don't have to—"

He tilted his head and regarded her the way one might regard a beloved relative suffering from senility. "I'm glad you *get* it, Summoner. But do you know how to hold your wrist yet?"

She blushed, realizing that she'd forgotten what was supposed to be the whole point of the proceeding. Hell, she hadn't been able to pay attention to how it was done when he'd spanked her with just his hand. How was she supposed to take notes while being beaten with a hunk of wood?

"Do you trust me?" he asked, standing as well.

"I do," she whispered. "It's just…"

Kasdeya took her by the shoulders and pushed her toward the bed. "Lie down," he said gently.

With one final, skeptical look back at him, Alexandra crawled onto the mattress. Kasdeya pulled two pillows from the top of the bed and placed them under her hips.

She sank down into the feather bolster with a sigh of surrender. Kasdeya stepped back and breathed a gusty sigh himself. Alexandra's legs were parted, her ass raised. She knew the folds of her sex were completely bared to him. Moisture slicked her crease; it was kind of embarrassing, actually, but the sight had to be driving him wild. She widened her legs and squirmed a bit, beckoning him, encouraging him to forget the paddle, to just pull her hips up and back and plunge inside her body. Instead, Kasdeya turned away and rummaged through the top drawer of her night table.

Crap. So much for that plan.

Alex came up on one elbow and stared at him. When he didn't find what he was looking for, Kasdeya shut the top drawer and opened the bottom. "What on earth are you doing?"

"I'm looking for your *olisbo*. You must have one. Every female since the beginning of time has had one."

"I don't have any idea what an olisbo is, dark man, but I'm pretty sure I don't have one." Her ass was burning and felt twice its normal size. So did her sex. In an unexpected twist of matter over mind, Alex felt anxious for the kiss of the paddle all of a sudden. She knew it would probably bring her to orgasm, and having the orgasm she'd been hovering at the brink of for the last ten minutes felt very important. She was dying here, and he was messing around.

He slammed the drawer shut. "Olisbo," he said in obvious frustration. "A…" his hands waved in the air before he dropped one to his impressive erection. "One of these. Or rather, something in the image of this that you use to pleasure yourself."

Alex had dropped her gaze when he'd dropped his hand and her mouth went dry with longing. Why would he want to use an olisbo when he had such a pretty cock right there?

Kasdeya smiled and pumped his length, pulling the foreskin back to make the head shiny and fat. "Where is it?"

"Hmm?" Her gaze rose to his face and she blushed at the perceptive pride in his eyes. He knew how bad she wanted him, and he was still fucking around.

"Your—"

"Dildo. It's called a dildo."

"Dildo?" His lip lifted. "I think I prefer the Greek word. But all right, where is your dildo, Alexandra?"

"Why do you want it?"

He arched a brow at her and picked up the paddle to slash a stroke across her ass. Alex went rigid in surprise. The hurt was large, but a gush of fluid immediately followed the hot pain. It overflowed her body to dampen the pillow beneath her. He was right; it wouldn't take much of that before she was screaming her way through a climax.

"It's enough that I *do* want it." He raised the paddle again. "Now, where—"

"Bottom drawer of the dresser."

"Thank you." He walked over to crouch in front of the dresser.

While his hands sifted through belts and boxes of jewelry, Alex admired him. The fine, tight shape of his haunches. The sexy winged tattoo. That blue-black hair mussed and decadent around his shoulders. Good God, he was so gorgeous. "It's in—"

"I've got it." He swiveled around with a pink drawstring bag in his hand; Alex's centurion was an obvious and illicit shape inside. "Centurion" had been the dildo's name on the package, so that's what she'd ended up calling it.

Kasdeya's eyebrows rose at the weight of the thing and, once he'd undone the bag's string, his brows rose even higher, almost disappearing into his hairline. "My, my." He tugged free the large, glossy black implement and took in its length—about two inches longer than his own—and its girth—about the same—and shook his head in amazement. "Should I be jealous?"

Her cheeks were bright red. "Shut up," she mumbled, burying her face in the bedding again.

The intimately well-known sound of the centurion's vibrator purring to life tickled the air. Kasdeya laughed. "I'm definitely jealous."

She heard him pad over to stand behind her. "Spread your legs a little bit more, pet."

Alex didn't hesitate. She'd rather have her dark man buried inside her, but the centurion was a fine consolation prize.

His weight settled on the mattress and then the soft, blunt head of the dildo was shivering down her spine. When it got to just above her bum crease, it changed direction, describing lazy figure eights around the dimples set low on Alex's back. She moaned and tilted her hips, raising her ass even higher. The feel of Kasdeya's breath leaving him in a great whoosh to gust over her exposed sex made her shudder.

"Pretty, pretty little angel," he whispered into the skin of her thigh.

The vibrator skimmed lower, teasing the heat of her cheeks before delving between them. Alex stiffened as it played over her anus. The shivers there felt so strangely intense. Too intense. She relaxed again when it dropped into the hollow between her legs, only to go rigid once more as he immediately brought it down hard on the unsheathed bud of her clitoris. She yelped and tried to pull away but he smacked his hand down on her ass, holding her in place.

"Kasdeya, it's too much," she said with a gasp, wriggling to escape.

"Is it?" He bit her leg just under the left cheek and moved the dildo up to probe her entrance.

Alex wriggled again, but this time she was trying to get closer. "Please…"

Another bite—higher this time—and another dip of the dildo to torture the sensitive nerve bundle. The pain of his teeth, the too-strong buzz of the vibrator… "Oh. Oh God." Smack. "Oh fuck. Kasdeya, please. Please!"

One more bite, the hardest yet. His teeth sank deep as the black cock lunged, cleaving her in two. When it crashed into her cervix, Alex screamed.

* * * *

Kasdeya sat up quickly, shoved her legs together to trap the olisbo inside and straddled her, his knees tight on either side of hers. He didn't allow himself to be distracted by the massive orgasm she was writhing her way through, though his cock quivered and shook in sympathy, spurts of pre-come dripping down to slick her skin. Instead, he grabbed the paddle and spanked her, timing his blows to the paroxysms that coursed through her body. Alexandra's climax escalated and extended, tossing her against the spikes of what he knew was almost unbearable pleasure.

"Kasdeya!" she keened, throwing her head back and rocking her hips desperately to meet the smack of wood. "Oh, fuck, I can't stand it. Stop now... God, you have to stop."

His hand froze in the air, held motionless by her words. He snarled, knowing she didn't mean it but helpless to continue anyway. Alexandra's shudders slowly diminished until she lay limp and exhausted beneath him. "Why'd you stop?" she mumbled into the sheets.

He chuffed in amusement and swung his leg over her body. "I think we're going to have to get you a gag, Summoner," he said. "I certainly didn't *want* to stop."

"Oh, right. Sorry."

She moaned when he gripped the end of the dildo, easing it out, and succumbed to another full body quiver. "I'm afraid I didn't catch the wrist technique," she said with a dreamy half-smile, pushing the pillows away to turn onto her side and face him.

Kasdeya smiled back and lifted the paddle up in front of him. "It's simple." He bent his wrist back and then snapped it forward to smack the wood into his palm. "Keep your arm loose and use your wrist to deliver the blow. Nothing to it."

Alexandra gaped at him.

"What?" He was trying for an innocent expression, but he couldn't seem to stop grinning.

"You asshole!" She scrambled to her knees and lunged at him.

"What?" he said again, bringing his arms up in front of his face to defend against the slaps she was raining on his head and shoulders. He was laughing now.

"You know *what*, you absolute shit!"

She seized a handful of Kasdeya's hair, wrenching him off balance so that he fell backward. He grabbed her and pulled her on top of him, his grin still firmly in place. "You aren't honestly complaining are you, pet?" he asked.

She lifted her hips in the air, away from his rigid prick, and bent her head to kiss him, biting aggressively at his lips before sucking his tongue into her mouth.

Kasdeya stopped laughing.

"I am complaining, dark man," she said after she'd worked him over thoroughly with her lips, teeth and tongue. He leaned up to capture her mouth again but she darted back. "That was a shitty thing to do," she continued. Kasdeya's hands were on her waist, trying to bring her lower body closer. She smacked them away and crawled off, motioning for him to shift positions so that he'd be laying the right way on the mattress.

"You've never come that hard in your life." He moved up where she wanted him. "And you know it."

Alexandra bent over, searching for something on the floor beside the bed. She hissed as her red bum came in contact with the soft cotton sheets. "That's not the point," she said, clearly irritated.

"No. The point was to teach you how to use a paddle to maximum effect." He paused. "Oh, wait, I did that too."

She straightened, handcuffs in hand, and gave him a sarcastic smile. "Keep it up, smart-ass. You're just making it worse on yourself."

"Promise?" He cheerfully offered his wrists to her.

"No. Hands over your head. And, yes, I do promise." When he complied, she slipped the chain through two brass spindles and re-cuffed him. "Now, remember—don't try to get loose." She touched the tip of her finger to the end of his nose. "And whatever you do, Kasdeya…" She scooted backward a bit and touched the same finger to the tiny slit in his cockhead. It gaped for her like a mouth eager to be filled.

"…Don't…come."

Now he was worried.

Chapter 12

Kasdeya's eyes glittered as she lifted the paddle. "You have me facing the wrong way for that, pet."

"Really?" she asked with wide-eyed innocence, slapping the wood against her palm. After a few seconds, she mastered the relaxed wrist movement. She had to shake her head at how simple it was. The jerk. "Well, let's see."

He had one knee bent at an angle and Alex aimed a smack against his exposed outer thigh. The only sign he gave that she'd hit him was a tightening of his lips. He dropped the leg though.

"No, bend it again, Kasdeya. In fact, bend both knees, please."

He scowled but lifted his legs into the required position, feet flat against the mattress.

"Thank you, dear." She smiled sweetly. "Now, let your knees fall to the right."

He scowled some more and added a grumble or two for effect as his legs dropped sideways, stretching his muscles and highlighting his lovely, long obliques. Alex ran an appreciative hand over the elongated muscle. But just as Kasdeya relaxed into the petting, she shifted away to get better arm extension and brought the paddle down on his exposed left cheek. His body jumped but he said nothing, looking stoically off into the corner of the room.

Let him pout.

After she had reddened that cheek nicely, no mean feat on angel skin, Alex had him bare his right side. His breathing was a bit deeper, but other than that he may as well have been reading the Sunday paper for all the emotion he showed. With one final, bruising slash, Alex sat down beside him, propping a foot up on the mattress to rest her chin on her knee.

Alicia Steele

"Tell me, dark man, are you withholding your response from me for any particular reason?" she asked, idly smoothing her fingers up and down his flank.

His gaze rose to hers. "I—No… I'm not withholding anything." He looked away again.

"No? Then what am I doing wrong?" Her hand came over his cock and Kasdeya bit his lip. "If it wasn't for this monster between your thighs, I'd think I was boring you to tears."

"No," he said again.

She waited.

"I'm not sure how to react on this side of things," he admitted.

"Do you like it?"

He seemed to consider. "It doesn't really hurt the way I know it should."

Alex frowned. "You were complaining before that I hit too hard."

"Yes…but…" He sighed and shrugged. "I don't know what's wrong, Summoner. It doesn't feel intense enough, maybe?"

Not intense enough? "Lie flat again."

When he had, she took the very tip of his erection between her fingers, pulling it away from his stomach until she'd achieved an angle of about ninety degrees. Kasdeya's eyes widened. "Alexandra, don't you—" The paddle connected smartly with his penis. "Fuck!" he cried, stealing her declaration of choice without realizing it.

His head hit the mattress with a thump.

Alex took another swing and his cock shimmied, darkening even further as blood rushed to the surface to protect this most delicate of skin. "How's the intensity now?"

Teeth clenched and jaw flexed, Kasdeya didn't respond.

"Answer," she ordered, giving him a flurry of snapping smacks.

"It hurts!"

"Yes, of course it does. But that's not what I'm asking." One more blow and then she stopped to push his legs apart. Wide apart.

Kasdeya's face contorted. "Don't…"

She smiled and fisted his cock a few times, wringing an agonized groan of pleasure from his mouth. Kasdeya's dark head tossed against the floral sheets. His body was quaking and his cock was harder than she'd ever seen it, an angry reddish-purple stone. Alex felt an electrifying surge of authority. Her dark man was, very visibly, on the last dregs of his control.

"How's the intensity?" she asked again, running the edge of the paddle down his prick and over the crease of his balls.

"Intense. Very intense."

She gave his scrotum the tiniest of taps.

"Ungh," he grunted, spreading his legs even wider.

Alex looked up as a metal shriek gashed the air. Kasdeya had had his hands wrapped around the spindles, and while he still did, the brass rods were no longer attached to her headboard.

"Hey! I just got this bed." She smacked his sac again.

Kasdeya turned his face into his bicep. His moans were long, unbroken sounds of anguished pleasure.

Alex was so turned on she thought she might come just from watching him. "You're hands are to stay above your head, dark man. Understood?"

He nodded jerkily.

"Lift your legs higher."

With what almost sounded like a whimper, Kasdeya did, exposing himself completely. Alex rained smacks down on his balls, balls which tightened and swelled impossibly fuller, turning a lovely, deep shade of violet-blue. His moans rose to howls.

"Stop!" he finally roared.

Her hand paused. "Stop?"

Kasdeya was sucking in great, gasping breaths. His body shook as if with ague. "Stop," he said again. "I can't take any more." He raised his head to look at her, his eyes swollen and dark. "I'll come."

Alex smiled and threw the paddle across the room. "All you had to do was say so."

With a sigh of exhaustion, Kasdeya let his legs relax. They were still splayed though, as if he couldn't stand even the touch of his own skin against his bruised genitals. "Now you tell me," he whispered. His muscles clenched again as she crawled up between his legs and Kasdeya groaned. "No more, pet."

Alex laid her head on his thigh and blew warm air across his groin. "Just a little more." Her fingers trailed up his opposite leg to brush against his perineum. "I'll be gentle."

* * * *

Kasdeya half laughed, half cried at the feel of her tiny hand on his body. He was in agony. He didn't think his Summoner had any idea how far she'd pushed him, but he was also so close to orgasm that even this small caress could be enough. The ache that had settled between his legs was vast, a whirlpool of smoldering sensation. But that just heightened the stroke of her delicate fingers, making the caress feel extraordinarily sweet by comparison.

"If you touch me again, little one, I refuse to be held responsible."

"Okay." She inched her mouth over to press a tender kiss to his scrotum. "I absolve you of any responsibility," she said, flicking her tongue against the dark skin. "You can come now, dark man."

Kasdeya's body twisted in ecstasy, his spine curving until only his head and ass remained on the mattress. Alexandra's mouth opened wider, taking one hard orb inside, and a sob caught in his throat. It felt so sweet…

The ache was already beginning to fade, his accelerated healing kicking in. Perversely, Kasdeya mourned its leisurely ebb. Stars burst behind his tightly shut eyes, and he squirmed on the diabolical rack of pain morphed into pleasure.

* * * *

Alex's tongue laved both stone-hard spheres then she licked her way to the top of his penis.

"Now, please, now," Kasdeya mumbled desperately.

She glanced up to see her dark man's lips drawn back in a rictus grin, his hands crushed around a mangled brass spindle. Every muscle in his body was taut, creating a stunning, jagged sculpture of perfect masculinity.

"Now," she agreed, opening her mouth.

When she'd swallowed as much of him as she could, Alex hollowed her cheeks to create intense suction. Her tongue flicked rapidly from side to side. Kasdeya's shaft expanded against her palate. As the first luscious spurt of his uniquely sweet semen bathed her tonsils, Alex reached down and squeezed his balls just as hard as she could.

Kasdeya screamed, an inhuman sound of ravaged ecstasy, and his torso curled in on itself like a leaf touched by flame. He bowed over his Summoner where she was nestled between his thighs. Garbled words of devotion—*can't…yours…forever*—fell from his lips onto her bent head. They mixed with the salt of his tears.

Alex kept her mouth on him long after he'd been drained, enjoying the minute tremors that quivered through his muscles and the feel of his cock softening on her tongue. When both his cock and his body fell quiet, she shimmied out from underneath him to sit up.

Kasdeya remained hunched over, slumped in what looked like sleep. His hands, she was amused to note, were still over his head, the poor brass spindle twisted around his long fingers. When she grabbed the cuff key and freed him, Kasdeya summoned the energy to raise his head. The look he gave her stopped her heart. His eyes swam with emotion.

"You can put your arms down," she said, smoothing his tangled hair back from his forehead. He put them around her waist.

"We're never doing that again," he said with a sigh, nuzzling her neck.

She rubbed his back. "You didn't like it?"

"I liked it," he admitted, crushing her close. "Too much. Much, much too much."

Alex grinned and fell sideway, pulling him down as well. "Too much of a good thing? That's not really possible, is it?"

His expression grew pensive. "Yes, pet. It is."

Chapter 13

Too much of a good thing…

Too much good…

Good…

"Bloody hell," Kasdeya swore, throwing down the hammer and sucking his thumb into his mouth. A monkey could repair a kitchen chair but he, formerly one of God's most powerful generals and currently the Devil's closest friend and most trusted advisor, couldn't. Not today.

Good! She was too damned good. What was he doing with her? Warping her. Wanting her. He had no right. What the hell was he doing endangering her like this?

"Hey, sexy!"

Kasdeya turned at the sound of her voice to see his woman striking a seductive pose against the shed's door. Even though she was dressed in loose jeans with no makeup on, her beauty stole his breath.

"Hey yourself," he said, holding out his arms. With a child's unending trust, Alexandra took a running leap and threw herself at him.

"Guess who's taking the rest of the day off to paint a house?" she asked.

He smiled into her hair and swayed her body close against his chest. "You?"

"And…"

"And…someone else who wants to paint a house?"

"Well, someone who *will* paint a house, if he's told to."

Kasdeya gave her ponytail a tug. "You're taking advantage of me, Summoner."

"Mmm, yeah." She tilted her face up for a kiss. "But you love it."

* * * *

The next few days settled into a wonderful, predictable routine. They woke up together, went to work together—where Alex spent way too much time mooning out her office window, watching as Kasdeya played the much-needed handyman for Dovescot—came home and had dinner together, worked together some more on their own house—it didn't feel like just hers anymore—and then collapsed into bed together to make love, sometimes until early morning, when they'd fall asleep in each other's arms for a few hours before starting all over again.

The only hitch had been the detective that showed up two nights ago asking about Darryl Grier. "What was the fight at Dovescot about? How was it resolved? Has he ever threatened you before? Have you had any contact with him since that night?"

Darryl was officially missing now. Imagine that.

If it had been left up to Alex, she'd have probably been hauled off to jail right then and there. She really did suck at lying, and she knew guilt had been stamped across her face, plain to read. Kasdeya had pulled some sort of Jedi mind trick though, and Detective Stevens had left satisfied that Alex hadn't had anything to do with anything. Alex still couldn't figure out how her dark man had accomplished that, but was darn happy that he had. Having a fallen angel as a lover definitely had its perks.

* * * *

Alex walked into the living room and stopped to admire the way Kasdeya's T-shirt had rucked out of his jeans while he stretched to paint the molding, treating her to a gorgeous expanse of tattooed brown skin across his lower back.

He was standing four steps up on an aluminum ladder, which put his tight little ass at perfect bite-height. Alex's mouth watered at the thought.

You'd think she wouldn't still be so damned horny for him. They made love two or three times a day. But every morning she woke up wanting him more. Needing him more.

She'd lain awake most of last night, watching him sleep, and had decided there was no way she could let him go. She loved Kasdeya, and if the Powers came and he had to run, she was going to run with him.

Today, she'd made arrangements to have Rose take over for her at Dovescot if she *did* have to leave suddenly. Alex didn't want to walk away from everything she held dear but she would if she had to. For Kasdeya, she would.

Rose had been angry. She'd demanded an explanation or else she was going to "shirk her responsibilities and quit too, and there would be *no one* to run the fucking place." Alex had made another tough decision and had decided to give her friend the explanation she was demanding. Minus

Kasdeya's full name, and with a pre-sworn oath of secrecy, Alex had told Rose the truth.

At first, Rose had voiced serious concerns regarding Alex's sanity. The word "loony bin" was tossed around once or twice. But after Alex had called Kasdeya in for a small demonstration—fending off *his* demands for an explanation all the while—Rose had had to admit that a man with fourteen-feet wings was hard evidence to dispute.

Alex hadn't told Kasdeya the truth though…or not all of it. Yes, she'd told him that she missed her friend terribly and was tired of lying to her—true. But she hadn't told him that she was willing to toss her entire life over to be with him—even though that was true as well. Problem was it would have been such an obvious declaration of love on her part when her dark man was showing no signs of making any declarations of his own. Time and again he'd whisper that he wanted her, needed her, but the word "love" had never crossed his perfect lips.

Hopefully, nothing would come of her illicit planning. It had been eight days since the picnic and there had been no sign of the Powers, thank God…or whoever.

After they'd kissed and made up, Alex had invited Rose and a few other friends and family over for drinks tomorrow night. The idea of a party made Alex smile. Their first guests as a couple. How remarkably *normal* of them.

Now if they could just get the living and dining rooms finished.

The front hall was already done, painted a dark terracotta that complimented the hardwood floors. The downstairs bath was also painted, and the cream and brown stripes against her antique silver mirror looked marvelous now that it was hung again. The dining room was mostly finished in rich russet gold and the living room was half done in deep forest green. They'd been working very hard.

And it was definitely time for a break. Alex tiptoed closer to her dark man. Just a little break. A "quickie" break, if you would.

"Hey, pet," he said over his shoulder. "Can you pass me some sandpaper? We missed a spot."

Alex frowned. She had been trying to sneak up on him every day but had no success. It was starting to get annoying. When she glanced down at the floor, trying to locate a still usable piece of fine-grit, her gaze happened upon a trim brush lying across the pint of cream molding paint. With a smirk, she bent to grab it.

"It's on the—" As he started to swivel toward her Alex used the nifty wrist technique he'd shown her, but now never let her practice, to flick a spatter of paint into his glossy back hair. His body stiffened and he slowly completed the upper body turn. "You did *not* just throw paint at me."

"Never!" she exclaimed in mock indignation, drawing back her arm for another flick. Paint droplets splashed against his cheek.

He started down the ladder. "Woman, you'd better run."

The doorbell rang.

"Saved by the bell, la la," Alex sang, skipping away. "Keep painting, you lazy bugger." She laughed at his grumble as he remounted the steps.

Alex was still laughing when she opened the front door, head turned back toward the living room, her braless breasts shivering under the loose paint-flecked shirt she wore. She swiped at some green paint on her chin as her face came forward and froze in the gesture, fingers pressed against her bottom lip.

The man's mouth curled into a knowing smirk at her reaction, the small movement of his lips highlighting the deep hollows under his wickedly high cheekbones. He took a long drag of his cigarette while his gaze traveled boldly down her curves, then back up.

"'Ello, luv," he offered in a thick Cockney accent, letting the cigarette fall and crushing it under the toe of his Doc Martin boot. He splayed his hand across the door, long golden nails gleaming, and pushed it open wider to step into the house. His ankle-length black trench coat trailed intimately across her bare legs as he came beside her. Instead of continuing past, he plucked her hand from where it was still pressed against her lips and pressed it against his own.

"Be a dear," he said, his voice mellow, low and rich with inflection. "Tell Kasdeya he has a visitor."

His unusual amber-gold eyes were less than an inch from her own, looking at her through the smoky fan of his lashes while his mouth pursed against her hand. This close, his scent of leather, smoke and just a hint of spicy musk was an undeniable aphrodisiac. His short ice-blond hair tickled her cheek, soft as an animal's fur. Alex unconsciously leaned into his slim body, seeking more contact.

"Who is it?" called Kasdeya from the room behind them.

Alex gasped and stepped away, only just realizing how close she had been to... Well, how close she had been.

The mystery man chuckled, still in possession of her hand, and gave her a playful nip on the edge of her thumb before releasing it. All the hair on her body stood up at the bite. So did her nipples. His eyes dropped to them. Alex flushed and took another step back. She comprehended all too late that she might have committed suicide simply by opening her front door. Was this one of the Powers? Funny, he didn't seem any more angelic than Kasdeya did.

Alex opened her mouth to reply that she had absolutely no idea whom she had just let into her house, and that maybe Kasdeya should get his butt in here, when the gorgeous blond beat her to it.

"It's an old friend, Kas. Do come and say hello, won't you?"

Kasdeya cursed viciously and they listened to him trip down the steps of the aluminum ladder. When he emerged into the hall, he slapped the air with the back of his palm. "Come here," he barked at Alex.

Normally, Alex would have bristled at such an imperious summons, but somehow the moment didn't seem right for an argument. As soon as she was close enough, Kasdeya grabbed her wrist and tugged her hard into his side, turning her so that she was almost entirely shielded from the other man's view.

"Shaitan," he said, his voice arctic. Alex shivered at the sound of it.

"Kasdeya." By contrast, Shaitan's voice was warm as honey and vibrating with suppressed amusement.

Alex's eyes widened. He wasn't a Power, he was—holy crap, the *Devil* was standing in her front hall. She shifted to peek around Kasdeya's bulk and when he again moved to hide her, she smacked his back. "I'm not a child to be protected, dark man," she said. "Move, please."

And, of course, he could do nothing but obey. With a furious look thrown over his shoulder, he reluctantly stepped to the side.

Shaitan's brows twitched up at their exchange. He seemed surprised that Kasdeya had backed down so readily. "Interesting," he said, slipping out of the duster to reveal a skintight, black mesh shirt tucked into skintight, faded black jeans. An inverted silver cross, strung from the finest of chains, glistened between his well-defined pecs. He retrieved a battered pack of Pall Malls from his coat pocket before tossing it over the stairs' newel post.

Alex saw more silver peaking through the loose webbing of his shirt, decorating both of his tan nipples. She drooled a little bit despite herself. She was madly in love with her dark man, but *sweet Jesus*!

"So, boys and girls," Shaitan said with a sardonic grin. "Let's have a cuppa and talk this out, shall we?" He flourished his arm, indicating that they should lead the way.

* * * *

"No," said Kasdeya. "Absolutely not." His fist pounded the top of her kitchen table and Alex jumped.

She was standing at the counter making coffee for Kasdeya and herself—her dark man had developed quite a fondness for the stuff—and a mug of Earl Grey with three sugars for the Devil. Out of the corner of her eye, she watched Shaitan raise his chin to the ceiling and blow six perfect smoke rings into the air before he responded to her lover.

"It's only fair, brother," he said mildly. "I'm trying to cut you a break here. Your other option is to return and finish the sentence."

Alex felt Shaitan's gaze traveling over her body, an almost physical sensation. She turned around with his tea, her hands shaking so badly that scalding liquid sloshed over the cup's side as she handed it to him.

Shaitan's fingers steadied hers on the warm china, making the simple gesture of taking the cup from her into a sexually charged caress. "Thanks," he said, tipping her a roguish wink.

"You're welcome," she mumbled. She snatched her hand back, turning to grab the coffees and set them down on the table before pulling out a chair for herself. Kasdeya impatiently kicked the chair back in and hauled her into his lap. His arms were ultra-possessive around her waist.

Alex relaxed against him. She could feel his angry desperation, and so if he needed her in his lap then that's where she'd stay. "Does someone want to clue me in?" she asked, reaching for her mug. "Who's Shi-Liu?" She turned her head to catch Kasdeya's thunderous black gaze. "And what exactly is being offered in lieu of your punishment?"

Kasdeya's jaw clenched and he looked at her for a long moment before shifting her a little to the side to reach for his own mug.

After almost thirty seconds of charged silence, Shaitan snorted and stubbed out his cigarette in the small ashtray Alex had provided. "You want me to tell her?"

"No."

"Well, she's gonna have to know soon, brother. Either that, or say good-bye to the lovely lady." Shaitan stood and stretched, his arms flung high over his head, back and neck arched like a diver. The mesh shirt pulled out of the waistband of his jeans, revealing a sharply chiseled stomach and the sexy ridges of narrow hips.

When she caught herself staring, Alex quickly looked away, right into Kasdeya's eyes. He was frowning. His gaze flicked from her to Shaitan and back, and each time it did, his brows drew down farther.

"I'll give you two lovebirds a bit of privacy," said Shaitan, picking up the ashtray in one hand and his tea in the other. "Oh, and Kas? I'm only asking for one night, not the week you'd actually owe me."

Alicia Steele

Kasdeya sneered at his Prince but Shaitan just shrugged. "You have ten minutes," he said, shouldering open the swinging door. "After that, I'll want an answer." He stepped through but almost immediately popped his head back in. "Oh, and I imagine it goes without saying, but I'll say it anyway. If you decide the answer is no, all communication with this lovely little Summoner will cease. Immediately."

"Get out," Kasdeya growled.

Shaitan's head disappeared. A second later, the TV clicked on. The sound of a sports match made its way into the kitchen.

Alex waited for Kasdeya to say something but he remained silent, his forehead resting in the center of her back. The seconds ticked away.

"Bloody hell!" Shaitan yelled. "Learn to kick a fuckin' ball, mate!"

"I think we're down to about seven minutes," Alex said, twisting in his arms to see Kasdeya's face.

Kasdeya sighed.

"Who's Shi-Liu?"

He looked like he wasn't going to answer again and Alex's voice became commanding. "Tell me. Tell me everything," she said. "What does Shaitan want?"

Kasdeya pushed back from the table, lifting and turning her body until she was straddling him. "He wants you," he said, his expression grim.

"Me?" Alex willed away the fission of excitement his words evoked. "Why on earth would he want me? We've never even met before."

He barked a humorless laugh. "It doesn't matter, pet. He wants you because you're mine. Because I..." He trailed off and ran an agitated hand through his dark, paint-spattered hair.

"Because you took something—someone—that was his," Alex said, drawing the obvious conclusion.

"I didn't take anything that wasn't offered," he said defensively. "Shi-Liu was bored. Shaitan hadn't been around for months."

"But who—"

"Shi-Liu is a succubus. She's also his first concubine. The closest thing Fallen have to a spouse."

Alex pushed his arms away and slipped off his lap. "A succubus?" she asked, moving to lean against the counter. "I thought—"

"You thought that Brethren and humans were the only residents in my brother's kingdom?" He gave a rueful shake of his head. "Not at all. Shi-Liu, for example, is a fire elemental. She was forced into human form to pleasure a sorcerer about three thousand years ago. She killed him, of course. They always kill the ones who make them."

Alex knew it would be *way* too easy to get distracted by this fascinating bit of information. She also knew that that was exactly what he was hoping would happen. Nevermind. There would be plenty of time for random Q and A later on. The only question that mattered right now was, "Why'd you do it?"

Kasdeya folded his hands on the table and looked down for a long moment. "You have to understand," he said softly. "Fallen don't love, not the way you do—the way mortals do."

Alex winced. There it was. He didn't love her. He *couldn't* love her.

He raised his head to look at her again, unaware of her inner pain. "Shaitan and I had argued, and I know Shi-Liu is resentful of how much time he spends away. Months—sometimes years. It was just so easy, and I—"

"And you thought, 'What the hell, let's do his wife?'"

His massive shoulders lifted in a shrug. "Yes, I guess I did. It's a game we play, the Prince and me. I knew he'd punish me, but by then it would be too late. I'd have already had her. His Shi-Liu. His untouchable flame."

"But the punishment…"

"A thousand years wasn't what I expected," Kasdeya admitted, biting the corner of his lip. "He must care for her more than I'd originally thought." He frowned, looking troubled. "Still, it's really not that long, and I knew I'd win free at some point." He toyed with the handle of his coffee mug and shook his head. "It's all part of the game, Alexandra. It's just a power play."

Alex fiddled with the button at her throat. Thinking about it like that, what Shaitan wanted made perfect sense…in a strange, twisted way. "Now he wants a night with me to get even with you."

Kasdeya scowled and nodded.

"And if I say no?"

"Then he takes me back."

"If I summon you right away, then maybe—"

He gave his head another shake, this one violent. "No." He ran both hands through his hair this time. "He can prevent us from ever communicating again. He *will* prevent us from it. He has that power." Kasdeya leaped to his feet, almost overturning the table. Coffee sloshed out of the cup, staining his jeans, but he didn't seem to notice. "Alexandra… Little one… I can see that you're attracted to him." He reached for her but Alex ducked under his arms.

"He's beautiful." She hugged her own torso. "But I would expect nothing less of the Devil."

Kasdeya waved his hand negligently. "'Devil' is a term like 'demon.' It doesn't truly apply to us."

"Oh, well, that makes it okay, doesn't it? You want me to do it then?" she asked, turning her back to him. "You want me to fuck him?" She was both horrified and aroused at the thought.

"No!" Kasdeya put his arms around her, despite her struggles, crushing her against his chest. "But I don't want to lose you, pet. I *can't* lose you!" His harsh, fraught voice assaulted her ear. "The thought of you with him…" He twisted her in his arms and buried his face in her throat, hugging her so tight that she couldn't breathe.

"Two minutes, people," Shaitan hollered. "You wanker!" Alex assumed the last bit was directed at the TV.

Kasdeya pulled back to look at her, his face tight with emotion. "I can't… I can't tell you I want you to do this. But I don't want to lose you." His knuckles skimmed down her cheek. "I never want to lose you, Alexandra."

If Fallen couldn't love, then that was the closest thing to a declaration she was going to get. But that was all right, she had love enough for both of them. And she couldn't lose him either. Alex tried on a small smile. "He is *very* attractive."

Her dark man scowled some more, but she saw the relief in his eyes, followed swiftly by a flash of jealousy.

"Don't say another damn word," he said, lowering his mouth to hers.

* * * *

"Sit," Shaitan directed, pointing to the tiny pink chair in the corner of Alex's bedroom.

Kasdeya eyed the chair, unsure if it would take his weight, but he gingerly sat.

"Take off your shirt, mate, and just relax." Shaitan sat on the edge of the bed and unlaced his docs. "You're going to be there for a while. Alexis, you—"

"Alexandra," Kasdeya corrected, his voice tight.

Shaitan raised his gaze from his boots, a cocky smirk gracing his face. Kasdeya pried his fingers off the chair's upholstered arms. Shaitan knew her name. He'd just been playing, Kasdeya knew, trying to piss him off further. Usually, Kasdeya didn't rise to the Prince's bait so easily.

"Arsehole," Kasdeya mouthed, lifting his T-shirt over his head.

Shaitan laughed, and when Kasdeya's eyes were clear of the fabric, he mouthed back, "Prick."

A smile tugged the corner of Kasdeya's mouth. If it were anyone but Alexandra his brother was planning to ravish, he'd be having a grand ol' time. Shaitan and he had shared many women over the centuries, always with this same sarcastic banter as part of the foreplay. His brows drew down again. But it was his woman this time, and he refused to be caught up in Shaitan's lighthearted games.

"Alexandra," Shaitan said, his voice filled with humor. "Why don't you have a quick shower, get that paint off and then put on something pretty?"

"Something pretty?" she echoed from where she was standing in the doorway, looking pale and anxious.

"Sure." Shaitan pulled off one boot and glanced around the room. His gaze lit on the paddle resting forgotten on the night table. He leaned forward to grab it. "Something that goes with this, maybe?" he said, taking a few swats at the air. "Kinky heels, naughty underwear…"

Alexandra was now bright red. It didn't take much to get her blushing like a rose, and the Prince's snarky words were more than enough.

"Just have your shower, pet." Kasdeya leaped to his feet and strode to the dresser. "I'll find something." He wrenched open the top drawer to paw through her underwear.

She threw him a look of gratitude and ran across the hall to the bathroom.

"Don't forget to scent your pubic hair, love," Shaitan called cheerfully, his head bowed over his other boot. "I do so love a perfumed pussy." The bathroom door slammed shut.

Shaitan never saw the punch coming. It laid him out flat in the center of the mattress. "Oy!" His eyes glinted fire at Kasdeya as he bounced back up, body coiled and ready to fight.

"You *will* treat her with respect, Shaitan," Kasdeya hissed, shaking his fist. The gesture looked unintentionally ridiculous with his hand chockfull of lacy lingerie.

Shaitan's gaze dipped to the frilly threat and one pale brow arched. He seemed to be fighting off another smirk.

Kasdeya swore and dropped the panties, but the moment was gone—along with his anger. Shaitan simply didn't understand how he felt about her. And how could he be expected to, really? Kasdeya himself didn't understand how he felt about her.

"Please," he said, turning back to the dresser. "Don't try to humiliate her. Treat her well. You owe me that much."

The sound of Shaitan's boot hitting the floor was loud in the itchy stillness. "You care for her," he said. It was an observation, not a question. "This mortal—this *human*." He imbued the last word with the same arrogant disdain Kasdeya had always felt for it—for them.

"Yes," Kasdeya said simply. "I do." He continued rummaging through Alexandra's lingerie, running his fingers through the silk and cotton. The light vanilla scent of her perfume wafted up from the delicate garments to soothe him.

The mattress creaked and then Shaitan's hand was on his shoulder. "Do you love her, Kas?"

Kasdeya took a deep breath and turned to face him again. "Can I? I've been laboring under the assumption that such a thing was impossible." He tapped his finger against Shaitan's chest, right over the unholy cross. "Isn't that what you've always said?"

"No," said Shaitan. "I never said it was impossible for the Brethren to love." He plucked a thong from the dresser: a tiny black one with a rhinestone heart on the back. "This'll do," he said, pushing the drawer closed. He shoved the underwear into his jean pocket and then opened the closet door.

Kasdeya stood stock still, feeling like he'd been pole-axed. "What do you mean, you never said that?"

"Just what I said," said Shaitan, his voice muffled by the closet's interior. He popped his head back out, a broad smile on his face, and waved the thigh-high boots in the air. "Been having fun, brother?"

"Gimme those." Kasdeya grabbed for the patent leather heels. "And start talking."

Shaitan whipped his prize out of reach. "I like these. She can wear them. And by 'start talking,' I assume you're still on the 'love' thing? Well, what I actually said, boyo, was that God hadn't given his first children the ability to love. He did, however, give us the ability to learn and grow." He shrugged. "I've always assumed that, given the right circumstances, any of us could fall in love. In order to do so though, we'd have to care for someone more than we care for ourselves." Shaitan laughed. "And let's face it, that doesn't happen amongst Angels or Fallen very fuckin' often."

Kasdeya opened his mouth but Shaitan held up a finger. "Hold that thought." He walked across the hall and tapped on the bathroom door. "Hurry up, sweetheart. No procrastinating now. Your clothes are outside the door, handpicked by your lover."

Alexandra's reply didn't reach Kasdeya's ears, but the high, nervous pitch of her voice did.

When Shaitan re-entered the room, he crossed to the bed and tossed the sheets on the floor, placing the paddle on the edge of the mattress. Then he pulled out a red disposable lighter from his back pocket and lit the candles still sitting on almost every available surface.

"Is this really necessary?" Kasdeya asked, watching Shaitan move confidently around the room. "I'm sorry for Shi-Liu. I am. Ask for anything else."

Shaitan seemed to lose his sense of humor for the first time since he'd entered the house. "No," he hissed, yellow eyes flashing as he whirled to face Kasdeya. "You took something from me, brother. And I—"

"Something you love?" interrupted Kasdeya.

The fire faded from his Prince's eyes. "Rose-tinted glasses much, Kas?" Shaitan slapped at the light switch by the door to plunge them into shadowy, golden gloom. Then he threw himself backward on the bed, arms wide, gaze fixed on the ceiling. "To be honest, I don't know if I love her. But I do care for her. And you hurt me, Kasdeya—both of you." Shaitan punched his chest. "Ripped my fuckin' heart out."

Kasdeya sat down in the ridiculously small chair again. "Sounds like love to me. But tell me, brother, where were you while we were ripping your heart out? Why was she with me in the first place?"

Shaitan sat up and stared at him. Incredulity, anger and humor chased each other across his handsome face. "You dare?"

"I'm just saying that if you care for her so much, maybe you should be there with her instead of here ripping *my* heart out."

"This will hurt you, Kasdeya?" Shaitan asked in a sibilant whisper.

"Yes."

"Good," Shaitan snapped with sudden malice. "Never forget how it feels, brother. And if you touch Shi-Liu without my consent again, I'll kill you."

Kasdeya leaned back in the chair. "And how would you accomplish that, brother?" he asked sarcastically.

"Don't tempt me, Kasdeya. Where there's a—"

Alexandra stepped through the doorway into the tender, flickering light of the candles. Her pink bathrobe was wrapped tight around her body, falling softly to mid thigh. It was an odd contrast with the shiny black boots slicked up her legs.

"Showtime," Shaitan murmured.

Her face was red. "Thanks for the clothes choice, dark man."

"He lied," said Kasdeya. "He does that." His gaze was hungry as it traveled over her body, his cock thickening at the sleek sexiness of the boots and at the sparkle of anger in her eyes. She was magnificent. "I didn't choose what you're wearing any more than I chose to put you in this position in the first place." He jerked his chin toward Shaitan. "Take it up with him, pet."

Her gaze turned to Shaitan and her cheeks got even redder. Shaitan smiled, unfazed by Kasdeya's words. He *did* lie—all the time. Everyone knew that. "C'mere, love."

With hesitant, mincing steps, Alexandra walked toward him, coming to a halt about two feet from the edge of the bed.

"Take it off," the Prince said, gesturing to the robe.

Alex undid the robe's belt, but then stood there fiddling with it, unable to meet Shaitan's gaze. His smile softened as he took a good look at Kasdeya's Summoner for the first time.

Kasdeya's scowled at the sight of his appreciation. His Prince seemed to have just realized how lovely Alexandra was, though how Shaitan could have missed it until now was beyond him. She was thin and supple, with delicate features and that gorgeous cupid-doll mouth. Her damp toffee-brown hair was drying into a shiny waterfall, framing her face like a halo. She looked so sinfully angelic in those ridiculous yet utterly sexy boots. She *was* an angel. More beautiful than any he'd ever known.

Alexandra was nervous—obviously—and angry. But her nipples were hard little pebbles under the thin robe, and her respiration was high from more than just anxiety.

"Look at me, little one," Kasdeya said. She half turned to do so, and his heartbeat quickened at the look of pained uncertainty she wore. The burning need to comfort and protect her welled up in his chest once again. "No. Face me."

One spiked heel caught in the bedding Shaitan had tossed on the floor and rather than just facing him, she ended up falling to her knees in front of him. Kasdeya smiled. Even better. "Take the robe off," he whispered. "But look at me while you do. Look only at me."

When she started to stand, he gave an almost imperceptible shake of his head and sat forward, catching a handful of hair to keep her down. He liked it when she knelt at his feet. Shaitan could bloody well come and get her.

Alexandra pressed a quick kiss to his wrist then pulled her head away. She leaned back on her heels and slowly spread apart her robe. Her gaze remained locked with his.

Kasdeya moaned at her beauty. Her skin glowed golden in the candlelight, her breasts, tipped with perfect, tiny pink nipples thrust up proudly at him. Never mind angels—she was a goddess.

Shaitan stood up from the bed. The movement caught Kasdeya's eye and his gaze flickered to his Prince before settling back on his woman. Kasdeya undid the button on his jeans and eased the zipper down. "Now touch yourself for me, pet," he whispered, freeing his cock. He stroked himself while waiting for her to comply.

* * * *

Alex was nervous, but at the same time so aroused that she could hardly breathe. Her gaze was locked onto her dark man's hand as it moved up and down his magnificent length. In response to his whispered command, she cupped her left breast, pinching the nipple. Her other hand slipped down to press her pubic mound through the thin satin thong. When she moaned, he did too, and his fingers moved just a little bit faster.

Knowing Shaitan was watching made the moment that much more erotic. Then she felt the blond's presence right behind her and Alex's muscles tensed. Her hands fell still on her body.

Kasdeya pointed to his eyes and she nodded. Even when Shaitan's fingers skimmed over her shoulders, easing down the robe, Alex kept her gaze trained on her dark man.

The Prince tugged her hand away from her breast and pulled the sleeve down her arm. When the pink fabric had settled in a puddle on the floor, he lifted her hand back into its former position, his palm hot on the back of hers. It was Alex's own fingers on her skin, but it was Shaitan directing them. He clenched his fist, making hers clench as well, trapping her breast painfully. His breath was moist on her cheek.

After a moment, Shaitan reached for her other hand, where it still rested between her legs. The robe came off completely and Alex, knowing where this was heading, pressed her thighs tight together.

Shaitan immediately let go of her breast and pushed her forward. The move was so unexpected that Alex had fallen onto her elbows, head between Kasdeya's feet, bum high in the air, before she was aware of what had happened. A stinging slap landed on her raised ass and she gasped.

Kasdeya growled a deep, threatening rumble. Alex's head snapped up but he wasn't looking at her; he was looking at Shaitan.

The Prince grabbed a handful of Alex's hair to tug her back up against his chest. Kasdeya was still growling, the sound growing choppier and more threatening. Shaitan growled right back, directly beside her ear, sounding even more menacing than her dark man. Alex quivered.

She'd never thought of herself as the type of woman who wanted men to fight over her. In fact, she'd always looked down on those women as manipulative and the men who quibbled over them as stupid. But these two demi-gods getting snarly with each other—over her, no less—was enough to completely soak the crotch of her panties. And the burn of Shaitan's handprint, still fiery on her ass cheek, wasn't helping her maintain her cool.

"Stop it," she said, her voice more husky than she would have liked.

"Tell your lover to back the fuck off." Shaitan tightened his hand in her hair and pulled until her neck was arched and her head rested against his shoulder. "The deal was that you'd be cooperative. I was simply reminding you of it."

Kasdeya was half out of his seat, looking ready to grab Alex from Shaitan's arms and throttle his Prince. That would ruin everything. Shaitan would surely take him away if Kasdeya couldn't control his temper. In a flash of insight, Alex knew that that was exactly what Shaitan was hoping to accomplish. He wanted to continue to punish Kasdeya.

The Prince was obviously very angry about his concubine. Much more so than Kasdeya seemed to realize.

"Kasdeya, sit!" she instructed.

Kasdeya bared his teeth but sat back down. Alex turned her head to give Shaitan a narrow look. His golden eyes glittered fiercely at her from less than an inch away.

"It won't work," she whispered. "I won't let him lose control like that."

He had the audacity to smile. "Maybe not, but it'll be fun trying," he said, so low that there was no way Kasdeya heard him. "And if I distract you enough…" He let the sentence hang, the implication clear. Kasdeya wasn't the only one being punished tonight. She seemed to have earned the Prince's ire as well—maybe for letting Kasdeya out of his prison? Or was it something else that was making Shaitan look at her with such cool calculation in his eyes?

"You seem to have him well bound, mortal. I'm impressed," Shaitan said at a normal volume. "As long as you keep him leashed, we shouldn't have any problems."

"Shaitan," Kasdeya warned.

"Shut up, mate," Shaitan said cheerfully, his good humor seemingly restored. "Why don't you just sit like the little lady told you to and keep your mouth shut?" He turned his head to lick up the long line of Alex's throat before releasing his hold on her hair. "Now where were we?" He put one hand back on her breast, and the other between her legs, pressing the satin into her wet crease.

She shuddered. She couldn't help it.

"Ah, right there." Shaitan squeezed both hands hard, his gaze never leaving hers. When she tried to turn her face away from the intensity of his stare, his fingers quickly left her breast to cup her jaw and keep her twisted into him. All she could do was shut her eyes, but when she did so, the feel of his fingers between her legs became much too intense. Especially when he left off teasing her through the panties and moved up the little bit required to sneak his hand inside. He laughed when he discovered just how wet she was.

Alex flushed and again tried to turn her head away. Shaitan's hand against her cheek held firm as his lips settled over hers. She flinched, but his kiss wasn't at all what she'd expected. It was soft. Without thinking about it, she parted her lips for the languid exploration of his tongue. His mouth formed a smile against hers when she sighed and leaned into him rather than trying to escape. His tongue seduced her tenderly, slowly, and his fingers on her sex were just as lazy with their gentle, soothing strokes, as if it really were a cat he was petting.

He was being coy with her clit too, barely grazing it before moving away. Alex brought one of her hands up around his neck and slid her fingers through his silky, platinum hair to hold him still while she deepened the kiss. Her hips lifted and her other hand trapped his between her legs, pressing him harder against her.

Kasdeya cursed.

Alex whipped her head back, eyes wide at her betrayal. That was when Shaitan decided to up his game. He tweaked her clit and dropped his fingers back to her breast, pulling and twisting the hard little nub he found there.

Alex grunted, her hips twitching and sex clenching. Her gaze found Kasdeya's, abject apology written across her face. He looked furious. But his hand was wrapped tight around his cock, the large purple head swollen and slick with excitement.

"Kasdeya," she whispered, lifting her arms to him.

"Little one," he groaned. "I want—"

"Yes, I—"

"No," Shaitan said. "That wasn't part of the deal."

"Please, my Prince…"

"Oh, please…"

Alex and Kasdeya's pleas merged into one moaning entreaty. Shaitan chuckled. "Well, all right, since you both asked so nicely." He took his hand out of Alex's underwear and slid it under her ass, lifting her up. "Go ahead. Bend over and take that big beast into your mouth. I'd love to see you do it, actually."

Alex's mouth filled with saliva. She shuffled forward on her knees, reaching to catch Kasdeya's hips in her eager hands.

"But…" Shaitan continued, no longer directly behind her.

Kasdeya's gaze left hers and his expression turned thunderous. "No."

Alex glanced over her shoulder. Shaitan stood beside the bed. In his hand was the paddle.

"I don't think that's your decision to make, brother," Shaitan said.

"And if I say no, I can't touch Kasdeya, right?" Alex asked.

"You got it." Shaitan grinned at her and grasped the neckline of his mesh shirt, ripping it violently off his body. Silver nipple rings gleamed. "Don't say no though. I think this is something we'll all enjoy." He carefully lifted the inverted cross over his head and walked forward to hang it on the closet door's handle.

Alex turned back to her dark man. He was still glowering at Shaitan but when he dropped his gaze to her, his eyes were warm. "Nevermind, pet, I'll survive."

Her hand circled his on his cock. "I want you to do this with me. And it's not like I hate being spanked."

He smoothed her hair away from her temple. "Little one, I didn't really spank you. Not to hurt. Not the way—"

"Enough talking." The Prince was behind her again. "We're losing our forward momentum here. Give me your answer, Summoner."

"No," Kasdeya said.

"Yes," said Alex.

Shaitan laughed. "'Yes' it is." His voice dropped an octave, becoming smooth and intimate. "Before I start, love, I'd like to see your tongue on my brother's cock. I want to watch him fuck those pretty lips of yours."

Another gush of liquid soaked her panties at his words and, with no hesitation, she leaned forward and took Kasdeya's cockhead into her mouth.

* * * *

Kasdeya grabbed her hair and thrust, tossing his head back in pleasure. Alexandra was going to regret her decision. He knew it. But he couldn't tell her to stop again. It felt too damn good.

"Yes," he hissed. "Deeper."

She moaned around his length, bobbing her head until he hit the back of her throat.

"Mmm," Shaitan murmured. He'd come around her body to see better and now knelt beside the chair, one hand holding back the curtain of Alexandra's hair. He looked up and caught Kasdeya's eye. "She's good. I can't wait for my turn."

"Don't...hurt...her," Kasdeya panted, twitching in bliss as Alexandra's mouth worked him over.

The blond smiled a wicked grin and stood once more. "I won't damage your precious woman, Kas." He took up position at Alexandra's rear and jerked his chin toward his brother's groin. With a resigned sigh, Kasdeya gently pushed her away.

"Wha—" she started to ask.

Thwack!

Sure enough, her teeth snapped shut at the impact. Tears sprang into her eyes.

Thwack!

"Jesus!" she cried. When she tried to gain her feet, Shaitan bent over and pushed on her lower back, keeping her down.

"Giving up so soon, Summoner? That's too bad. I'm sure my brother will miss you terribly."

"She can be with you, Shaitan," Kasdeya said. "Just you, like you'd originally planned."

"No. We have a new deal, her and me. She—"

"She's fine." Alexandra spread her legs a little farther apart to brace against the strength of his blows. "She's just fine, you sadistic fuck, so go ahead."

Shaitan let out a great big belly laugh. "S... Sadistic fuck! Oh, that's rich." He wiped his streaming eyes. "Well, you know what they say, love, if the shoe fits"—he sniggered some more—"and this one certainly does, then I guess I should wear it."

Kasdeya was trying not to laugh too, but it *was* funny, calling Shaitan sadistic. No! Really?

* * * *

Alex saw the smile flit across her lover's face and it infuriated her. This was so *not* funny! She dug her nails deep into his hips.

"Do it." She glared at Shaitan over her shoulder. "Just do it, already."

The Prince grinned and raised the paddle. "Your wish, my lady, is—"

He extended his arm.

"—my—"

Alicia Steele

Thwack!

"—command."

She felt a shout try to slip past her lips and muffled it with Kasdeya's prick. Alex looked past the sleek, bronze muscles of Kasdeya' stomach and pecs to see that the smile had been wiped clean off his face.

She lost track of how many times the paddle fell. Her ass had gone from warm pain to hot agony to something beyond that. She was screaming continuously around her dark man's cock, the vibrations making him groan in tune with her shrieks. Kasdeya tried to soothe her, petting her head and shoulders, and though she appreciated the thought, it wasn't really helping.

Her slavish devotion to his shaft had him riding the cusp of orgasm every few seconds, but each time she felt that tell-tale swell against her tongue, Alex lifted her head away. There was no way he got to come while she was being tortured. No fucking way. And she wasn't going to forget that he'd laughed at her either. Oh no, Kasdeya was going to get his.

But then the inevitable started to happen—Alex pushed back into the whacks, rather than trying to wriggle away from them. Her entire rear-end throbbed and pulsed. Hot. So hot. Her clit was pulsing too, sending skittering shocks of tangled pain and pleasure signals throughout her body.

The next strike had her clawing at Kasdeya's thighs. Her body tensed and she lifted her head, sobbing in pleasure. Just one more smack would do it.

"'Bout time," Shaitan mumbled. The paddle dropped with a loud clatter. "I'll give you this, Summoner—you're a hell of a lot tougher than you look." He fell to his knees behind her and tugged the thin strip of satin from between the lips of her engorged sex. "Keep suckin', love, you can come together," he said as he lowered his mouth to her soaking wet core.

Alex bent her head to take Kasdeya deep into her mouth at the same moment that Shaitan smacked his palms on her raw ass cheeks and spread them wide. When the Prince's tongue found the firm pebble of her clit, lashing it with aggressive glee, she started to come in long, shuddering pulses of pleasure. She screamed around her dark man's cock again, but this time she didn't pull away when he bulged against her palate.

Kasdeya hollered and reared up, hands firm on the back of her skull. Jet after jet of sugary come scalded her throat.

One of Shaitan's hands left the red-hot fire of her bottom and he thrust two fingers deep inside her body, fucking her with short, hard strokes. Without coming down even slightly from the first, she climbed another climactic summit. Kasdeya slipped from her open mouth, still dribbling, as Alex thrashed and sobbed in his lap.

"Oh God, stop," she moaned. "Stop."

Shaitan didn't stop but he slowed, easing her through the spasms of ecstasy. His tongue laved her skin, his cool, slick saliva soothing the burn.

Eventually, she became quiet, breathing heavily into the sex scented curls of Kasdeya's groin.

"You'll do, love," the Prince said, his fingers easing out of her body. "You'll do."

Chapter 14

"I can appreciate what you see in her, brother," Shaitan said around the cigarette clenched in his teeth. He dunked the tea bag a few more times and then used a teaspoon to squeeze out as much of the muddy brew as he could against the side of the cup. "She's phenomenal."

Shaitan stepped on the foot pedal of the garbage and flipped the sopping tea bag inside, his movements practiced and casual. Kasdeya watched him in annoyance. When he'd arrived, Kasdeya'd had to relearn everything about Earth; so much had changed in only one hundred years. Shaitan, on the other hand, made it a point to set foot on this plane at least once a year. "Just to keep my hand in," was how he'd always explained it. Kasdeya vowed never to let so much time pass between visits again. The language, the technology, everything was so different.

And if there was one thing Kasdeya hated, it was feeling inept. He was going to get a cellphone too, damn it. Everyone had one—even the High Prince of Hell. He'd been astonished when Shaitan had fished the tiny silver device out of his coat pocket before following Kasdeya into the kitchen. What did Shaitan need a cellphone for?

Shaitan tucked the phone between shoulder and ear, listening to his missed messages as he stirred way too much sugar into his tea. He grunted and snapped the thing closed, pausing to flick his cigarette butt in the sink before taking a seat across from Kasdeya at the table.

"Shi-Liu's getting edgy." Shaitan pulled another smoke out of his pack. "Wants to know where I am." He didn't bother to use a lighter this time, touching it to the edge of one golden fingernail instead. The end of the cigarette glowed red.

"Yeah? Well, why don't you run along home to her then?" asked Kasdeya before draining his coffee.

Shaitan blew a cloud of smoke in his face. "Not yet, mate. I haven't fucked your woman yet."

Kasdeya grimaced and slammed his coffee down hard enough to chip the tabletop. Somehow, the cup didn't break.

The Prince just crossed his legs calmly and sipped his tea. "Careful, you'll wake Sleeping Beauty, and she's gonna need to be well rested for round two."

They'd left Alexandra curled in the center of the bed, so deeply asleep that she barely seemed to be breathing. Kasdeya had had to carry her the short distance as his beautiful little angel had hardly been able to stand. Yes, she needed rest, but not for more sex. At least, not for more sex with Shaitan.

"Call it off, Shaitan. You've already—"

"What? I've already what?" the blond snapped. "Given her two orgasms and then watched you pant and moan your way through one? Is that what you were going to say, Kas? 'Cause that's all I've done. One night is what we agreed upon, brother, and it's only"—he glanced at the clock on the stove—"twelve-thirty. I've got hours yet. So lay off. I'm not going anywhere 'til the damn cock crows."

Kasdeya leaned back in his chair and tucked his hands behind his head. "Cock-a-doodle-doo."

The Prince choked on his mouthful of tea, coughing and laughing at the same time. "Yes, you *are* a cock. But I'm still staying."

Kasdeya smiled. "It was worth a try."

Shaitan leaned back as well, suddenly serious. "What's your plan here, Kas?"

"My plan?"

"Don't play dense, man, it doesn't suit. They're going to come for you. Soon. If I can find you, the Powers won't be far behind." He took a long drag on his cigarette, looking around at the partially plastered walls and the paintbrushes sitting on the counter. "I can't help but wonder why you're playing house. You should have started to move days ago. Take the Summoner with you, but get going."

Kasdeya ran a hand down over his face. "It's not that simple, brother. She has a full life here. I—"

"Are you brain dead?" Shaitan interrupted. "When Uriel gets his hands on you both, her life will end—quickly and, hopefully for her sake, not too painfully. It's you he'll want to visit pain on. What are you thinking?" He took another drag. "And speaking of her life, did you want me to contract her while I'm here?" He stubbed out the cigarette to hold up his hand in front of Kasdeya's face. The first two fingers were crossed.

"No funny business, I swear," he said solemnly. "Or not much, anyway. Maybe a yearly stipend or something. She really is phenomenal."

Kasdeya slapped the hand away. "After tonight, you're never touching her again, so get that thought right out of your head. As for her soul..." His shoulders slumped. "I don't think Alexandra will sell. She's too good a person."

Shaitan shrugged. "Lots of good ones fall, brother. You should know that better than anyone. If you love her, how can you stand by and watch her die? These human lives"—he snapped his fingers—"go like that."

"I never said I loved her," Kasdeya mumbled, dropping his gaze.

"Oh, Kas," Shaitan said with an indulgent grin. "You surely did. I'll leave a contract before I go. Make her sign it. Don't let her slip away." He motioned to the half-decorated room. "And stop with the holly-homemaker crap. She's not safe here. You're not safe here. Either sign her up and bring her home or run."

"I've set up a guard."

"Great!" said Shaitan sarcastically. "That'll work super, as long as neither of you ever leave the house."

Kasdeya's brows drew down.

"Oh, you do leave the house?" the Prince continued. "Well, then, you must know a globe-encompassing spell. Do share. Not to mention the fact that she calls you by name all the bloody time. Has she said it outside of the house, Kasdeya, in front of anyone else? Is your name, even now, being bandied about Earth? Tripping off of mortal tongues and flying straight to immortal ears?"

Thoughts of Melynda and her coven flitted through Kasdeya's mind. "I'll protect her."

Shaitan reached for his hand, curling his long white fingers around Kasdeya's long brown ones. "Who are you trying to kid? You can't protect her from the Powers, brother. Not on this plane."

* * * *

Alex woke to the lovely feel of strong male hands traveling over her skin. She turned into his chest and offered her mouth up for a kiss. He obliged, and it was sweet, and soft, and good and...it wasn't Kasdeya. With a gasp, Alex pushed away, using Shaitan's muscular white torso for leverage. She encountered an equally muscular body behind her.

"Oh," she said, "I thought—"

"He was me," Kasdeya finished for her. "Well, he's not, pet." He slid his hand under her arm to palm her breast. "So roll over and try again."

When she tried to do so, Shaitan caught at her hip. His hard cock rubbed against her, clearly felt through his jeans. "One more for me, first." He gave her a charming, lopsided grin. The coldness she'd seen before was completely gone from his eyes, replaced by a fond, golden warmth. "After all, he gets to kiss you every day, and I only have tonight."

"Uh... I..." she stammered.

"Oh, go ahead, pet." Kasdeya pressed his prick—also denim covered—into her ass, where Alex was surprised to feel only a slight tenderness, not the agony she'd expected. Her boots were gone too. They must have healed and undressed her while she slept. The question "Why am I the only one mostly naked here?" died on her lips as Kasdeya rolled her nipple between his fingers. She arched into the caress.

"He's right." Kasdeya trailed kisses along her throat. "He only has you for one night. I suppose we can humor the bastard."

Shaitan chuckled and his gaze lifted over her shoulder. "Too kind, brother. Too kind."

"I live to please you, my Prince," Kasdeya said, with a chuckle of his own.

What the hell? Alex felt like she'd woken up in an alternate reality. Were these the same two fellows that had been at each other's throats only a few hours ago?

"What say you, Summoner?" Shaitan leaned in until his lips brushed hers. "Can I steal another kiss?"

Kasdeya swirled his tongue into her ear, and plucked more aggressively at her nipples. First one, then the other.

Alex moaned into Shaitan's mouth, her hips twitching against his groin. Her tongue delved between his lips. He smiled and sucked on it, letting her explore as she liked. His hand skimmed down her thigh, lifting it and setting it on his hip so he could rock his hardness against her crotch. She moaned again and threaded her hands through his short, soft hair.

"All right." Kasdeya gave Alex's ass a slap. "It's my turn now, cut it out."

Alex turned only her upper body, her sex still pressed tight to Shaitan's cock, and tugged her dark man's head down to hers. Kasdeya was much more demanding, thrusting his tongue hard inside her mouth, claiming her. His hand left her breasts to wrap around her neck, holding her close for his kiss.

Alex didn't have long to mourn the loss of his wicked fingers though. In a single, crisp maneuver, Shaitan shifted backward, tugging her lower body with him to create a space between her and Kasdeya, then rolled her onto her back, his body between her thighs. He slithered down a bit to replace his brother's fingers with his lips. Alex wrapped her legs around the Prince's waist, grinding into his naked stomach. Her fingers clenched tighter in his hair, pressing him closer still.

Shaitan bit at the stiff, saliva-slick peak of her nipple, making Alex buck beneath him. "Eager, love?" he purred.

Her mouth was still full of Kasdeya's tongue, so all she could do was moan louder in affirmation.

Kasdeya pulled his head back, his black eyes flashing with desire. "You're still all right with this, pet?"

She nodded and petted his cheek. "And you? You don't mind—"

"I mind." He kissed her palm. "But I don't want you to mind. He's my sovereign. You're my lover. You're both important to me. Let's just try to wring some mutual pleasure out of the situation, all right?"

Alex bit her lip to keep from moaning in his face as Shaitan slipped his hand into her thong. She nodded a tad too energetically.

Kasdeya quirked one dark brow. "Distracted, are you?"

The Prince flicked her clit and she whimpered, chewing on her lip so hard she tasted blood. She nodded again.

Kasdeya smiled and smoothed her hand down his torso to the waistband of his jeans. He let her go for a second to undo the button and lower the zipper, then he directed her fingers inside. "I'd like to be distracted too."

Shaitan laughed softly into her skin, making her breast quiver. "Hold up there, ya greedy bastard." He gave Alex's nipple one more lick before lifting himself off her body. "It's my turn and you know it."

Kasdeya sighed, rocking his hips in time to his woman's strokes. "I suppose you're right."

Alex gave him one final squeeze and a quick, deep kiss. "I love you," she whispered against his cheek. Then she sat up to face Shaitan, not wanting to see Kasdeya's expression in the wake of her admission. If he didn't feel the same way, fine. But she wanted him to know that no matter what happened tonight, he was the only one in her heart.

                              * * * *

It took every ounce of will Kasdeya possessed not to pull her back shouting, "Mine! Mine! Mine!" like a crazed fool. She'd said it! Kasdeya felt delight, terror and a thousand other emotions too muddled to decipher in the maelstrom her words had incited. She'd actually said it. Not in the heat of ecstasy, but with cool, calm knowledge of what she was admitting.

She loved him.

And against all odds, he loved her too.

And—God damn it!—the woman he loved was about to fuck someone else.

Kasdeya squeezed his eyes shut against the sight of his Prince taking Alexandra in his arms. It was just for one night. Just one…fucking… night. Yes, "fuck" really *was* a versatile little word.

* * * *

"I want to see you in this sexy underwear before I rip it off," murmured Shaitan between kisses as he maneuvered them both to the edge of the mattress. "Stand up, love."

She did, resisting the urge to cover her breasts as she took position in front of him.

The Prince whistled and lifted her hands from her sides, holding them wide. "You're bloody gorgeous, Alexandra, no lie. You've outdone yourself, Kas," he said over his shoulder.

Alex's gaze flicked to her dark man's. Kasdeya was lying with one hand clamped over his eyes, his mouth turned down in a frown. It was evident that he couldn't even bear to look at her. She should have kept her stupid mouth shut. Now everything was ruined. Her lip trembled and she looked away, tears welling.

"Oy. What's gotten into you?" Shaitan asked. "Sorry, love, but there's no way I'm seducing a crying woman. Even the Devil has to have principles."

* * * *

Kasdeya had been doing his level best to ignore them both but at Shaitan's words he snuck a quick peek. Why was Alexandra crying? Shaitan caught his gaze and made an exaggerated chin motion towards the Summoner. Alexandra had big silvery tears rolling down her cheeks, the sight of which made Kasdeya's own waterworks turn on. He slapped his palm back over his leaking eyes, embarrassed at how emotionally out of control he felt.

"Look at your woman, brother," Shaitan said, exasperation hardening his tone. "Isn't she gorgeous?"

"She is." Kasdeya's hand didn't move away from his face.

"Look at her, idiot!" snapped Shaitan. "Tell her, not me."

Kasdeya looked. His gaze was soft, full of love. "You're gorgeous, little angel." His voice cracked on the last two words.

Alexandra let out a tiny, hiccoughing sob.

"Oh, for fuck's sake." Shaitan threw up his hands in disgust. He nudged the Summoner out of his way and stood to wrap a friendly arm around her shoulders. "All this emotional bullshit is killing me, folks. Let's get it over with once and for all so we can have a proper little orgy sometime before dawn, okay?" He gestured to Kasdeya. "C'mere, mate."

Kasdeya crawled to the edge of the mattress and tried to stand but Shaitan pushed him back down. "Give me your hand." Kasdeya frowned as he placed his palm in Shaitan's. "Put your hand over his," Shaitan instructed Alex. She obeyed. "Good. Now, brother, repeat after me. 'I love you, Alexandra.'"

Alexandra gasped. "You can't make him—"

The hand on her shoulder lifted to clap itself over her mouth. "Say it," Shaitan said in a bored drawl.

Kasdeya laughed at her big, round eyes peeking at him over his Prince's palm. "I love you, Alexandra."

"Mmm-hmm," Shaitan said. "Now say, 'And I want to spend eternity with you.'"

Kasdeya smile turned into a frown. His Prince was playing games again. But Alexandra's eyes clouded over at his hesitation.

"And I want to spend eternity with you," Kasdeya repeated softly. His gaze held hers, trying to make her understand the absolute truth of the words, even though they weren't his own.

She looked unsure for one more second, but then he must have reached her, because elation replaced uncertainty. Shaitan removed his hand. "Say, 'ditto,'" he whispered in her ear.

Alexandra laughed—a wonderful, joyous sound. "Ditto."

The Prince nodded. "Fine. When we're through, I have some papers for you to look over, love."

"Shaitan," Kasdeya warned.

"Shut up, brother. This is yet another instance where it's her choice—not yours. But right now…" He turned Alexandra to face him directly. "Right now, I think its past time you started thinking about pleasing the fella who can keep you both apart if he's in a pissy mood." He leaned his forehead against hers. "And he's starting to feel a tad pissy."

Kasdeya chuckled, feeling much better about things all of a sudden. His Prince had done him a favor. Who knows how long it would have taken him to work up the nerve to tell Alexandra how he felt on his own? And his earlier thoughts on the sex still stood. They should all try to wring as much pleasure as they could out of the situation. "Go ahead, little one," he said. "Show him how wonderful you are. Make him live to regret that he'll never have another night with you."

Shaitan grinned. "That's what I'm talking about."

"By the way," Kasdeya said, leaning back on his elbows to watch, "those moronic nipple decorations aren't just for show. He likes it as rough as you can make it."

The Prince's brows shot up. "Kasde—"

* * * *

Alex wasted no time. She grabbed the rings and twisted them. Shaitan's lips peeled back from his teeth. His eyes squeezed shut. "Traitorous prick," he hissed at Kasdeya.

Alex changed tactics, tugging the jewelry violently away from his body. One knee came between his legs to mash against his groin. Shaitan shuddered. "Oh, I knew you'd fuckin' do," he groaned, gripping her waist with one hand and tangling his other in her hair.

This time when his lips met hers there was nothing soft about it. Their teeth clashed and their tongues dueled. The kiss was so forceful that Alex's lip tore, flooding their mouths with the tang of copper. Shaitan groaned again, a feral sound. Alex pulled at his nipples with all her strength but, of course, he was just as indestructible as his dark brother.

"What else, Summoner?" Shaitan broke away to ask. "What else have you got?" His eyes were darker now, still yellow, but rather than bringing to mind honey or amber, images of snarling wolves and screaming eagles flashed through her head. She glanced at Kasdeya. He shifted sideways and patted the mattress.

"Rough," he mouthed.

She nodded and looked back into Shaitan's eyes, allowing all her repressed, violent human tendencies to surge forward. She couldn't hurt him, and he liked it, so...

In a simple maneuver that he could have easily countered if he'd chosen to, Alex hooked her ankle behind Shaitan's and pushed. He fell backward onto the bed, bearing her down with him, but she immediately sat up, straddling his hips.

Shaitan smirked at her. "Now what? Got any more toys to play with, maybe? He lightly slapped her thigh. "I'm afraid the paddle doesn't do much for me."

Uncertainty crept back into her expression. Now what, indeed? She looked to her dark man for guidance.

"Toys?" he asked, moving up to rummage through the night table drawer. "Well, let's see..."

Alex already knew there wasn't anything suitable in there. Shaitan needed a bullwhip...or something.

When he turned back around, Kasdeya had the handcuffs, a blue scarf, lube and the centurion in his hands. Alex blushed at the wave of heat the big black cock inspired. "Here's some toys for you, sire," Kasdeya said.

She frowned. What good were those?

"Brother…"

Shaitan sounded odd, hoarse. She looked back at him, surprised to see him eyeing the collection with trepidation.

"Brother," Kasdeya mimicked. His lips crooked and he held out the handcuffs to Alex.

"These won't hold him any more than they'd have held you if I hadn't made a point of ordering you not to break them," Alex commented, taking the proffered item.

"Shaitan knows the rules of this game." Kasdeya's malicious grin grew by the second. "He won't try to escape. Would you like a safe word, my Prince?"

Shaitan's prick, an iron rod under her ass, gave a hard jump at Kasdeya's words. Alex's brows twitched up. Kasdeya seemed to know what he was doing; the High Prince of Hell was quivering with excitement. "I don't believe in 'em," Shaitan rasped. "You know that, Kas."

Kasdeya shrugged. "Had to offer." He shifted his gaze to Alex. "Cuff him."

She felt another salmon-like leap against her rear.

With a bemused expression, Alex took Shaitan's hands off her legs and raised them above his head. He was completely unresisting. He was also too far down on the bed, his feet were still flat on the floor. "Move up," she instructed.

"Make me."

Once again, she looked to Kasdeya for guidance. He gazed back blankly, motioning "go ahead" with his hand. No help there.

She thought for a second. "Keep your hands over your head for a minute?" The Prince nodded agreeably.

Alex put the cuffs down beside him and scooted backward to undo the button fly on Shaitan's tight black jeans. His cock, almost shockingly pink, sprang out. Underwear wasn't something these guys seemed to have much use for. Alex licked her lips at the long, thick length of him. Not as thick as her dark man's, but maybe a bit longer, and more than respectable, at any rate. She peeled the denim down his legs, gasping in surprise when his plump, full scrotum was revealed, decorated prettily by three more silver hoops.

When he was naked, she crawled up the bed to kneel with her back against the headboard, three feet above his head. Shaitan tilted his face back to regard her. The fingers of his outstretched hands were about eight inches short of her body.

In a single, sudden move, Alex reached down and ripped her thong off. Gemstones scattered over the sheets. She shook loose the remaining jewels and then leaned over to stuff the satin into Shaitan's mouth. He groaned around the gag.

The sound of Kasdeya chuckling made Alex look up. He grinned broadly at her from his side of the bed. "You're doing great, pet."

She smirked and held his gaze while she spread wide the lips of her sex. His smile became greedy as his gaze dropped. Both men watched her dip two fingers into her wet warmth and then bring them up to massage the raised pebble of her clit. After only a few seconds of this intense scrutiny, Alex was ready to come. She tossed her head back, canted her hips forward and let herself go, making every moan count, twitching and whimpering as the pleasure washed through her. Before the pulses had fully stopped, she felt Shaitan's hands between her thighs. He'd snuck up the distance required to touch her—still not close enough to cuff, but only short by inches now. Three long fingers thrust inside her and curved into her G-spot, and Alex enjoyed another climax before letting her head fall forward.

Kasdeya was now naked and much closer than before. He leaned over to kiss her, never stopping the rough fisting he was treating his lovely dark cock to. She kissed him back enthusiastically for a minute and then returned her attention to Shaitan.

"I didn't say you could touch me." She grabbed a handful of his white-blond hair and used it to wrench his head to the side.

His laugh was audible even through the satin. It stopped when she leaned over and bit at his exposed throat, clamping her jaw around the strained tendon.

She couldn't make out what he shouted, but if his bucking hips were any indication, he liked the sharp, oral attention.

Alex moved down his body, biting and sucking, until her breasts were in his face. He grunted, apparently pushing out the gag because she immediately felt his mouth on her nipple, biting back, making her cry out. Then he suckled the hurt away. She enjoyed the sensation for a moment before lifting her body off him. Alex picked up the sodden panties and rolled them into a ball. "If it comes out again, I'll stop. All you'll get from me is a plain ol' missionary screw. Got it?"

Shaitan sucked in his cheeks, clearly choking on a smart-ass retort, and nodded.

"Open wide."

He obeyed and she shoved the underwear back in his mouth. Then she went straight for his left nipple, catching the hoop in her teeth and pulling. He hollered and grabbed at her hair, but Kasdeya was instantly there, capturing his Prince's hands and bringing them back over his head. "Ah, ah, that's not allowed, either," Kasdeya said.

Shaitan twisted and groaned, caught between Kasdeya's hands and Alex's teeth.

Alex could feel her dark man's thigh pressed against her knee. He was sitting right beside them now to hold Shaitan's hands down, and her raised ass was only inches from his mouth. The thought made her groan, made her sex clench. Kasdeya groaned as well, and she felt his hot breath—a kiss, a nibble—on her hip. No time for distractions, though. She sped the Prince's seduction up, trailing nasty, hard bites down his torso until she hovered over his prick. She was straddling Shaitan's face now, her pubic curls brushing his chin.

Shaitan thrust his cock at her in mindless desperation, but the throbbing shaft, which was so close to her lips that each puff of her breath made it twitch, received no attention. Instead, she hooked her finger through the first silver ring in his scrotum and tugged straight back.

His cries became frantic and he buried his face in her body to try to contain them. The stifled screams shivered deliciously through her womb. Alex glanced back to gauge her progress. Kasdeya's biceps bulged as he held his Prince immobile. When he saw her looking, he stretched Shaitan's arms high. So close.

Alex nodded and picked up the cuffs, passing them back to him. He grabbed them with one hand and she heard a distinctive click. Before Shaitan had a chance to react, she took the tip of his cock between her lips. Her tongue dipped into the slit to sample the nectar of his pre-come, which was almost as tasty as Kasdeya's, and her finger renewed its persuasion on the silver hoop. After a few quick swipes, she moved one inch away. Shaitan could sense the warmth of her mouth, so very near. All he had to do was follow where she led. He did, bucking his hips higher up the mattress to enable him to thrust down her throat.

The satisfying noise of the cuff's chain being fed through the remaining bed slats was heard, and then another click. Job done.

At the sound of his confinement, Shaitan's whole body convulsed. Warm, syrupy pulses flowed over Alex's tongue. His release was so profuse that she couldn't swallow fast enough. After what seemed an eternity, the pulses diminished. Shaitan's breath was labored and uneven. He snorted through his nostrils, seemingly unable to gain enough air. Alex sat up and turned around to pull her panties out of the poor fellow's mouth.

"Don't think you're done, love," he gasped.

She was about to reply when Kasdeya chimed in. "*You're* done for now, brother. It's my turn." Her gaze rose to his and her breath caught in her throat. He looked half-crazed with lust, his chest rising on great pants of air. His pulse was so high she could see every thump of his pounding heart in his temples, throat and cock. She moaned and slid over Shaitan's body to crawl into his arms.

"No," Kasdeya said. "Straddle him again."

"What?" she asked. "No! I want you."

Kasdeya groaned and crushed her close, grinding against the warmth of her stomach. "I know. I want you too. Trust me." He gave her a bruising kiss then lifted her back onto his Prince's body.

Alex pouted, but dropped back onto Shaitan's lap, positioning herself above his still iron-hard cock.

"Don't you dare!" growled Kasdeya.

"Then—"

"Just wait a minute, pet. You'll see." He grabbed two pillows and shoved them under Shaitan's head, lifting it up about a foot. "Good?" Shaitan nodded, smiling. Kasdeya picked up the scarf.

"Oh, come now, Kas." Shaitan turned his face to the side "I've seen you up close before."

"Sorry, but not tonight, my Prince." Kasdeya grabbed a handful of Shaitan's hair to lift his head up even further and tied off the fabric. When the Prince's head dropped back onto the pillow, his eyes were completely covered. Kasdeya looked at Alex. "Move up and grab the headboard."

She did, ending up with her thighs parted around Shaitan's head. "*Oh.*"

"Yes, 'oh,'" Kasdeya confirmed with a laugh. He moved behind her, straddling the blond as well, and shifted her into the proper position, angling her ass toward him. Then he used his knees to walk her forward the tiny bit needed to push her breasts into the headboard and her sex into Shaitan's mouth. Her hands framed her head on the wall. "Ready?" he whispered.

Shaitan was already lapping at her engorged clit, making her tremble. Alex groaned, but nodded.

Kasdeya entered her slowly. Too slowly. Filling her so gradually that it seemed one long, never-ending thrust as she stretched to accommodate him. Shaitan, on the other hand, was being much too harsh on her clit. He'd trapped the sensitive bundle of nerves between his teeth and was flicking his tongue rapidly back and forth over it. She started coming even before her dark man hilted.

"Oh God," she cried, her body going rigid. Kasdeya slapped her ass, making the climax stronger. Silky fluid streamed down Shaitan's chin. "God, God, God," Alex panted on purpose. Each repeat earned her another smack.

* * * *

Kasdeya chewed on his lip, fighting off the orgasm with his entire being. Alexandra was coming so hard he couldn't have retreated from her body even if he'd wanted to. Her inner muscles had clamped down in a death grip, working every ridge of his cock, pulling and sucking and mauling. It was so bloody good. And she wouldn't stop calling on God, so he couldn't stop spanking her, which just made the blissful agony go on and on.

"Pet," he moaned. "Pet, stop now. Please." Her sex went through one more round of python-like contractions that had him grabbing the base of his prick in an effort to stop from flooding her womb. Then she suddenly fell limp. The only things keeping her up were the wall she rested against and his cock buried in her body. Her back wore a sheen of sweat. She couldn't seem to stop whimpering.

Kasdeya took a second to recover and curved around her, breathing deeply.

"Oh no," Alex breathed. "Shaitan… No." But her hips rocked the slightest amount, moving in time with the blond's tongue.

Kasdeya smiled against her back. He knew the routine. Now, his Prince would be gentle, and it was up to Kasdeya to provide the contrast. He took one more deep breath, not entirely sure he was up to the task. But nothing ventured nothing gained, they always say.

Kasdeya grasped her hips firmly, pulled back until only the flared head of his cock remained inside, paused for one second more and then slammed home.

"Kasdeya!"

And again. "Oh God."

Smack. Again.

"Oh…"

Again.

"Fuck…"

Again.

Alex's muscles twanged. She reared up, reaching back to wrap her arms around his neck. Shaitan raised his head to follow her.

Faster now: a blur of pleasure. Tears were streaming down her beautiful face. "I love you so damned much!" she gasped.

Kasdeya crushed her in his embrace. "Forever?"

"Yes!"

It felt like he'd been torn asunder so great was his release. It was as if his very life force cascaded out of his body into hers. He just held her tighter, drowning.

Chapter 15

They collapsed beside Shaitan, barely conscious. Alex was caught firm between their large, wonderfully male bodies.

"You two are something else," the Prince commented, turning his blind face toward where she snuggled against him.

Alex smiled into his shoulder. "Yeah, we are," she said drowsily.

"Hey, now." His grin was wry. "No falling asleep. Somehow, amidst the declarations of undying love and the multiple Earth-shattering orgasms, I still haven't been shagged yet."

"You fuck him," Alex mumbled to Kasdeya as her eyes drifted shut. "I'm too damn tired."

She must have dozed, but not for nearly long enough. Alex was still exhausted when the sound of Shaitan groaning roused her. He sounded all riled up. It was a very sexy sound—certainly worth cracking an eyelid for. Just one lid though, sweet unconsciousness beckoned after all.

"This is not what I agreed to, boyo. I… Oh… Oh, yeah…"

Alex blinked both eyes open. Then blinked again. Kasdeya was kneeling between Shaitan's thighs and he was…

She sat up fast. No, he wasn't. But he kind of was.

The centurion was being slowly and methodically worked into the Prince's ass by her dark man.

"Wha—" she said, but Kasdeya held a finger to his lips, his eyes twinkling with mischief.

"Kasdeya," Shaitan groaned. "You know I'm quite fond of this, you're way up there on my top ten favorite fucks list, but I really must in—" His words choked off as Kasdeya slammed the dildo the rest of the way home. The blond gasped. "Bloody hell," he moaned, planting his feet on the mattress and rising to meet the intrusion.

"You must what now?" Kasdeya asked, pulling the toy almost all the way out.

"I must insist that Alexa… Ahh, fuck!"

"Hmm?" Kasdeya was laughing openly now.

Alex leaned over the Prince's body to see better. She'd never had anal sex, or seen it performed, and was surprised to find herself not only interested, but turned on as well.

"That Alexandra fuck me!" Shaitan finished in a rush before Kasdeya could interrupt him again.

"If you insist, sire." Kasdeya motioned Alex into the space between Shaitan's legs. She came eagerly, slipping just in front of him. "Rough," he whispered in her ear, taking her hand and placing it on the dildo.

She wasn't rough though—not at first. Hunkering down on her elbows, she timidly drew the centurion out, astounded at the way Shaitan's body stretched to accommodate its girth. Just as hesitantly, she started to push it back in again. But then, the shocking feel of one well-lubed finger breaching her own ass made her arm twitch, and she accidentally pushed the dildo all the way home.

"Harder, Kas," Shaitan hissed.

Alex realized that Shaitan thought it was her dark man's cock stretching his body. The thought was unbearably erotic. The image of the two gorgeous males entwined—one pale white and blond, the other dark bronze and black—flashed through her head, making her groan. She worked the dildo faster.

Kasdeya kept pace with her, sawing back and forth into her virgin pucker. His other hand was playing with her clit. Then there were two fingers in her body. The burn was extreme, the pleasure more so. Her body tensed as another orgasm threatened.

"Not yet, pet."

Suddenly, she was empty.

Alex whimpered at the loss and her hand fell still, holding the centurion locked in Shaitan's ass.

"Bloody hell, don't stop!" hollered the blond.

Kasdeya moved to Shaitan's head and whispered something to him. Shaitan nodded once and then, easy as pie, snapped the cuff chain. He ripped off the scarf, leaning up on his elbows to smirk at her. "What are you doing, you naughty girl? Don't you know it's not wise to try and deceive the Devil?"

He looked so damned cocky, but Alex knew something he didn't. With a smirk of her own, Alex flipped the switch on the bottom of the toy and leaned her full weight into it.

Shaitan hollered and thrashed. "Call her off, Kas," he yelled, grabbing his balls in one hand while trying to fend her off with the other. "Call her off!"

Interestingly enough, he didn't attempt to remove the cock himself.

Kasdeya gently pulled her away, leaving the dildo where it was. The flanged base ensured it would stay put for a minute, but he did flick it off. "I'm afraid he won't stop pestering until he's had you, pet. So let's just get that over with, all right?" He turned her in his arms and spread her legs over Shaitan's. Kasdeya gave her a single, deep kiss and then pushed her flat. Now she was lying with her back pressed to Shaitan's front. She frowned up at her dark man. What was he doing?

The Prince's hands came around her torso, cupping her breasts. "Now you're going to get it," he said, licking her throat.

She was about to ask him what he meant when she felt Kasdeya position Shaitan's cockhead against her wet folds. Her dark man took hold of her hips and pulled her toward him and, just like that, Shaitan was engulfed by her slick inner walls.

"Mmm." It was hard to tell who moaned that time.

Kasdeya slid her back up and then tugged her down again. She was so damp with sweat that she slipped easily over the blond's skin. It was strange to be moved by someone else, to have no control over the pace or depth. But this was an entirely new angle for her, rubbing entirely new spots, and it felt damned good. Plus, she really was tired, and if her dark man wanted to manipulate her like a puppet, that was fine with her. She let her eyes drift shut as she enjoyed the new, languid sensations.

Then Shaitan's cock left—her vagina, anyway. Now it was pressed against her sphincter. Alex's eyes shot open again. "No."

"Yes," Kasdeya disagreed in a low, soothing voice. He scooped some of her abundant juices out, distributing them lower over Shaitan's prick and her tiny hole.

"Kasdeya." She struggled but the Prince held her firm.

"Little one," Kasdeya murmured, spreading himself over her body and easing his rock-hard cock in where, only moments ago, Shaitan's had been. "This is mine." He held himself up with one hand and dipped the other between their bodies to clasp her mound. "Shaitan has agreed to take you this way, so that this can *stay* mine. I will never allow another male's seed to bathe your womb." He bent his head to hers, stopping a hairbreadth above her lips. "Don't worry. You'll enjoy yourself, pet. I promise." He rocked his hips to stroke her from the inside while Shaitan's prick nudged harder against her ass.

"If I say stop?"

"We'll stop."

Shaitan laughed. "You won't want us to stop, love."

Kasdeya took a firm hold of her hips and very slowly eased her down again. When she whimpered at the unfamiliar ache, he stopped and drove into her, pulling her attention back to her sex. The Prince moved one hand in the tight space between her and Kasdeya to tickle her clit. His other hand remained on her breast, the nipple caught between his fingers.

"Relax, Alexandra," Shaitan whispered, fondling her earlobe with his tongue. His nipple rings scraped her back as Kasdeya pulled her down a little bit further. The firm, round head of Shaitan's cock popped inside. It seemed smaller than she knew it to be, but it was still plenty big enough to hurt.

"Oh... I can't," she moaned, pushing at her dark man's chest. "I can't."

Kasdeya leaned over further, ignoring her ineffectual attempt to move him, and suckled her throat. "You can." He jabbed into her again, hands biting deep into the flesh of her hips. Shaitan's fingers were powerful on her clit, on her breast. They were both kissing her neck, licking, biting... and Kasdeya was thrusting, thrusting...and suddenly Alex realized that indeed she *could*. Indeed, she had.

Time seemed to stop as Shaitan hilted. Their bodies paused, hips motionless, hands still, as if all three were balanced on a great precipice. The great plummet toward that mini-death was inevitable, but for one second, the anticipation of the fall was more important than the fall itself.

"Right," said Shaitan after a moment. His voice was husky. "Let's do this." His prick swelled in her ass, expanding slowly to chafe against the sensitive inner walls of her colon. Kasdeya's cock answered with its own jolt against her cervix. That trick Kasdeya did with his tongue—she realized they could do it with every part of their body.

"No bigger," Alex begged the Prince. She already felt full to bursting.

"All right," Shaitan agreed, spreading his legs wider around Alex and Kasdeya's to brace himself. "Get ready for the ride of your life, love." His hand left her breast and caught in her long, tangled hair, turning her face to his so that he could ravage her mouth. His other hand renewed its movement on her clit.

Kasdeya started to move again too. Every time he retreated, Shaitan would drive forward. Their motions were smooth and practiced. Alex had a brief thought as to why that might be. How many times had they done this?

But soon, all thought was obliterated in the roil of sensation rushing from where she was so deliciously impaled between the two demi-gods. She groaned against Shaitan's lips, one hand coming to rest on his jaw. Her other hand found the back of Kasdeya's skull. All she had to do was twist her head a fraction, and then it was his tongue filling her mouth. Both of them were kissing her, taking turns, until it became impossible for anyone to know whose tongue was whose. The bed was rocking with their motion, shimmying across the wood floor.

Shaitan's breathing became ragged, as did the movement of his hips. "Come, love," he gasped. "I can't last much longer." His fingers were a blur on her clit.

"I don't know if I can," she said. "It's too much."

Kasdeya leaned away from her body, changing the angle of penetration. One of his hands left her waist to delve between their entwined legs. There was a soft click, then the muted sound of the centurion whirring to life deep inside Shaitan's body. The Prince's cock vibrated.

"You bastard!" cried Shaitan. His hips bucked, driving him deep into Alex's body. The gush of his release followed, coating her insides in what felt like a torrent of hot, thick liquid. His hand spasmed on her clit at the same time that Kasdeya hammered into her G-spot.

Alex convulsed, almost tossing her dark man off with her manic thrashing. The orgasm was too severe, drawing scream after scream from her as pleasure flayed her nerves. Her nails raked lines into Kasdeya's back.

The manic milking her body was treating him to soon catapulted Kasdeya over the threshold too, and the feel of him bathing her womb pushed her even higher. Her voice finally gave out.

Shaitan was cursing and gnawing at her throat. The strength of her climax seemed to have wrung another one from him as well. Kasdeya was groaning into her shoulder, whispering words of love and lust, as he came…and came…and came.

It took a long time for their moaning to subside.

* * * *

"That may well have been the best shag of my life," Shaitan said some time later. "And I'd love to bathe in the glow a bit more, but you guys weigh a ton, and this thing in my arse is driving me batty. Get off."

Kasdeya laughed and lifted his head from where it rested on Alex's body. "We weren't too heavy a minute ago."

"Well, you are now. Plus, if ever a fuck deserved a celebratory smoke, it was that one."

With an amused shake of his head, Kasdeya wrapped his arms around Alex and rolled them sideways. Shaitan sat up, reached down to tug the dildo out and flicked it off before tossing it aside. He moved to sit on the edge of the bed, bending down to fish his cigarettes out of his jeans. With his back fully to her, Alex noticed something she hadn't before: Shaitan had a winged tattoo as well. It was very pale, white and cream against alabaster skin.

The guttering light of the candles didn't provide enough light to see it properly though, so Alex reached over Kasdeya's body to turn on the bedside lamp. She turned back to look again. In the clearer illumination, she could see that each feather was outlined in a fine thread of glittering gold.

"Your wings are beautiful."

Shaitan smiled over his shoulder, a cigarette clamped between his teeth. "Thanks." He held up one still-manacled hand. "Keys?"

"Drawer," Kasdeya said.

"I miss *your* wings," Alex said to her dark man, shifting up to sit against the headboard.

Kasdeya rolled onto his stomach. "Why didn't you say so?" In a flash of movement too fast to track, the tattoo morphed back into huge raven wings. They fanned the air gently.

"Wings are a fuckin' nuisance, always getting in the way." Shaitan finished uncuffing himself and then leaned back beside Alex. "Smoke?" he asked, holding out the pack to her.

"She doesn't—" Kasdeya said.

"Sure," she said, taking one. She'd quit two years ago, but what the hell? One wouldn't kill her.

The Prince gave his brother a smirk and lit it for her with his forefinger. Alex didn't even bat an eyelash at the trick. "Kas?" Shaitan leaned over to sway the pack hypnotically in front of Kasdeya's face. "Peer pressure, mate. Everyone's doing it."

Kasdeya snorted and laid his head in the cradle of his arms. "You know my answer, sire. It's a filthy habit, even for Brethren." He opened one eye to nail Alex with a disapproving look. "And they can't die from it."

Alex rolled her eyes and blew a cloud of smoke into the air above his head.

They lounged in compatible silence for a few minutes.

"Don't you want to see my wings?" Shaitan asked, stubbing out his cig and giving her a pout.

Alex laughed and grabbed the tealight that was serving as an impromptu ashtray to snuff out her own cigarette. "I thought they were a nuisance."

"They are. But mine are much nicer than his."

"Beg to differ." Kasdeya didn't even bother to open one eye this time.

Shaitan shifted away from the headboard to give himself room. Two enormous white wings snapped into existence behind him. "See? Nicer, no?"

She cocked her head and made a big show of looking between them. "Well, the gold gilt *is* pretty." Kasdeya raised his head and scowled at her. "But I think I prefer the drama of black."

"Yeah, Kas is a drama queen, all right."

"Don't be a sore loser, brother."

"Bah, she has no taste. I mean, she fell in love with you, right? So something's obviously off with her." Shaitan's wings disappeared and he turned around to pull on his jeans. "Well, it's been a slice, folks. But the sun's coming up, and all good demons should be home in bed."

"Fallen," Alex corrected absentmindedly. Her head was resting against the wall and she was almost asleep. She'd never been this tired or sore in her entire life.

The Prince looked up from buttoning his fly. "He's sure got you trained," he said with a laugh. "But some of us like the moniker 'demon.' It has a certain roguish appeal, don't you think?"

"Hmm-mmm," she mumbled.

Shaitan chuckled again. "Can't fall asleep just yet, love. You and I have to have a quick chat first."

"Shaitan," Kasdeya said, dire warning in his tone.

"Out." The Prince jerked his chin toward the door.

"No."

"That's an order, Kasdeya."

"That's unfortunate, my Prince."

Alex blinked in surprise. The mood had shifted from lazy to charged awfully fast.

"Kasdeya, you will—" Shaitan said, his voice hard.

Alex could plainly hear more punishment lurking in his cold tone and could see it even plainer in his cold eyes. "Come on guys, you just made up," she said, trying to lighten the mood. Neither glanced at her, their gazes were locked on each other. "Kasdeya, what can it hurt? Just give us a few minutes."

"Little one, I'd really rather not," he said, still not turning away from Shaitan.

"Give us a few minutes, dark man, please," she said. It wasn't quite a command. Not yet.

When Kasdeya finally looked at her, Alex made her expression just as stern as the Prince's. Whatever Shaitan wanted to talk to her about it wasn't worth losing Kasdeya over. Kasdeya read her resolve in the thin set of her mouth, the tight line of her shoulders and, with a snarled oath, he threw himself off the bed. The door slammed in his wake.

Alex sighed. "What's on your mind, Shaitan?"

Chapter 16

A few minutes turned into more than an hour.

The Prince had carried Alex into the bathroom and bathed her, dried her, brushed her hair, brought her back to the bedroom, sat her in the pink chair and changed the sheets. Let it never be said that the Fallen treat their lovers like less than royalty. She'd thought this slavish dedication to her comfort was unique to Kasdeya, but Shaitan cared for her with the same offhand devotion.

The entire time he'd pampered her, he'd talked. Alex had asked few questions; she'd been too shocked—too dismayed—at what he was revealing. Kasdeya had made the threat seem relatively minor. That couldn't have been further from the truth.

Uriel *would* come gunning for Kasdeya, Shaitan told her. It was only a matter of time. It was the Powers' job to rid Earth of all demonic influence but, apparently, Uriel had a special hate-on for Kasdeya in particular. Seems he'd taken the fall of his comrade in arms as a personal betrayal. The former friends were now the bitterest of enemies and her dark man had gone up against Uriel many times. He'd also lost many times. Not to say he *always* lost, Shaitan had hastened to reassure her; Kasdeya was a damned fine warrior. But he *often* lost, and when he did, he lost big.

Uriel was God's best. On his own, he was almost impossible to beat, and if other Powers fought with him… Well, if that happened, the unfortunate Fallen never stood a chance. Why on Earth hadn't Kasdeya told her the risk he was taking by staying here?

Shaitan blew out the few remaining candles that hadn't drowned themselves. "He loves you, Alexandra," he explained, answering her unspoken question as he carried her the short distance back to the bed. "He's afraid that if he makes you choose between this life and him, he'll lose in the contest." He tucked the blankets under her chin and sat down beside her. "Will he?"

"Of course not," she replied indignantly.

Shaitan cocked his head and studied her. "Well, if that's true, Summoner, then contrary to Kas's opinion, you should be eager to sign this." He produced a rolled parchment sheet out of thin air and handed it to her.

Alex sat up and untied the black cord binding the document. "Contract to…" She stopped reading aloud as she skimmed the script. Her eyes became narrower with every word. Then she threw the vellum as far from her as she could. "You've got to be joking. No way."

"Alexandra," said Shaitan, leaning across her to retrieve it. "I just heard you profess undying love for my brother. 'Forever' is what you promised."

"Yeah, but…"

"Sweetheart, 'forever' actually means something to us." He took her hand in his and curled her fingers around the vellum. "And it's not the paltry fifty years or so that you have left before you're whisked away to eternal boredom." He gave her hand a pat. "Think about it, Summoner. If you run now—today—you'll probably be able to evade the Powers… for a while. But every minute you delay in signing this you run the risk of dying. A car accident, an aneurism, skewered on the end of a huge, fiery sword… Who knows what fate has planned for you?"

"Well, we can go to, uhh…to Kasdeya's home," she offered weakly. "I assume he's allowed back now?"

"The word you're looking for is *Hell,* love. And, yes, he may come back. The punishment's been met." His fingers stroked up her arm and he leaned in closer. "And quite spectacularly too, I might add," he whispered, running his tongue along her ear.

Alex shivered and ducked away. "Don't distract me, Shaitan."

He grinned. "Am I able to? How wonderful."

She gave him a quelling look. "As I was saying, we can always go to *Hell* if we have to. That's an ability I seem to have."

Shaitan sat back and sighed. "Yes, you are the Summoner, so you can visit my domain at will. But that will only make your time together shorter."

"What do you mean?"

"You've plane-traveled before, I assume? To the Prison."

She nodded. No harm in telling him now.

"Have you never noticed how fatigued you are when you return?"

Alex bit the end of her thumbnail and thought back over the last month. Yes, sure she was tired… "But that's because we stayed up every night making love."

He smirked. "Did you? The lucky bastard. That might explain some of it then. But no, Summoner. The reason you were so exhausted is because your own life force energy is used when you travel the planes."

"My own…" Jesus, she'd spent more than a week going there every night. "Does Kasdeya know that?" she asked in a horror-struck gasp. "How much have I lost?"

"Kasdeya's never had any direct dealings with a Summoner, Alexandra, so no, I don't think he knew. I can't imagine he would jeopardize you on purpose." He popped a cigarette in his mouth, offering her the pack. She took one and he lit it for her. "And I have no idea how much you've lost. All the more reason to accept my offer."

She drew her knees up to rest her chin on them. "Okay," she said after a deep drag. "What exactly is your offer, Shaitan?"

"Eternal life, love. What else?"

She took another drag and studied him shrewdly. "In exchange for my eternal soul, I get eternal life?"

He propped his own knee up and rested his chin on it as well, bringing their faces within inches of each other. "Mmm-hmm," he answered in a cloud of smoke.

"And the catch?"

"No catch."

Alex snorted in disbelief and reached for the now overflowing candleholder-slash-ashtray. "No offence, *Satan,* but you're not exactly known for cutting straight deals. Your reputation, I'm afraid, precedes you."

"And my reputation is well deserved—never doubt it. But I'm not trying to trick you, Alexandra. For my brother's sake, for his happiness, I'm offering you exactly what I said. Eternal life. No strings." He slicked his tongue along his upper lip. "Plus, I'd love to have you living in my house someday when you get tired of earthly delights. If you two ever spat, I'm just a floor away, ready and willing to offer you succor."

"Kasdeya lives in your house?" she asked, surprised.

"It's a big house."

"And what would Shi-Liu say if I came to live with you?" Alex shook her head at the thought.

He grinned lopsidedly. "Don't know. But knowing her, it'll probably be something to the effect of, 'She's gorgeous, Shai-baby, let's get a bigger bed.'"

His words startled a snigger out of her. "Yeah, right. I'm sure she'd—"

Just then, his pocket started singing a tinny version of *Star Wars'* *Imperial March*. How apropos. "Speakin' of," Shaitan said, fishing his phone out and glancing at the screen. He butted out his cigarette, took her face between his hands and planted a loud smacking kiss on her lips. "I've got to run. When you decide to accept my offer, give me a shout. My number's all sixes." He smiled. "I just couldn't resist. Or you can summon me the old-fashioned way. Even I'm not immune to the call of a Summoner."

Another, less comedic kiss followed.

"Don't wait too long though." He squeezed her in a hard, fast hug. "'Cause you never know, love. You just never know."

Chapter 17

Their first party as a couple was also going to be their last party as a couple. Alex was so friggin' depressed. She wandered her house disconsolately, running her hand over antiques she'd spent years collecting and framed pictures of family and friends.

After Shaitan had left, Alex and Kasdeya had had a talk. A long, way past due talk. And, after much inner angst, Alex had decided that discretion was probably the better part of valor here. Why ask for trouble? If she didn't leave, the chances were good that eventually the Powers *would* show up. And then what?

If Kasdeya were hurt in the fight, he'd have to go home to recover, probably for "a good long while," he'd said, looking embarrassed, and she'd go with him, losing her house, job and most likely her soul in the process. Who knew how long she could stay in Hell until her own life force was used up and she was forced to accept Shaitan's offer? That was something both Kasdeya and Alex agreed was to be avoided at all costs.

To up the ante just a bit, he'd told her that though the Powers weren't allowed to harm mortals, that rule didn't apply to humans who willingly comported with demons. A la, the Summoner. So, yeah… No house and friends, or her soul and maybe death.

It was a tougher decision than it probably should have been.

Alex had skipped work, needing the time to pack and, frankly, to wrap her head around the life-altering decision she'd just made. She'd stop and say good-bye to Dovescot before she left in the morning. Right now, it was ten minutes and counting until her friends would arrive, and Alex was still trying to figure out how to say good-bye to *them*.

"Knock, knock," called Rose. The front door swung inward without any actual knocking having occurred. "I come bearing skanky wine!"

Alex rounded the corner from living room to front hall; saw her best friend standing in a shaft of late-afternoon sunshine with red hair wild around her face, a big grin on her lips and a box of year-old wine in her arms; and promptly burst into tears.

Rose dropped the wine. "Oh, honey, what the fuck?" she cried, holding out her arms.

"Leaving...tomorrow... Don't know when... Let Jen have...stupid house..." Between having her face crushed into Rose's chest and sobbing hysterically, Alex knew that she wasn't being at all comprehensible.

Rose let her have a good long cry before she took Alex's head between her palms and pulled back to look down into her tear-swollen face. "I have no idea what you just said. Try again in English."

Alex took a calming breath. "Sorry," she mumbled, bending down to retrieve the box.

"Don't apologize, Alex. Just tell me what's going on."

"Sure, come on in. We'll crack this open and I'll tell you all about it." Her breath was still hitching on every second word, making her sound like a three-year-old after a tantrum.

"We're not actually going to drink that." Rose pulled a face as she reached behind her to shut the door. "I brought it as a joke."

Alex turned the box over. "It says it's still good for three months yet."

"Oh God. No." Rose drew a brown bag out of her big glittery purse. "*This* is what I'm drinking." She ripped the paper off dramatically and kissed the bottle's red wax seal. "One hundred and one proof caramelized rum straight from Jamaica, baby." Rose's affectionate arm wrapped around Alex's waist as she steered her into the living room. "By the way, I don't know if this is the right time to drop this into the conversation, but the house looks amazing. When you're all done crying, I definitely want the grand tour."

Alex smiled, but almost immediately started to tear up again. She was going to miss Rose so damned much.

* * * *

"Feeling calmer?" Rose asked.

Alex drained her second rum and Coke. "Yeah, I guess I am." She poured another slug of liquor into the tumbler.

"So where is Prince Charming?"

"He's gone to drop off some of my things and to bring someone back to help you."

"Drop your things off in..."

"Hot storage." She grinned a tad drunkenly at her wit. "Otherwise known as Hell."

Rose rolled her eyes. "And bring someone from..."

"From Hell, yeah." Alex picked up a cheese tray and shouldered open the kitchen door. "Thanks for playing, Rosie. Get those chips would ya?"

"Hey, now." Rose grabbed the bowl and hurried after her. "Hot lovin' with impossibly sexy demons sounds great and all, but I don't want to have to ditch *my* life when the Powerpuff Boys come calling."

"You're a laugh riot." Alex lobbed a piece of cheddar at her friend. "No, he said it wasn't a Fallen he's bringing. Must be just a regular dead guy."

Rose grimaced, dropped her bowl on the coffee table and attempted to extract the crumbly cheese from her hair. "That sounds *so* much better. Please tell me he's not a rotting corpse. I don't think I can work with a rotting corpse. I have a real problem with maggots."

"Get a grip, Rose. Kas wouldn't bring back a zombie to work with you. I'm sure he's maggot free. His name's Samuel, and he's supposed to be a whiz with all things mathematical, a.k.a financial. Maybe he can keep Dovescot in the black."

Rose snorted. "I thought miracles were the other side's forte." She finally succeeded in removing the cheddar. "Listen, Alex, are you sure about all this? I mean it's only been, what, three weeks, and—"

"Four and a half."

"Whatever. Four and a half weeks then, and you've fallen in love with a demon, have to now run for your life to stay with said demon or, alternatively, you could just sell your soul to the Devil and go live in Hell with said—"

"He's Fallen! Would you quit calling him a demon?" Alex collapsed on the sofa in a huff.

"Whatever!" Rose said again. "Alex, could you try to focus? You've worked hard for this house, for Dovescot... Is this *really* what you want? To just walk away from it all?" She sat down beside Alex and took her hand. "I mean, I'm not saying... I'm just saying, ya know?"

Alex blew out a big breath and squeezed Rose's hand. "I love him, Rose. Is this what I wanted to have happen? No, obviously not, but..." She dropped her gaze. "But I love him."

The sound of tires crunching up the gravel drive threatened to cut the conversation short. "And hey, it's not all bad," Alex continued. "All the money in the world, traveling anywhere I want." She stood up and gestured to the walls. "As of this morning, the house is completely paid off, courtesy of 'said demon.' Plus Dov—"

"Yeah," Rose cut in. "It's really great of you to let Jen rent your place for so cheap. There's been no sign of Nicole's deadbeat father, so Jen needs all the help she can get. I can't wait to tell her she can stop looking for something just a little less roach-infested than all the rest."

Alex did her best not to flinch at the mention of Darryl. Luckily, the doorbell rang, giving her an excellent excuse to turn away. "I'd give it to her for free if I thought she'd take it. Just put the money back into Dovescot." She headed for the door and tossed over her shoulder, "Now, remember—DotCom millionaire, secret engagement, trip around the world."

"Yes, dear." Rose came into the hallway behind her and leaned against the wall. "'Isn't it exciting that our own sweet Alexandra has officially joined lifestyles of the rich and famous?' I've got it."

"I knew I could count on you, babe."

* * * *

"Oh. My. God!"

Alex craned her neck to see what Josh was exclaiming over now. She loved her brother dearly, but his exaggerated flamboyancy could sometimes be a bit much.

Kasdeya was standing in the arch between the living room and front hall, looking around in bewilderment. It was supposed to have been a small get-together, but Alex had encouraged her friends to call over other friends and so on…and so on. It was now pretty much standing-room only at Casa de Alexandra. If she was going to have a good-bye party, she was going to have a *huge* good-bye party, darn it.

"Hey, big boy," she hollered gaily, waving from where she was holding court in her favorite wing chair. "Over here."

Kasdeya nodded and turned his head to speak to someone behind him.

"Oh. My. God!" Josh said again. "*That's* your rich Greek, Lexie?" He left off playing with the stereo, leaving it on *Who Let the Dogs Out*—a song which Alex had once thought cute, but now hated—to make a break for Kasdeya. Alex leaped up to intercept him, or rather, she meant to leap up. Really, she kind of levered herself up with one arm, sat back down and then, with the help of Sandy and a cute boy Alex had never met before, finally found her feet. Too late.

"Well, well, well," she heard Josh croon. "So *you're* the stud whisking my sister away from us."

Through the crowd, Alex caught a glimpse of Josh pressing his body against her dark man's. Jeez. Not again. Joshua had this really annoying habit of hitting on her boyfriends, something straight men didn't usually take very well to. "I'm just separating the wheat from the chaff, darling," he would blithely respond whenever Alex tried to tear a strip off him for it. "If they can't deal with a gay brother, best to get that out there right from the start." Problem was it was easier to deal with a gay brother when he wasn't plunked in your lap with his tongue in your ear. It wasn't so bad now, but in college, her younger brother's shenanigans had scared more than one macho frat boy right out the door.

"That would be me, yes," Kasdeya said, amused.

"Could I interest you in a matched set?" Josh asked in his best sultry-sweet twinkie voice.

Alex navigated past the people blocking her line of sight and saw Kasdeya put his arm around her brother's waist to steady Josh as he attempted to climb his body.

"For God's sake," she exclaimed in exasperation. "Joshua Brannigan, you leave him alone!"

Kasdeya held up his finger to her and winked, then he bent down low over Josh's body. Josh was only five inches taller than Alex, with the same hair color and the same slim build. For the first time, Alex got to see how dwarfed she must look against Kasdeya's imposing bulk.

With a small smirk lifting the corner of his lips, Kasdeya whispered something into her brother's ear. Josh's eyes opened really wide. He seemed to swoon against her dark man's chest.

Kasdeya said one last thing before easing Josh away and giving his ass a playful slap. "Now, please, go turn this music off, Joshua. It's pitiful."

"Y… Yes, I'll do that," Josh responded, strangely subdued. As he came abreast of Alex, her brother stopped to lay his flushed face against her shoulder. "Honey, if you don't marry him, I will."

She turned her head to watch him stroll away. What the…? "What did you say?" Alex asked, moving closer to press her own body against Kasdeya's. He had that effect on people. Such gorgeous muscles simply needed to be pressed against.

"I'll never tell," he murmured, bending over her in the exact same manner he'd just done to her brother. Only he was going for Alex's mouth, not her ear.

Being a little—okay, a lot—drunk, Alex quickly lost focus on anything but the feel of his hard body rubbing against her own and his agile tongue plumbing the depths of her mouth. When she lifted her leg around his hip, he laughed and pushed it back down. "Not that I don't want to, pet, but you seem to have filled the house up with people."

"I was depressed…and lonely." She stuck out her bottom lip and smacked his shoulder. "Where have you been? It's been hours."

* * * *

Kasdeya squinted down at Alex. She looked charmingly mussed, hair a little wild, purple blouse half off her shoulder and partially untucked from the floor-length, black velvet skirt she was wearing. Yes, mussed and, perhaps...

"How much have you had to drink, little one?"

"Lots. Lots 'n' lots." Alexandra twirled one finger in the air in blasé abandon. She was so bloody adorable. "It all goes back to the lonely, depressed thing." She ignored the way his hands had slipped down her spine and were now stealthily creeping over her ass. "So answer the question, dark man. Where were you?"

"Had a bit of a problem with the timeline, pet."

That was a lie. Now that he was back in the Prince's good graces, besides having access to Hell's almost unlimited coffers, he had some of the best mathematical minds ever born at his disposal. Samuel could have had him back mere seconds after he'd departed this morning.

The real reason he'd delayed his return was exactly *because* Alexandra had been so depressed. Every time he'd looked at her with her beautiful blue eyes red-rimmed and swollen and her proud little chin trembling, he'd been too tempted to tell her, "Nevermind, pet. We'll stay." But that wasn't an option any longer. For her safety, they *had* to move—as soon as possible. It had been foolish in the extreme to wait as long as they had. It would seem that love could make even the Fallen act foolishly.

"Oh," Alex said with another pout. "I didn't think of that. Well, but how will I get my stuff back? If I need it?"

"Shaitan will send it along. I spoke to him about that before I left." Kasdeya squeezed her firm bottom, lifting her up so that her feet were dangling, the better to grind against her. He ducked his head for a kiss.

"House full of people," she reminded him, squirming to get down. Of course, that just made him hold her tighter.

A man cleared his throat behind Kasdeya and he glanced over his shoulder. Oops. "Sorry, Sam." He regretfully lowered his Summoner back to the floor and stepped aside so that she could see the newcomer.

"Samuel, Alexandra. Alexandra, Samuel."

* * * *

Alex's ears felt hot—a sure sign that her face was fire-engine red. This poor fellow had been standing there the entire time waiting for an introduction while they'd been... "Dumb ass," she whispered out of the corner of her mouth.

Kasdeya had the audacity to laugh and give her bum another squeeze. "You can be very distracting, pet."

She ignored him and held out her hand to the tall chestnut-haired man in front of her. "Samuel, a pleasure."

Samuel inclined his head over her hand, air kissing the back of her palm. "Just Sam is fine, my lady. And the pleasure is all mine, I assure you." He straightened and pushed his thin wireframe glasses higher on his nose. Large gray eyes twinkled merrily at her.

"Then just Alex is fine as well, Sam," she responded with a smile. What a charmer he was, and not a single maggot in sight.

"Hey, Alex, where're your paper towels, I dropped... Oh." Rose let the kitchen door swing shut behind her. "Hello, Kas. I was wondering when you were going to join the party."

Alex knew Rose was pissed at Kasdeya for having left her alone to cry the day away, but you wouldn't have known it from the breathy voice and hundred-watt smile her friend was currently treating him to. Honestly, you'd think these people had never met a demi-god before. The thought made her giggle, and at the realization that she was giggling, Alex giggled harder, because she *never* giggled.

Kasdeya fondly shook his head at her and pulled her into his side. "Hello, Rose. If you have a moment, dear, there's someone I'd like you to meet."

Chapter 18

"C'mon, pet."

"G'way."

Kasdeya's hands gently stroked her bare back. "I think you'll find you're not in as much pain as you should be, Alexandra. But you'll have to open your eyes to find out."

"No deal." Alex buried her head further under the sheets, which had all somehow ended up around her shoulders.

Kasdeya chuckled and tore her defense away.

"Jerk." Alex cracked open one eyelid. Hmm. He was right. It really wasn't that bad. Minor headache, no nausea. Still, she sat up very carefully just in case the hangover god should come storming back with a mocking laugh and a steel-shod tread. But nope, she was good. "Hey, thanks!"

"You're welcome. Now get up. You told Rose we'd be at Dovescot for lunch."

"I did?" She gathered the sheets back around her body and rubbed her temple, trying to massage the last little ache out. "What time is it?"

Kasdeya glanced at the clock. "Eleven twenty-seven."

"What?" She grimaced. "Why on earth didn't you wake me sooner?"

"I'm afraid it took me a fair while to tidy the house, little one, and even longer to tidy the night's excesses from your unconscious body."

Alex blushed. "Sorry. Did I end up behaving very badly?"

He scooted closer to kiss her bowed head. "If you did, no one else was in any condition to comment. Anyway, I rather enjoyed having a sexy wild-woman trying to tear my clothes off every opportunity she got."

"Ugh." She covered her face with her hands. "On second thought, don't tell me. I really don't want to know."

He grinned. "As you wish, pet. Hurry, have a shower and pack anything else you might need. I'll wait for you downstairs."

* * * *

They walked into the office to find Samuel typing happily away at the computer and Rose lying as if dead on the floor in front of the desk.

"Hey." Rose lifted her wrist about an inch off the floor in weak acknowledgement. "Thanks for the donation, Kas."

"You're very welcome."

"Oh yeah. I meant to tell you about that." Alex's heels clicked across the hardwood floor until she hit the rug Rose was lying on. "With Sam's help, you might even be able to turn a profit and branch out."

Rose winced and curled into a fetal ball. "Could you keep it down?" she whispered. "And yeah, Sam seems great."

"Sam is great," the man himself interjected, never stopping his muted tap-tapping on the laptop's keyboard.

Rose winced again. "And as soon as I don't feel like old gum on someone's shoe, I'm sure he'll be able to teach me a lot."

Alex knelt down beside the redhead, who still hadn't opened her eyes. She looked up at Kasdeya hopefully. "Can't you do anything?"

"We're not under the guard here, pet. The outlay of power would be small, I suppose, but it may still be noticed."

Her face fell. "I see." She gave Rose's shoulder a squeeze. "Honey, is there anything *I* can do for you?"

Rose made what seemed to be a gargantuan effort to sit up. "No, I'll live. I'm just waiting for that handful of aspirin to kick in. Should be any minute now..." Her eyes squinted open. The slitted orbs were bright red, making the green of her irises look neon in comparison.

"By the nine hells." Kasdeya sighed and came down on one knee beside them. "Moderation, ladies. You may have heard of the concept?"

"Judge not lest—" Rose's eyes bulged. She clamped a hand over her mouth, trying to scramble to her feet.

Alex turned another pleading look on Kasdeya.

"Yes, pet, all right." Kasdeya grabbed Rose's elbow with one hand and placed the palm of his other flat on her forehead.

"Kas!" Rose pushed at his arm. "Let me go! I'm gonna...be..." Her voice faltered and she stopped trying to escape. Less than a minute later, she opened clear eyes. "Holy shit," she said with a feeble smile at Alex. "He's a handy fellow to have around, isn't he?"

"I realize you aren't completely well," Kasdeya said, standing, "but you should be able to function now."

Rose used his outstretched hand to gain her feet. "Yes. I'm feeling much better. Thank you, Kas."

His answering smile was tight. "We really can't stay long," he informed Alex.

"Right," Alex replied, standing as well. "Why don't you take a break, Sam? Come join us for lunch."

"I'm fine, thank you." Samuel was leaning close to the computer screen. Blue light reflected in his spectacles. A lock of chestnut hair had fallen across his busy eyes.

Rose reached over and hit the hibernate button. "Don't be an anti-social schmuck, Sam."

Alex stifled a gasp at her friend's words. She was used to Rose's abrupt, "tell it like it is" ways, but Samuel seemed so genteel, so polite. He must be horrified by her.

But Samuel looked up with a warm, shy smile. A hint of color rose in his cheeks. "Yes, all right," he said softly, catching Rose's hand as she went to withdraw it and pressing it to his lips.

Now Rose's cheeks were pink.

Alex and Kasdeya exchanged a surprised look.

* * * *

An hour later, Alex was leaning against the hood of her car getting ready to leave. "It's too bad I missed Jen."

They'd said good-bye to everyone and had a few laughs and a few tears, all in less than sixty minutes. Kasdeya was becoming increasingly anxious to get underway.

Now it was just Rose and Alex. Samuel and Kasdeya were exchanging a few words at the rear of the car, both seeming to understand that the girls needed privacy.

"Yeah." Rose shook her head. "Jen said to tell you how grateful she was though, and that she'd take care of everything as if it were her own. I know you've taken a real load off her mind." She fingered her shirt's collar. "Here's hoping this thing with Nicole is nothing. Those two have been through enough."

Alex crossed her arms and frowned. "She didn't tell you what the CAT-scan results were?"

"No, just that they wanted to run some more tests today. She got the call and high-tailed it out of here early this morning."

Both women became silent, considering the implication of that. It didn't seem good.

"Ladies." Kasdeya opened the bug's driver-side door.

Rose got a little teary, which in turn made Alex's eyes fill. "Hey," Alex said, hugging her friend close. "Kas says we can visit whenever we like.

And on your vacation, no place is off limits, anywhere you want. We'll see each other real soon, Rosie."

Rose clutched her tighter. "I know, I know. I'm being a baby. I'm going to miss you, is all."

"Me too, hon." Alex pulled the valet key off her key fob and pressed it into her friend's hand. Rose was going to pick the car up from the airport for her. She gave the redhead one more quick squeeze and then pulled away. "Good thing you have Samuel to distract you from the pain, huh?"

Rose's smile turned wicked. "Good thing."

* * * *

Kasdeya tossed Alex's duffel bag onto one of the sateen sofas in the living room of their five-star hotel suite. "Never again!"

"It wasn't that bad," Alex said, though the fourteen-hour flight, with only one quick stop to stretch their legs, *had* been something of a trial. Even in first class.

Alex tipped the bellboy and closed the door before turning to admire their new accommodations. She'd told Rose it wasn't that bad too. Sure she had to leave her home, but she was being compensated by getting to travel anywhere she wanted. Who didn't want to do that? But in her heart Alex hadn't really believed it.

Until now.

"Would you look at that?" she exclaimed, walking through the gorgeous room past the delicate antique tapestries on the wall and the huge vases of flowers adorning every polished surface. When her heels left the intricate parquetry floor of the foyer, they sank at least two inches into plush champagne carpeting. She hardly noticed. It was the amazing, three-hundred sixty degree *view* that had grabbed her.

She slid open the terrace doors and clacked her way over white terrazzo tile to lean against the steel balcony. "God," she said with a sigh, lost in almost trancelike adoration. Notre Dame was right there! She turned her body. The hotel overlooked the Jarden des Tuileries and tiny colorful sailboats skidded happily along on the park's manmade lake. In the long distance, the Eiffel Tower stood tall and impressive. She knew a walk to the corner of the terrace would give her a completely different view, this time of the Sacred Heart, the Opera and The Louvre.

An ancient children's rhyme, "I see Paris, I see France..." flitted through her mind and a huge grin took over her face. Did she ever!

Kasdeya came behind her. "Do you like it, pet? This suite came highly recommended."

"Like it?" She shook her head in wonderment, jostling his chin where it rested on her hair. "I love it!" She turned and threw her arms around his neck. "I love you!" Alex tossed her head and kicked her legs so that he had to support her full weight.

Kasdeya took the hint and obligingly stepped back to swing her around in a wide circle. "And I love you, Alexandra. France wouldn't have been my first choice, however. Spain, Greece, someplace hot. But if you're happy, I'm happy."

"I'm happy."

He stopped spinning to kiss her. "How happy?" he murmured against her mouth.

She nipped at his lips. "Very, very."

"Show me."

Her breath caught as she remembered the last time he'd asked her to "show him" how happy he'd made her. She moaned and slithered her tongue into his mouth.

Kasdeya's fingers traveled down the front of her blouse, parting the semi-sheer lilac material with supernatural speed. He palmed one breast, plucking at the ripe little nipple through the ivory lace of her bra and…

A discreet knock sounded on the suite's door.

"Damnation!"

"Crap!"

They both laughed.

"Go ahead and get that, dark man." Alex tugged the halves of her top back together. "I should call Rose, anyway—let her know we got in okay."

Kasdeya sighed and adjusted himself within the now tight confines of his khakis. "Don't forget where we were, pet."

She smoothed one finger down the clearly defined ridge of his hard-on. "How could I?"

Kasdeya glanced down at himself and frowned. His black polo shirt morphed into a loose, long dress shirt, concealing his aroused state. As he answered the door, Alex took a seat on one of the plush sofas and picked up the phone. She dialed the number for both Dovescot and Rose's, but there was no answer. She bit her lip and did the calculation again. Maybe she'd gotten it wrong?

"It's six forty-five PM in Paris so that makes it… No, I'm right," she grumbled. "It's quarter to ten in the morning there. Why isn't anyone answering the damned phone?" She left a quick message telling Rose they'd arrived alive and giving her the suite's unlisted number. When she hung up, she felt unaccountably uneasy. Alex sat there a minute staring at the phone, willing her friend to call back.

"Problem?" Kasdeya wheeled over a linen-draped cart sporting a large, covered stainless steel tray. "Compliments of the management," he replied at her questioning look. "When you pay well, you're treated well."

She lifted the polished lid. "I guess so!"

Creamy artichoke soup served with foie gras mousse tempted her palate. Also present were tiny lamb chops and roasted scallops adorned with truffles, apples, celery and chestnuts. There was another course of soft, runny cheese with fresh greens and, lastly, the coup de grace: two small custard dishes of silky crème brûlée.

"No, no problem," she said in response to his question. "At least, I hope not." She grabbed a bowl of soup and headed onto the terrace to eat it. It was still a good two hours until sunset, and she wanted to spend as much time as she could enjoying the incredible view. "I can't seem to get a hold of Rose, is all."

Kasdeya rolled the cart after her. "I'm sure everything's fine." He picked up one of the custards.

"You can't eat dessert before dinner."

"Watch me." He grinned and leaned against the balcony rail next to her. "I figure I'll need the energy for when you show me how happy you are."

Alex finished her spoonful of soup and put the bowl aside. "Better share then, dark man, because I'm horny *and* tired, and it's up in the air which need will end up being slaked first."

He spooned a huge dollop of custard onto her tongue. "You're tired because that was a trip even my brother couldn't have devised to be more hellish. So again I say, 'Never again.'"

"And again I say, 'It wasn't that bad.'" She plucked the brûlée out of his hand, which made Kasdeya pull a face. "You're the one who said I'd freeze to death flying long distance with you, and I can't summon a place I've never been," she reminded, licking at the caramelized ridge along the edge of the dish. "So…"

"I'll get you an anorak and some sealskin boots." He picked up the second dessert. "You've been here once now, so I don't expect to have to travel in such a barbarically cramped way again."

Alex smacked the end of his nose with her spoon. "It was first class, you big baby."

"First-class torture."

"Well, I want to see Egypt next, so we'd better pick up that anorak."
She finished the custard, dropped her dish on the cart and sidled closer to
Kasdeya, holding her mouth open like a baby bird. Kasdeya granted her
the tiniest lick of his brûlée.

"Miser," she said with a mock pout. She rested her head against his
shoulder, cuddling happily into his custard imbued floral-cinnamon scent.
"That was the first I've heard of being able to fly with you. Why haven't
we done that before?"

Kasdeya shrugged and ate the last bite over her head. "I suppose it was
a matter of not wanting to draw attention. Not to mention the fact that
your decrepit old house seemed to consume most of our time."

She tilted her face up to his. "Shut up, my house is lovely. And we
could have gone somewhere else."

He pursed his lips. "All right, then, how does 'I didn't think of it'
work for you?" He gave her a wry smile and brushed back a wisp of hair
that had blown across her cheek. "I've never had a human lover before.
I suppose I was expending so much effort pretending to be mortal that I
just didn't consider the possibility."

"Hmm." Alex pretended to mull it over. "Yes, the concept of you being
fallible does work for me."

Kasdeya twirled the wisp of hair around his finger and gave it a tug. "I
thought it might, wench. Is dusk soon enough for your first flight?"

"I guess it will have to be." Alex sighed theatrically. "I'm sure we can
find *something* to amuse ourselves until then."

Kasdeya bent close and licked the lobe of her ear. "I'm sure we can."

"Dinner first though." She wriggled out of his arms to pick up a plate
of lamb. "I have to keep up my puny mortal energy, you know."

Kasdeya adjusted himself yet again. "Tease," he admonished, but his
eyes were full of tender humor. He took the plate from her hand—the
better to feed her himself.

Chapter 19

Alex was nearly asleep in her dark man's arms. They were enjoying the pool-sized tub in the suite's massive white-marbled bathroom. She sat in Kasdeya's lap, her thighs spread around his. His cock, nestled between her legs, prodded ever so gently, but he made no move to complete the joining. Instead, he seemed content just stroking her breasts and belly and raining bubble-light kisses along her throat. "You awake, pet?" he murmured into her damp hair.

"No."

"Mmm, too bad. It is dusk, after all."

Alex's eyelids fluttered. Dusk. That meant something. Dusk. Images of birds and gorgeous angels filled her mind. Dusk…

"Flying." She willed her lids open and smiled sleepily up at him. "For that, I'm awake."

He smiled back and twitched his hips. "Only for that?"

Alex shifted, catching the crown of his penis inside of her body before lifting herself out of the bath. "You had your chance, Kasdeya."

Kasdeya jumped out after her, sloshing hot, sudsy water around the room. "That better not have been my only chance, little angel." He grabbed a bath sheet and brusquely rubbed her down before lifting her in his arms. "Or I might decide not to take you after all."

She laughed. "If you're gonna play *that* way, then let me just say it had better be a *damn* fine flight, sir, or I might decide not to take *you* after all."

His brows rose at her threat. "Oh yeah?" He turned sideways to navigate them both through the door.

"Yeah."

Kasdeya picked up his pace, striding across the hardwood floor of the bedroom. "Yeah?" he asked again.

Alex held on tighter; he was practically jogging now. "Uh, yeah…?"

The terrace doors were wide open to the purple night. When they hit the terrazzo, he was at a full run. His skin flashed alabaster white for one second then darkened to the same dusky plum as the sky. Massive black wings slapped the air. Once. Twice. Before she'd had a chance to ready herself, they were airborne.

"Whoa," Alex gasped. She turned her body into his, squeezing his neck hard enough to throttle him.

Kasdeya shook his head. "No, pet, you have to look. You issued the challenge. Now you must enjoy the consequences."

He manipulated her body until she was straight against him, head tucked under his chin, toes tickling his shins. When he tried to turn her around though, she fought the maneuver with a death grip. "Kasdeya, I'm naked!"

"You're scared," he corrected.

"And naked."

Kasdeya alit in a dark corner of the park and set her on her feet. Alexandra quaked against him. He chucked her under the chin to tilt her face up. Her eyes remained tightly shut. "Open your eyes, Alexandra."

"Now I'm naked on the ground."

He laughed. "I love you, pet," he said, pressing kisses to her closed lids, her nose, her mouth. Then he gave her ass a wicked pinch.

"Hey!" Alexandra's eyes popped open to glare at him.

"Good," he said smugly. "Now look at yourself."

Still frowning, she did, and gasped at what she saw. Her skin and hair were the same smoky violet shade as his.

"How—"

"Nevermind how." Kasdeya gave her one more kiss before turning her body around, the way he'd been trying to in the air. He created a binding wrap that circled Alexandra from under her breasts to just above her hips. It wrapped snug around them both, locking his torso to her back. "Better?"

Her tense muscles relaxed. "Much. She turned her head but could only reach his clavicle, so that's where she kissed him. "Thank you."

He ducked his own head and ended up kissing the tip of her ear. "You're welcome. Let's fly then, angel of mine."

* * * *

Paris is very well lit at night.

On one hand, that was great; everything was in stark, sodium vapor relief, visible even from high up. But on the other hand, it meant they couldn't get too close. Still, it was awesome. Swooping through the air in her dark man's arms was the most amazing thing Alex had ever done.

It was also really freakin' cold. He was right—even clothed she could never have born more than a day in the air.

After they'd circled the Eiffel Tower twice, winged over the Arc de Triomphe close enough to brush the horse's backs with their bare feet and admired the elegant domes of Sacre Coeur, Alex had to call a stop to the fun.

"Kasdeya, this is great and all..." She wasn't sure he could hear her over the chattering of her teeth. "But I'm freezing to death."

"I'm sorry, pet. My fallibility is showing again." His torso against her back warmed, feeling like the world's hardest heating blanket. Kasdeya let go of Alex's hands, which he'd been holding wide apart to smooth out their gliding maneuverability, and his palms slid over her forearms, up her biceps and shoulders and then back down to cup her bare breasts. "Better?"

Alex laid her head back against his breastbone. "Getting there," she said, pushing as best as she was able into his palms.

"Mmm." The binding holding them together loosened enough for Kasdeya to lift her higher and lick her throat. One hand crept down her body to the apex of her thighs. "How 'bout now?" He teased the crisp curls before dipping one finger between her lips to rub her clit. His cock was lengthening velvet against her backside.

"Not quite..." Alex spread her legs, bending her knees to bring her calves up behind him and then locking her ankles in the small of his back. She felt her dark man's breath quicken. "Almost..." With a wriggle and another slide, his erection popped between her legs.

"Pet, I'm not—"

"Not quite..." One more wriggle. "Ahh." She sighed. "Now I'm better." Just the crown of his cock was inside so Alex kept on wriggling, inching her way down his long shaft.

Kasdeya sucked in a breath. They stuttered in the air, falling several feet before he corrected the plummet. Alex shrieked and—in a spasm of panic—brought her legs together, catching him tight inside her body.

He shuddered in response, his breath hot and heavy against her temple. "I was going to say, 'I'm not sure this is a good idea,'" he moaned, pushing her down harder with one hand while fingering her faster with the other. "But I'll be damned—again—if I'll let you stop now." They took another alarming dip as he hilted. Alex moaned, so lost in pleasure that she barely noticed this time. Kasdeya's big palm was flat on her stomach, holding her still for the roll of his hips. "I do think we should land, however," he said. "You wanted to see the Louvre yet, yes?"

"Yes." They started plummeting once more in a barely controlled descent. Alex looked down, quivering on the edge of climax, to see the Louvre's left roof rushing toward them. "I mean, no!" His cock was chafing her G-spot, and her clit throbbed under his skilled fingers. "No," she cried again, riding the first ripples of pleasure. "No, no, pull up!"

"What... What's the matter?" Kasdeya paused in mid-air. Only his hips kept moving, churning, driving Alex crazy.

"Wait... Don't land," she panted, trying her best to make coherent conversation while coming so hard. "...Alarms... Oh...God."

"Alarms?"

"Yesss."

* * * *

Her sex was tight and hot around him, spasming erratically as currents of electric ecstasy continued to spark under his finger. "If any place has... an alarmed roof...it's this one... Trust me," she said.

"Ahh." Kasdeya waited until she had finished quaking before he made the safety band disappear and flipped her in mid-air to face him. Alexandra didn't even flinch. Hell, she didn't even open her eyes. She just wrapped languid arms around his neck and snuggled closer. Kasdeya smiled at her sudden aplomb and drew her legs around him once more. He found his home deep in her body before ascending. "Back to the hotel, then?"

She didn't answer. She was busy.

Kasdeya let his head fall back, enjoying the way her delectable little mouth was nipping at his Adam's apple, the way she was rubbing her warm and slippery body against his.

Now that her own needs had been met, Alexandra was riding him with an indolent lack of urgency. Love overwhelmed him at that moment, flying high in the air with his woman lazy and trusting in his arms...but so did lust.

"Pet," he moaned, cupping the back of her skull to keep her mouth right where it was—now suckling under his left ear, which he loved. The pair described large looping circles in the air high above Paris as his concentration narrowed down to just her. Her mouth. Her body. Her.

"Yes?"

"Please..."

Alexandra laughed and chewed on his earlobe, knowing darn well what he seemed incapable of vocalizing.

"Ever fucked in church, dark man?" She looked up at him and waggled her brows. "Or on one, for that matter?" Her eyes twinkled like blue, star-filled pools.

Alicia Steele

"Can't say as I have, Summoner. It sounds sinful."

She shimmied her body, making him gasp. "Doesn't it just? Follow the river." She jerked her chin to the right. "Notre Dame's that way."

In less than a mile and less than two minutes, they were there. Kasdeya was desperate by the time they arrived. Alexandra was still teasing, purposely giving him just a little less than he needed. Thus, he was perhaps a bit rough when he slammed her body into the cathedral's cold and gritty metal roof. Gargoyles snarled at them from every niche. None wore a snarl as fierce as Kasdeya's.

"You look every inch the demon, Kasdeya," she said, a half-smile playing over her lips.

He hooked her knees apart and lifted them up over his shoulders. Kasdeya's great wings thrashed the air behind him, holding them aloft while his hips drove forward, impaling Alexandra to the icy lead. His hands caught hers and slammed them over her head. "I *feel* every"— another deep thrust—"inch"—his teeth caught at her throat—"a demon." He paused, quivered. His breath stopped, caught somewhere deep in his chest.

"Come, dark man." Alexandra undulated against him. "I want to feel you come."

One large hand held both her wrists together. The other dropped. "Come with me."

Kasdeya palmed her mons, giving it a squeeze before moving down. She bucked against his fingers, groaning as his mouth slanted over hers, his tongue mimicking the renewed plunge of his cock. Soon, molten seed bathed her womb, burning her from the inside out.

Kasdeya wobbled in the air, allowing them to slip a few feet as his orgasm took precedence over staying aloft. "You are my life, little one," he gasped, devastated by pleasure. "My life. I would die for you." Kasdeya gazed down into her face, contorted in bliss and so, so beautiful, and said again, "I would die for you."

Alexandra clutched him tighter, too overcome by her own pleasure to reply.

Chapter 20

"Ignore it." Kasdeya pulled the sheets up over their heads and popped Alex's already thoroughly suckled, achingly sensitive nipple back into his mouth.

The phone chirped again. Alex groaned, gently pushing him away. "I can't. It's Rose. Only she has the number."

"Call her back." He clung to her thighs when she attempted to leave the bed.

She laughed and slapped at his roving fingers. "Stop it now, Kasdeya."

But he didn't stop. If anything, his hands became more insistent in their efforts to thwart her. Alex frowned. Why wasn't he...?

"You didn't summon me this time, pet," he said, in answer to her perplexed expression. He shifted himself between her legs once more, grinning at his success in frustrating her departure, and smugly trailed kisses along her belly. "I came back from Hell of my own free will."

Oh, yeah. Well, that was easily remedied. Alex opened her mouth, the words ready on her tongue.

"Don't!" He yanked her down underneath him, thighs spread wide around his hips. "We're equals, Summoner." Kasdeya slid into her body as smooth and as hot as a knife into butter. Alex gasped at the sudden fullness and clutched his shoulders, the summoning spell driven completely out of her head. The phone stopped ringing. "Equals," he purred, pausing on the down stroke, buried so deep she felt his heartbeat in her belly. "It has to be that way, little one. Don't you agree?"

Alex looked up into his face. Her heart fluttered at the pleading in his eyes. "Mmm," she said, stopping to moan as he thrust again. "That depends. Will you still let me tie you up without trying to escape?"

He smiled. "I will."

Her head tossed with another hard plunge. "And can I paddle you?" She twisted frantically beneath him, trying to get the deal done before he brought her to climax yet again. This had to be the sixth or seventh time that morning. Her body was a tightly strung high-voltage wire ready to snap in a cascade of fiery sparks at his slightest whim.

"Oh yes." One large hand slipped down her side and a ringing slap echoed through the room. "Right after I paddle you." He gave her flank another sharp smack—one that pitched Alex into orgasm. "Deal?" He fucked her even harder as her sex compressed and pulsed around him.

She grabbed his hair and held on for dear life. "Deal," she agreed on a guttural moan before sinking her teeth into his collarbone. His howl of gratification had the leaded glass windows shivering in fear.

* * * *

Alex held out her cup for a refill, the phone caught between her ear and shoulder as she dialed for their messages. Kasdeya shoved the rest of a croissant into his mouth and knelt up to tilt the carafe over the delicate porcelain. Alex shut her eyes, inhaling deeply of the rich, dark aroma. Fresh black coffee and pastries in bed—could life get any better?

She opened her eyes to see a creampuff being held in front of her lips. She pushed the last digit on the number pad and obligingly opened her mouth. With a chuckle, Kasdeya pressed the entire creamy, crumbly mess in between her lips. Pale golden flakes and powdery sugar rained down on her breasts. Her dark man was in instant attendance to clean her up with his tongue.

"Hey…" Rose said on the recorded message. "I have no idea what time it is there, so if you're asleep, I'm sorry." Rose didn't sound like herself. She sounded depressed and tired. "Listen, Nicky's tests came back and it's… Oh, Alex, I wish you were here. You're so much better at handling shit like this than I am."

Alex pushed Kasdeya away. He sat back with a frown, but when he saw her concerned expression, he moved beside her and put his arm around her waist. His eyes asked a question that Alex didn't have the answer to yet.

"It's a tumor," Rose went on, her voice cracking. "An anaplastic den… roden… Ah, fuck! I don't know what the hell it's called. Inoperable brain tumor is what we're talking about." She let loose a choked sob that just about tore out Alex's heart. Her own throat ached with tears repressed. Poor little Nicole. Poor Jen.

"They're gonna give her chemo," Rose continued, "but you know, the outlook isn't great. Three to five years…"

There was a long pause. The only sound was Rose's hitching breaths. "Honey," she finally whispered, "I know a brain tumor is in no way related to a hangover but…can he do *anything*?"

Alex's gaze sought out Kasdeya's. Could he?

"I'd just hate to see her die if she doesn't have to," Rose said. Alex listened to her friend pace over wooden floors. "Okay, sorry to piss all over your honeymoon. You can call me at your place. I've hired a nurse to stay with them and administer her treatments at home. No one can seem to get a hold of her father but apparently he doesn't have any money to help anyway. Thank God for Kas's donation.

"Anyway, I'm heading over there to get Nicky's bedroom ready to be lived in." Rose gave a tiny laugh. "She's chosen the turret room. No place to put her bed, but she doesn't seem to care. Tonight we're painting it the most god-awful shade of pink I've ever seen." She gave another laugh, this one bitter. "If the chemo doesn't have her violently ill, the paint surely will. Call me. I hope… Well… Yeah, just call and let me know. Love you, babe."

Alex hung up the phone, sitting numb for a moment.

"What—"

"We have to go back." She threw off the covers and scrambled for her jeans. "Right now. Get your clothes on."

"What—"

"Rose is a wreck. Nicky's sick. That fellow you killed—she's his daughter."

"The people you're letting stay at the house?" Kasdeya ran one hand through his tangled hair. "What—"

"Cancer. A brain tumor." Alex was shoveling toiletries into her purse. "Can you heal that?"

Kasdeya frowned. "I don't know. Minor healing is all I've—"

"Now's the time to find out." She ripped open the closet. "For God's sake, Kasdeya, get dressed!" Hangers clanged as she indiscriminately pulled down the clothes she'd hung mere hours before.

"Alexandra, slow down. We need to—"

"Just get dressed!"

"I am dressed!"

She glanced over her shoulder to see him occupying the exact same space, now clad in a light sweater and slacks. Shit, she'd forgotten he could do that. "Okay. Good. Then could you go get our stuff out of the bathroom?"

Kasdeya uncurled from the bed, all grace and serenity. The sight of him strolling calmly toward her set her teeth on edge. Did he feel no urgency here?

"Little one," he said. "Even if we could get away with going back, the power required to heal her would surely draw—"

Alex shook her head impatiently. "But Uriel can't kill you, right? It's impossible to kill you." The zipper on her suitcase wouldn't budge. She wrestled with it, cursing vehemently.

Kasdeya's hands settled on her shoulders. "He can kill *you*," he said with cold finality.

"But we'll be in the house. It's guarded." She sagged back against him, letting the case fall. "Kasdeya, she's just a little girl. If it comes down to it, I'm willing to trade my life for hers."

Kasdeya's fingers tightened, biting deep. He tugged her around to face him. "I'm not. And besides, we don't even know if it will work."

"We have to try." Alex held his gaze, resolute, and he held hers just as steadfast, but she thought she saw him weaken when her lower lip trembled at the thought of that sweet child only having three pain-filled years to live.

A few seconds later, Kasdeya said with a defeated sigh, "If the Powers show up, leave. Summon yourself away. Promise me that or I'm not doing it, no matter how dejected you look."

"I promise."

"I'm very serious, pet." Kasdeya narrowed his eyes and leaned forward until their noses were touching. "If I have to worry about where you are, I *will* lose this battle."

"Don't worry about me, dark man," she said. "I'll be gone. You have my word."

* * * *

Kasdeya and Alex coalesced in the middle of the living room, scaring Rose—clad in very cute Hello Kitty pajamas—shitless. "Jesus Christ, Alex," she cried, falling to her knees to pick up the coffee cup she'd dropped. Bitter brown liquid now liberally decorated the valuable antique rug. "How did you do that? And what if Jen or Nicky had been in here? Christ!"

"Nice to see you too, Rosie," Alex said with a weary smile. "Having a sleepover?" Kasdeya supported her full weight. The strength seemed to have drained right out of her the minute they'd solidified.

"Yeah, Jen wanted the company, though she hasn't slept a wink. Sorry 'bout that welcome, you just scared me." Rose's face sagged with tiredness and grief. "I *am* glad to see you. Fucking ecstatic, actually. Some first week on the job, huh?" She braced against the coffee table to stand, the coffee forgotten. "Want it back? The job?"

Kasdeya swung Alex up in his arms. "No, she doesn't. She wants a bed, and I want to see the girl. The sooner I attempt to heal her, the sooner we can leave."

"*Can* you heal her, Kas?" Rose asked.

Kasdeya started up the stairs. "We're about to find out."

* * * *

Alex paced the hall while Rose kept Jen calm downstairs. It had been almost three hours, and even though she'd slept through two of them, she was starting to feel a jittery pulse of panic at every additional minute that trickled by. God knew what Rose was saying to Jen to keep her away. Alex and Rose had both assured the frantic mom that Kasdeya was going to do his best to help Nicky. He just needed some time alone with her. Jen had allowed it, but Alex got the impression that Jen would have allowed anything that offered even a smidgen of hope.

Finally, Alex could take it no longer. She crept into the bedroom, which was still dark even though it was a little after seven in the morning. A big storm was brewing. Wind howled eerily around the old house. Thunderclouds had set up camp in front of the sun.

Kasdeya sat hunched over Nicole where she lay asleep. His hands engulfed her fair head and his eyes were squeezed shut in concentration. Beads of a faintly luminous, opalescent liquid that Alex could only assume was the Fallen version of sweat dotted his brow. Funny, she'd never seen her dark man sweat before.

Alex crept forward on cat feet, trying to assess the situation without breaking his focus. She must have made some sound though, because Kasdeya sighed and sat back, turning reddened eyes to her.

Alex's heart sank.

"I've encapsulated it," he rasped as his hands fell away. "I believe I've shrunk it as well. But frankly, I have no idea how long either measure will last. It isn't permanent." He rubbed at his temples as though in pain. "The problem, pet, is that Father has called this one home. It would take a greater power than mine to thwart her fate."

Thunder rumbled in the distance, ominous and fitting.

"I see," said Alex quietly. She looked out one of the long, narrow windows just as the first fat drops of rain struck the windowpane. "I appreciate you trying, dark man." She sighed. A streak of lightning seared the sky, very near. The clap of thunder that followed sounded as if it had originated in the room. "I guess it was a long—"

The next lightning bolt was so close Alex was blinded.

"Alexandra," Kasdeya cried, his voice full of urgency. "To me." She turned her head in his direction but could only make out a streak of shadow leaping toward her. The room appeared a negative of itself as her eyes struggled to adjust.

Another lightning strobe followed. It somehow seemed to explode up from the floor between her and Kasdeya.

Alex couldn't see a damn thing. "Kas—"

A strong male arm wrapped around her waist, hauling her off her feet. Alex clung to his body, waiting for her pupils to contract.

"Let her go, Uriel," Kasdeya said from somewhere behind her.

"What…" Alex trailed off as a starkly handsome, cruelly arrogant male's face came slowly into focus. The angel had mahogany brown skin, full ox-blood-hued lips and a wide, flared nose, but his most striking feature were his large almond eyes, tilted up like a cat's. The irises were the most unusual shade of julep green Alex had ever seen. Tawny golden wings rustled restlessly against her side.

Uriel was as beautiful as either Kasdeya or Shaitan. But where the Fallen were sensual looking—gorgeous decadence—Uriel's beauty was the beauty of a wasteland. Pitiless.

Someone had got it wrong. Here was a real demon.

Alex struggled in his grip, her gaze darting around fearfully. And where the hell had he taken her? She could still make out Nicole's bedroom, but everything looked see-through and vague, like it wasn't quite real. Uriel's waist-length black hair, adorned in hundreds of braids tied off with jet beads, clicked like the skittering of insect legs as he bowed his head to look at her.

"Summoner," he said, his voice gentle. "I *am* sorry for the path you've chosen. It pains me to see a soul fall so very low." One of his hands came up to her jaw, forcing her head back.

"Flee!" her dark man howled.

In a completely upside-down view, she saw Kasdeya draw a great black sword out of thin air. It matched the black of his wings, once more in evidence behind him. Panic twisted his face.

Flee. Yes, that was the deal. It had happened so bloody fast that she hadn't had time to gather her wits. But now she shut her eyes and visualized her office in Dovescot.

"No," Uriel said, his tone still kind. "I'm afraid I can't allow that." The pressure on her jaw intensified. There was an instant of horrific, searing pain. As if from far away, Alex heard an odd crackle. The crunch and snap was almost exactly like the sound of walking through autumn leaves. She loved that sound.

"No!" Her dark man's screech of anguish made her wince.

It was okay. She felt okay. When she tried to tell Kasdeya that, though, no sound came out of her mouth. Weird.

Uriel must have let her go because suddenly she was free falling. The view bounced when she hit the ground but somehow, she didn't feel it. *Dovescot*, she told herself firmly. Kasdeya wouldn't be able to fight if he was worried about her.

But Alex couldn't seem to bring the image into focus. Everything in her mind was wavery and dim.

She felt the sensation of wind on her face and opened her eyes to discover that Uriel had kicked her out of the way, tossing her through the air with sickening ease. Another muted snap when she landed. And still Alex felt nothing. Everything *outside* of her mind was going wavery and dim too. Suddenly, Alex realized she wasn't okay at all.

"Summon Shaitan," Kasdeya sobbed, using his sword to try and hack his way to her. Uriel evaded his frantic thrusts. The angel's own sword, seemingly made of pure white fire, wove through Kasdeya's defenses with no apparent effort. He appeared to be toying with the Fallen, scoring gashes on every part of his body without bothering to deliver a killing blow. Tears and phosphorescent sweat covered Kasdeya's face, and blood sheeted his perfect body, making him look like some sort of gorgeous, tragic martyr.

Fight, dumb ass, Alex thought with what she realized was a distressing lack of urgency. Kasdeya was being brutalized and all she felt was mild concern. The battle seemed so surreal. Not very important at all.

"Shaitan!" Kasdeya screamed again, barely seeming to notice as Uriel slashed through his left wing. Blood and feathers sullied the air. "Pet, please!"

Shaitan? Shaitan... Right... Okay. It was too much effort to keep her eyes open. "Shaitan," she tried to say, but no words escaped her mouth. The sound of fighting receded; all that Alex could hear now was the hum of a vast, rushing sea. *"Shaitan..."* She called him with her mind, slipping down, down into the soothing water. *"I*—Kasdeya—*summon*—needs—*you*—"

Before she surrendered completely to the darkness Alex heard, as if from a far distant shore, "Oh, bloody hell!"

* * * *

Pain!

"No, no, no," Alex whimpered, trying to crawl away from the agony. Her body, she couldn't move her body. Her eyelids trembled.

"Yes, yes, yes," Shaitan said. "Come on, love. I can't hold you here for long. You're too close to death."

She reluctantly opened her eyes. Her neck, head and shoulders were a barbed wire web of torture. Everything below them was numb.

"Probably not a good time to say I told you so," he said, "so I'll resist the temptation."

Shaitan picked up her right hand and brought it to his mouth, sinking his teeth deep into the meat of her palm. Alex looked on in horrified fascination, still feeling absolutely nothing. He tilted her hand so that blood ran down onto her thumb. "All right, Summoner, you can't sign this," he flourished a scroll, "in the traditional way, but with verbal assent and a blood print, it will still bind. So, do you offer your soul to me in return for eternal life as previously discussed?"

Alex looked past him to Kasdeya, who was getting his ass handed to him by a huge, brown-skinned angel. Then she looked past them to the smoky outline of what was formerly her home office but was now the bedroom of a dying four-year-old girl. For a second, everything bled out to faded sepia before snapping back into solidity once more.

"Alexandra," Shaitan said, his voice strained. "I need you to say yes *now*." He had her thumb hovered over the vellum. One word and it would be done. She brought her gaze back to his and opened her mouth.

* * * *

"What the fuck do you mean, 'no'?" Kasdeya heard his brother exclaim.

No? He automatically turned toward them, giving his opponent a clear shot at his back. It was an opportunity the angel was loathe to waste, and the tip of Uriel's fiery sword emerged from between his second and third ribs. Kasdeya knew he had a half-second or so before the pain kicked in. He strained to hear what Alexandra was saying as he stumbled to his knees. All at once, fire seemed to consume every ounce of air in his lungs.

Uriel withdrew his blade and kicked Kasdeya over onto his side. "Really, Kas." His lip curled in disgust. "That was your most pathetic effort to date. Have you forgotten everything I taught you?"

Kasdeya ignored Uriel. His full attention was trained on Alexandra and Shaitan. They were only about twelve feet away, just far enough that he could catch nothing of their conversation.

Shaitan shook his head, and then shook it again more emphatically. He turned his troubled gaze on Kasdeya.

Kasdeya held out one hand to the pair even as Uriel straddled him, raising his glowing sword for the killing blow. With a grimace, Shaitan finally nodded. The Prince held her hand for one second more, and then, with his thumb and forefinger, closed her eyelids.

"No!" Kasdeya cried. His outstretched hand curled into a tight fist of pain. Squeezing his eyes shut against the sob of anguish trying to rip its way up his throat, Kasdeya moved his hair away from his neck. "Make sure you sever it completely, Uriel." He gagged on the blood in his mouth. "I don't want to wake up for a very long time."

Uriel squatted and wrenched Kasdeya's head up. "I don't take requests, Kas." He smashed Kasdeya's face into the ground, breaking his nose in two places. "Truly pathetic. I had thought that such an outpouring of power on your part meant you were ready for battle. Why else would you do something guaranteed to attract my attention? But no." He stood and kicked Kasdeya in the ribs again, encouraging a larger gout of blood to splash from the Fallen's lips. "I see it was just one more example of your stupidity. I should have known." He turned away, his body fading before his voice did. "Enjoy your recovery, Kasdeya. I suggest you not be so eager to seek me out again."

Chapter 21

"You're awake? Good. Get up. Kasdeya needs you."

The words were enough to propel Alex into an upright position before she'd even had a chance to take in where she was or who was speaking. There was the sound of heavy drapes sliding along a metal pole. Ruddy red light beamed into the room through a large circular window across from the bed. She raised a hand to shield her eyes from the eerie crimson glow. "Holy shit!" Alex felt her neck and shoulders frantically. "I'm healed?"

The woman at the window snorted. "No," she said in a silky, smoky voice. "You're dead, imbecile." Alex couldn't see her well against the light, but her hostess was apparently a bitch with a nice voice.

Memory came flooding back. Ah yes, her deal with the Devil. She sighed and swung her legs over the edge of the mattress. Since she was dead, Shaitan better have held up his end of the bargain. Alex was surprised when her feet didn't touch the ground and looked down to see she still had a good eight inches to go. She was forced to hop off the royal-sized bed.

Dead.

She was dead.

Good God, she was dead! Alex's knees wobbled. She leaned against the bedpost, trying to calm the panic attack she could feel coming on. Her hands clenched, crushing the thickly brocaded gold comforter. Dead! "Is Shaitan around?" she gasped.

The speaker moved forward. She was a stunning, daintily petite Oriental girl. The sight of her temporarily drove Alex's dread away. Ankle-length black hair swayed around the elfin beauty's lithe form as she stalked toward Alex clad in a formfitting crimson cat-suit that showed off her serpentine curves and left her firm, brown-nippled breasts entirely uncovered. She snicked across the plush carpet on heels at least six inches high. A haughty sneer twisted her luscious red lips.

"And what," the woman asked, stopping in front of Alex to cast a depreciating eye over her naked body, "do you want with my Shaitan? Do you plan to fuck him again?" One fine, high eyebrow arced even higher.

Christ, she really didn't need this right now. Alex straightened, ignoring her nude state, and mimicked the woman's conceited stance. She'd always been the shortest gal on the block, but she had half a head on this one, something Alex used to her advantage as she leaned forward right into the broad's space and said, "Well, I don't know, Shi-Liu. Do you plan to fuck *my* man again, sending Shaitan off into another jealous rage that can only be cured in my arms?"

Shi-Liu's pretty mouth pursed. She tilted her chin up, narrowed scarlet, sharply slanted eyes and leaned in even closer until the tops of her high, round breasts brushed the bottom of Alex's. Waves of heat radiated off the shorter girl's body, and a not entirely unpleasant sunburn sensation quickly settled into Alex's exposed skin.

"I tend to never say never," Shi-Liu purred, "but I have no plans in that direction at this time." Her mouth was a fraction of an inch from Alex's. Suddenly, Shi-Liu snapped her head forward, catching Alex's bottom lip between her sharp little teeth.

Alex held herself perfectly still, even as the tang of blood washed her taste buds. If she pulled back, her lip would not only be punctured, it would be torn. The idle thought that it didn't seem fair she could still be hurt when she was dead drifted through her mind. Then again, this *was* Hell, right? There wouldn't be much point to the place if the souls sent here couldn't be hurt.

Shi-Liu waited one second more and then, with a self-satisfied smirk, loosened her hold to dart her tongue inside Alex's mouth, lapping at the wound she'd made. Sharp black nails scratched up Alex's spine and snarled in her hair to keep her close. But that was okay; Alex wasn't going anywhere. A point was being made, and Alex could make points with the best of them.

Alex's hands closed over Shi-Liu's seemingly frail shoulders and she took her turn with her teeth, sinking them hard into the smaller girl's tongue. Shi-Liu went rigid, but then she laughed. Her super-heated little body rubbed against Alex's, small breasts mashed into her own, and a very odd thing happened: Alex felt aroused. When she tried to pull away, Shi-Liu's claws tightened and her now-free tongue became ruthless, coaxing Alex's lips wide apart. The nymph was stronger than she looked.

"Ooh boy," said someone with a gruff English voice from the doorway. "If that ain't a sight worth creaming your jeans over, I don't know what is."

Shi-Liu gave Alex a final, crotch-dampening twirl with her very hot, very nimble tongue and turned her head toward Shaitan, laying her cheek coyly on Alex's shoulder. The heat rising from her body abated slightly, mellowing to a comfortable level. "You're right, darling. She *is* something special. Kasdeya has done well."

"Uh, thanks," Alex mumbled, thoroughly befuddled by the unbalanced little creature cuddling against her. She awkwardly petted the girl's back. "Speaking of my dark man…" She turned to the Prince, who was lounging against the doorjamb bare chested and barefooted in dark red, skintight leather pants. "How's he doing?" She did her level best to keep her gaze on his face and not on his chiseled abs. "Where is he? Shi-Liu said he needs me."

A cloud seemed to cross Shaitan's features. "It's only been a few hours, love. He's still deep in a healing trance. But he'll recover. We always recover. I believe having you close will speed up the process though."

He walked further into the opulent crimson and gold room. "Come here, you flirt," he said with an amused smile, holding his hand out to Shi-Liu. The Oriental woman slipped out of Alex's arms and sashayed into Shaitan's, leaving Alex with no cover for her nude body.

Shaitan, of course, performed an immediate and thorough inspection. "Nothing wrong with your self-image is there?" Before Alex could ask what he meant, Shaitan gestured to a large gilt armoire angled into the far corner of the room. "Clothes are in there, Alexandra," he said. "But don't feel you have to dress on my account."

Alex threw open the armoire's doors and gasped in surprise at the leather, lace, silk, velvet, even plain old cotton. Every outfit she'd ever dreamed of owning was neatly lined up before her.

Shi-Liu smiled. "Did I do all right, Summoner? I had to guess at your size, but I'm rarely wrong."

Alex ran a reverent hand over the fabrics. "They're beautiful."

"Good," Shaitan said, suddenly all business. "Get dressed then. We'll wait for you outside."

* * * *

Alex walked the labyrinth of corridors flanked by Shaitan and his first concubine. Everything was so different here. The glimpses she'd had outside showed an alien landscape that was majestic and beautiful, but strange. An enormous red sun hung low in the sky, making the forest of black trees that surrounded the castle seem to strain toward the occupants. And yes, it was a castle, with thick stone walls, a bottomless moat and real live gargoyles that wheeled around the castle's upper reaches like a flock of giant birds.

And everyone was so *attractive*. She was much more attractive too. Alex had had to sit when she'd first looked at her reflection in the mirror. She still looked like herself, only…so much better. No more wrinkles. No more freckles. Her skin was now as smooth and white as Kasdeya's. Her tits seemed perkier, her stomach flatter and her hair… Good God, her hair was as silky and shiny as any Pantene model's. If people knew what dying did for your appearance and self-esteem, Alex was sure they wouldn't be so terrified of the prospect.

Still, as beautiful as she felt—especially in the fitted, blue velvet gown she'd chosen—she was nowhere near the flawlessness of the rest of the castle's residents. Everywhere she looked, she saw eye candy. The lavish gilt furniture and priceless artwork on display in the predominantly red and black rooms seemed nothing but a natural backdrop to the supernatural splendor of the Fallen.

"Hey." Shaitan gave her ass a smack. "If you're going to ask questions, pay attention to the answers."

What had she asked? Alex groped for the thread of their conversation as two stunning, utterly naked male Fallen strolled by. Bare assed seemed to be the uniform of choice in Hell. Alex was feeling decidedly overdressed.

"Samuel isn't dead," he said again. "I would have explained this to you before but I was on a bit of a time constraint, as you'll recall."

"Not dead? But—"

He shrugged. "He got the same deal I offered you, Summoner. Eternal life. No strings." Shaitan squeezed her hip and leaned in to say, "He's not an idiot though, so he took it."

Alex snapped her teeth at his nose and he pulled back, laughing. He laughed harder when Shi-Liu smacked her ass this time, making her yelp. Alex stopped walking and motioned the two together before taking up position on their left, beside Shaitan. Everyone was so damned slap happy. At least this way she'd only have to deal with *his* hands.

"I thought you didn't offer that deal to just anyone," she said as they resumed their journey. Where was Kasdeya? They'd been walking for at least ten minutes.

"I don't. But the kid's a bloody genius. He's got it so that there's no lag between this plane and any other for my cell and email. The coffers are

Alicia Steele

three times the size they were just five hundred years ago thanks in large part to him, and—"

"Five hundred?"

"Mmm-hmm." Shaitan nodded. "He made the deal five-hundred-some-odd years ago."

Alex rubbed her forehead. "And because he's still alive, he can go to Earth. And because I'm not, I can't."

He looked at her sympathetically. "In a nutshell." Shaitan stopped walking when he saw the stricken expression on her face and pulled her into his arms for a bear hug. Shi-Liu plastered her hot little self against Alex's back, and Alex strangely didn't mind. "My friends, my brother…"

"Oh, sweetheart." Shaitan smoothed down her hair. "Samuel's working on a way to get your friend Rose down here for a visit, and if anyone can see it done…" He took hold of her skull, tilting her face up to his. "We'll figure something out."

Alex nodded, but a single tear trickled down her cheek. "How about my deal? Is Nicole—"

Shaitan smiled. "One miraculous recovery, as ordered." He swiped his thumbs under her eyes, catching the next droplet before it had a chance to escape.

Alex nodded again, a snapping movement. "Okay." She shrugged them both off. "Okay, that's great. Amazing. Thank you. And that *was* the deal, as you say. I just… I just didn't realize I couldn't ever…" She scrubbed her cheeks with rough hands. "If you're going to bring people down for a visit, Shaitan, I'd like to see my brother too, if that's at all possible."

Shaitan managed to frown and wince at the same time. "I don't know, Alexandra, even one—"

"I'm all he has left. Our parents died when he was just thirteen." Alex stroked her hands down his chest and tilted her head demurely. "*Please*, my Prince." Then she remembered the woman standing just behind her and snatched her hands back. But a quick peek showed that Shi-Liu, rather than being annoyed at her obvious flirting, was looking amused by the situation. Alex turned her gaze back to Shaitan, throwing in a few eyelash bats for good measure.

The Prince's nostrils flared on an exasperated breath. "I'll think about it!" He stalked off down the hallway. "Let's see *my* brother well first, all right?"

The succubus caught her hand as Alex started after him, twining the Summoner's fingers through her own. "Next time you ask him for a favor, darling?" Shi-Liu said in a low, humor-filled voice. Her other hand rose, palm up, then snapped closed in a vicious fist. "Go right for the balls."

A laugh was startled out of Alex. What the hell? Minutes ago, Shi-Liu had been furious at the thought of Alex anywhere near Shaitan's balls. What a strange, strange girl! Things really *were* different here.

* * * *

"Now remember," Shaitan cautioned, opening the thick oaken door, "no wound is fatal to a Fallen. He *will* recover."

Alex scowled. Why did he keep saying that?

Kasdeya's room was so dark she couldn't see a damned thing. "Light?" Alex asked, walking tentatively across what felt like cold marble.

A black-shaded lamp flicked on beside the bed, the same bed as was in his prison. The fallow glow didn't improve matters much, however, because the entire room was black—the floors, the walls, the furniture— but at least she could see her dark man's face now. It was a ghostly white smudge above the ebony sheets. Shaitan and Shi-Liu came to stand at the foot of the mattress as Alex sat down beside him.

She petted his lustrous hair away from his fine, high forehead. He didn't look *too* bad. His nose was purple and blue—clearly broken—and a single, ropelike gash trailed from his temple down the left side of his face and throat to disappear beneath the sheets. When she started to turn back the covers, Shaitan moved quickly to stand beside her. His steadying hand settled on her shoulder.

The gash continued down Kasdeya's torso, where it was joined by dozens more. A bloody New York road map, set on vellum of mottled plum and green, decorated her dark man's body, to say nothing of the four—no, five—pulpy red puncture wounds. The largest one was about the size of Alex's hand and covered most of Kasdeya's ribcage on the right side. Alex could hear the wet sucking of his indrawn breath, and the sound wasn't coming from his mouth. As if to add insult to heinous injury, his beautiful wings were ragged and dull, the left shorter than the right by half.

Alex covered her mouth in dismay. "Oh my God."

Shaitan squeezed her shoulder. "He will heal, Summoner. He just needs time."

Alex turned huge eyes up to him. "How much time are we talking about?"

Chapter 22

A whorish, hellish, horrific long time: that's what he should have said! Six months had passed. Alex was curled into Kasdeya's side, reading the latest Stephen King novel that wasn't due to be released until next summer. "Perks of the job," Shaitan had said when he'd tossed the foil-wrapped bundle to her a few weeks back. "I make an appearance in this one, so let me know what you think."

So far, *The Crimson King* didn't fit much with the Shaitan that Alex knew. But it was still a good read. Not good enough to distract her for very long though.

"Dark man," she whispered, laying the book aside to stroke her hands down his lifeless body. "You have to wake up now." As usual, there was no response. Alex sat up, tossing the deep blue comforter off them both.

The first thing she had done on learning that she was stuck here was redecorate Kasdeya's bedroom. His entire room had been black. Who lived like that? So damned macabre. Well, no more. The floors were now a pale-blond maple, the walls a gentle mossy green. Huge Monet canvases, like so many picture windows, rounded out the healing atmosphere she was very much trying to create. A reading area with a matching blue divan had been set up in the corner, but it was pretty much unused space since Alex spent most of her time in bed with Kasdeya.

Shaitan had offered her her own room—the one she'd first woken up in—but Alex couldn't stand sleeping apart from the man she loved, even if this *was* starting to feel way too much like a necrophiliac love affair. If she could have gotten her dark man's cock to play along, it would have done more than just *feel* like one. But unlike a mortal man, Kasdeya didn't experience random erections while he slept. Sadly, that lovely part had stayed as seemingly deceased as the rest of him.

Lucky for Alex, the centurion was among the things she'd had sent down here for temporary storage, along with such personal effects as her mother's antique writing desk, her entire CD collection and her home computer. Her little corner of Hell was feeling very homey indeed, and if her man would just wake up already, Alex knew she could be happy here.

It didn't really even feel like she was dead since Shaitan allowed Alex to phone or email her loved ones whenever the whim struck. Her brother and her friends still thought Alex was living the high life somewhere in Europe. Rose knew the truth, thanks to Sam, and it was a huge relief to have her best friend to talk to. But it would have been better to have a flesh-and-blood shoulder to cry on rather than the long-distance, late-night phone calls Alex made with disturbing and slightly hysterical regularity.

Shaitan and Sam were still working on the visitor situation, but there was some sort of "unbound soul" clause in the rules Shaitan and God had agreed to millennia ago. It was holding the whole process up. Shaitan assured Alex he was on it though, and that would just have to do. She'd make sure to ask for an update the next time she saw him, which might not be for a while; the Prince was a busy fella. He'd been gone for more than two weeks now, and the time before that he'd disappeared for three months. When he was away so long, Shi-Liu tended to get petulant and even more touchy-feely than usual.

Shi-Liu. Against all odds, Alex was becoming pretty good pals with the tiny firebrand. It was a weird friendship, to be sure. For one thing, Shi-Liu found women—Alex—attractive. At first, that had made Alex feel uncomfortable. A kiss on the mouth to say hello, a pat on the ass for good-bye—that was Shi-Liu on a good day. But the tiny Oriental woman seemed to realize that Alex didn't lean that way so she didn't push, and now, almost six months later, Alex sometimes found that she was the one leaning down for a kiss. It was just the way it was between them. "No big," as Rose would have said.

And for another, Shi-Liu was always parading "eligible" bedmates in front of Alex. She just didn't seem to *get* the concept of monogamy. Shi-Liu had admitted that the jealous routine she'd pulled when Alex had first arrived had just been a test of Alex's "mettle" when Alex had pointed out that Kasdeya would be just as angry as Shi-Liu had been to find out he'd been betrayed by the person he loved.

It turned out Shi-Liu took lovers all the time—with Shaitan's consent. This had confused Alex; wasn't that the very thing that had sent Kasdeya to the Prison in the first place? Then Shaitan had clarified: Shi-Liu took *female* lovers, thank you very much, and they always shared them. He'd then gone on to waggle his eyebrows and leer, saying, "A bigger bed's on order, Alexandra, for when you get tired of waiting for my lazy brother to wake up."

He'd only been joking. The Prince understood Alex's commitment to his brother, and although he flirted outrageously, it was always in a "wink wink, nudge nudge" way. He never made her feel uncomfortable the way his concubine sometimes did. Shi-Liu didn't *mean* to make her uncomfortable, she was just a sexual creature. Sex was what she'd been made for, it was what she liked, and she didn't mind showing or exuding that. Alex could see how Kasdeya had gotten into trouble there. Hell, sometimes Alex felt like she was close to getting into trouble herself. Six months was a long time. And though Kasdeya's wounds had closed, and the bruises had faded, there were still thick, raised scars crisscrossing much of his body.

Her dark man was showing no signs of waking up anytime soon.

Alex reached for the healing oil that was in permanent residence on the nightstand and rubbed some into those scars, running her fingers over the now familiar cables of flesh as the scent of growing things rose to tease her nostrils.

Shaitan assured her that he could wake up at anytime—that the healing didn't need to be complete. He also encouraged her to talk to Kasdeya, which she did every single day. Why wasn't he responding? Alex didn't care about the scars. She just wanted him to open his eyes for her, to smile for her. To kiss her.

Alex breathed a gusty sigh, corked the oil and tucked Kasdeya back in. She went to get dressed, though "dressed" had become a rather subjective term, as the Fallen's habit of nakedness had begun to seem perfectly ordinary. All Alex pulled on was a pair of white panties and a delicate white satin slip that ended well above her knees. A long black velvet cloak finished off the outré outfit.

Please, God, make him wake up soon.

It didn't escape her that selling your soul to the Devil and then praying for a Fallen's health was pretty much ridiculous, but Alex had always prayed and she saw no reason to change her habits now. God could just continue to ignore her if that's what he felt he needed to do.

"I'll be back soon, big boy," she said. "Holler if you need me." Ha-ha.

She shut the door carefully behind her and started the fifteen-minute journey up to Shi-Liu and Shaitan's apartment. Alex had arranged to get together for lunch with the succubus and then head to Hell's zoo, where every creature that hadn't made the ark was on display. Alex loved the unicorns; she could sit and watch the snowy white herd all day long.

Shi-Liu was friendly with the dragons, often bringing them yummy little tidbits, like fresh baby deer.

"Hey, Ink Spot," Alex said as an eight-inch, half-grown chimera circled above her head a few times before landing on her shoulder. "How's your daddy?"

Ink Spot cooed and burbled, snorting small puffs of smoke from his flat reptilian nostrils. Big, friendly green eyes blinked at Alex from a face so very ugly it was cute. This baby gargoyle—or "chimera," as Shaitan kept correcting her—had lost his mom, and the Prince had unofficially adopted the little black orphan. It followed him everywhere, meaning Shaitan must be back.

Alex's steps faltered. That also meant that Shi-Liu would most likely be busy for the next few days. Her heart sank. Shi-Liu and Shaitan were the only friends Alex had here. Admittedly, she hadn't expended much effort at being social between spending most of her time locked up with Kasdeya and fending off Shi-Liu's matchmaking efforts, but she *did* need companionship every once in a while, and she'd really been looking forward to this outing.

"Maybe he's back but they're not in bed yet," she mumbled, continuing on. She was almost halfway there now and it couldn't hurt to check. She wouldn't even have to knock because if they *were* in bed Alex knew, from past experience, that she'd be able to hear them well before she hit the front door.

* * * *

After holding her ear pressed to the door for a few seconds, Alex figured it was safe to knock. At the rap of knuckle against wood, Ink Spot chirruped in excitement, digging sharp claws through the velvet cloak. He didn't like being locked out.

"Come on in, Alexandra. We were just talking about you." The bolt was drawn and the door eased open.

"How did you know it was me?" Alex stepped into the ornate red room and hastily averted her gaze. Ink Spot seemed to have no such qualms. He flew over to alight on his master's bent knee as Shaitan lounged nude in front of a massive stone hearth. Shi-Liu, just as nude, twined around him like a vibrant gold-skinned snake.

"Oh, please." Shaitan chuckled, giving his pet a friendly cuff before motioning Ink Spot to his perch on the mantle. "That polite little knock? Anyone else would have pounded the thing down. There's a reason the lock is the size of your head, love." Shaitan flung his left hand out to her. His right was exploring his concubine's ass. "C'mere."

Alicia Steele

Alex sidled closer, undoing the clasp of her cape and letting it fall. "Put some clothes on first."

Shaitan rolled his eyes and created a pair of jeans, undone so that Shi-Liu could keep *her* hand right where it was. "Not over that modesty crap yet, Alexandra?"

"Just Alex, remember?" Kasdeya called her Alexandra, and it sounded odd now coming from anyone else's lips. She sat down beside the Prince but he apparently wanted her lying down; he grabbed her hair and pulled until she fell into the position he preferred, tucked snug alongside him.

Shaitan sighed in contentment, stroking her flank. "Alex is a man's name. You aren't a man."

"It's not a... Oh, nevermind." She was unwilling to get into this debate right now. Not again. "You were talking about me?"

"Mmm-hmm."

Alex glanced up to see his lips caught between his teeth, eyes shut. Shi-Liu's hand moved faster. "I can come back," she said, attempting to rise.

His arm tightened. "No need. I can do both." He opened heavy eyelids to smile at her.

Alex's stomach fluttered at the look of sensual pleasure he wore and her sex constricted, moistening the crotch of her panties. He was so sexy. And it had been so long.

Shaitan's nostrils flared. "You smell great." He nuzzled into her hair to find her earlobe—with his teeth.

Alex turned red. She knew he wasn't referring to her perfume. "Shaitan, stop it." She ignored the way her adulterous body was pleading with him to do the opposite. This had officially entered the realm of *way* beyond acceptable.

She pushed against his chest but her hand was caught fast and immediately lowered to his thick, hard cock. Her palm stroked before she could stop it. Naughty palm. Shaitan groaned and arched into the touch, though it wasn't Shaitan who had put her hand there.

Alex snatched her fingers away and frowned at Shi-Liu over the Prince's pale, muscular chest. "Would you two cut it out?" She rolled out of their reach and finally succeeded in sitting up. "I'm going to go. I don't know why you even let me in."

The massive iron bolt slid across the front door even as Shaitan groaned, thrusting hungrily into Shi-Liu's—

Oh, that was special.

Alex grimaced and drew her knees up to her chest, hiding her face in the V shape created. Did she *really* need to be here for a deep-throating session? What the fuck was wrong with them? This was just cruel. And she was now so wet she was dribbling onto the rug right through her underwear. Very nice.

When the slurping had subsided, Alex said, "I don't know what you hoped to accomplish with that. I thought you respected…" She raised her head to glare at them. "Nevermind. Can I go now?"

They were both looking back at her identical expressions of amusement on their attractive faces.

"Darling," Shi-Liu said, sitting up as well. "We wanted—"

Alex held up her hand. "*I* want to leave."

"No. Not yet." Shaitan buttoned his pants and then flipped onto his stomach, bringing his knees underneath him in an extraordinarily sexy feline maneuver.

Alex looked away. But she was hard pressed to continue ignoring him as he crawled toward her, swaying on all fours. When he was directly in front of her, he sniffed the air and smiled. "I think you might be in a good frame of mind to talk now. Horny *and* angry, right?"

Alex smacked him. "Fuck off, Shaitan. Does that answer your question?"

He laughed and plopped himself down beside her, producing a pack of Pall Malls out of the air. "Yep. It does."

Shi-Liu stood up, gloriously naked and gloriously unconcerned about it. "Anybody want anything?"

"I'll take a beer, love, long as you're up."

"If I'm being forced to stay, I guess I will too." Alex sighed, accepting a cigarette. "So, okay, I'm pissed off and horny." She took a long, angry drag. "What now?"

"Now, sweetheart," Shaitan said, "we discuss how to bring your lover back from the dead."

Chapter 23

"You're certain he can hear me?"

"Yes." Shaitan blew lazy smoke rings into the air. "I know he can."

"Then why isn't he responding?"

He slanted her a look as he accepted a frosty brown bottle from his concubine. "That's the burning question, isn't it? Unfortunately, it's one I have no answer to. I honestly thought he'd pull himself out of it the first time he heard your voice. Granted, his wounds will take longer to heal if he's awake, but I figure that's a price he'd be willing to pay."

Apparently not, Alex thought morosely as she took the other beer from Shi-Liu.

"It doesn't matter why." Shi-Liu sat cross-legged in front of them. "It only matters that he *isn't* responding. Our plan should bring him around. And if it doesn't…" She shrugged. "No harm, no foul."

Alex looked down and fiddled with the beer's loose paper label. "Yeah, but if it does…" She glanced up. "He'll be so angry. He might never forgive—"

"Bah." Shaitan waved off her worry. "Of course he'll forgive you. He loves you."

If that was true, then why wasn't he awake?

"Look," Shi-Liu said. "Shaitan and I have been turning this idea over for a while now. We *did* try to come up with less drastic measures, but we couldn't think of any. Can you?"

"If I could, don't you think I'd have tried them by now?"

"So what then?" Irritation hardened the succubus' velvet-flocked voice. "Is the thought so abhorrent that you'd rather wait ten years for him to wake up naturally?"

"Of course not," Alex said. "You know I don't find…" Shi-Liu's words kicked in a beat late. "*Ten years?*" She turned to Shaitan, who was throwing his concubine a dirty look. "He's going to be asleep for *ten years*? Why didn't you tell me?"

He smiled in pained placation. "Probably not ten years, love. He was much more grievously wounded the last time he tangled with the Powers."

Alex blanched. More wounded? He must have been—

"In pieces," Shaitan supplied, reading her horrified expression. "Uriel made a bit of an object lesson out of Kas the last time he interfered in a mortal's life." He scowled at the memory. "Twelve against one. If I'd gotten there just a bit sooner, I—"

"But you didn't," Shi-Liu said. "And this is entirely beside the point." She leaned forward to take Alex's face between her small, searing hands. Sharp nails rested in subtle erotic threat against Alex's cheeks. "You have nothing to lose, darling, and everything to gain. If he doesn't wake, he'll never know."

Oh, he'll know, Alex thought. *Because I'll have to tell him.* Still, Shi-Liu was right. Ten years was much too long to wait.

Shi-Liu smiled when she read her answer in Alex's eyes. "Good," she said, leaning in for a kiss.

The succubus teased Alex's lips apart with the tip of her tongue, something she hadn't attempted since Alex's very first day in Hell. Alex hesitated only a moment before accepting the advance. Might as well.

When Shi-Liu had kissed her with a skill both disturbing and breathtaking, Shaitan's concubine leaned back, saying, "Very good. I promise."

* * * *

"Kasdeya," Shaitan said imperiously. "Wake up." He was straddling her dark man's chest, one fist caught in his black hair. He'd tried this before and this time was no different. There was absolutely no response. The Prince hauled off and slapped his brother, leaving a red handprint on Kasdeya's fair skin.

Alex gasped. "What are you doing?" She attempted to grab Shaitan's arm but Shi-Liu held her back.

Shaitan didn't answer. He was watching Kasdeya closely for any reaction. When he didn't see one, he did it again.

"Stop!" Alex struggled against the smaller but infinitely stronger woman standing between her and them.

"Wake up, you wanker," Shaitan growled, raining a flurry of blows down on her defenseless lover's face.

"God damn it, let me go!" Alex yelled.

"Trust him," Shi-Liu said.

"Wake—" Shaitan stopped slapping to study Kasdeya again. "Ahh, there we go." He shifted off his brother's body and motioned the girls forward.

Alex rushed to check Kasdeya's face for damage. She felt his cheek and jaw bones carefully. "What the hell were you doing?" she hissed, rounding on Shaitan. "This wasn't part of the plan."

"It was part of *my* plan, love," he said. "Do you notice anything different?"

"He's still unconscious. I notice that."

"Look again."

She did. No, there was nothing. Wait a minute…

"He's frowning." Hope flared to life deep in Alex's chest. For half a year now, Kasdeya's face had been a perfect mask of non-expression. Now he was frowning. Alex laughed in delight. "He's frowning!"

"Ding, ding, ding! Give the girl a prize." Shaitan patted the mattress between his body and Kasdeya's. "Ready, sweetheart?"

Was she? She looked at him and then at Shi-Liu, who had scooted in close to Kasdeya's other side. They were both naked, both beautiful.

Shi-Liu winked and beckoned Alex forward with a curled finger. Her pretty mouth hovered ready over Kasdeya's ear.

Alex took a deep breath and pulled the slip over her head. "As I'll ever be," she said, crawling onto the mattress to join the unholy trio.

* * * *

"Shaitan has his arms around your woman, Kas," Shi-Liu purred. "He's naked, and she's only wearing a pair of virginal white panties that—"

Shaitan grinned and delicately took the front of Alex's underwear between his fingers. The sound of fabric ripping was shockingly loud.

"Nevermind," Shi-Liu said. "She's not wearing them anymore." The Oriental girl wriggled half on top of Kasdeya to get a better view of the proceedings. "Now Alexandra is kissing the Prince's throat…biting."

Alex was doing no such thing. She was just lying there, wondering if she'd lost her freakin' mind and trying hard to ignore the fact that Shaitan's prick was caught intimately between her legs. Alex craned her head to catch Shi-Liu's eye but Shaitan cupped her jaw and brought her face back to him.

"Pay no attention to the woman behind the curtain," he whispered, stroking his thumb over her lower lip. "It's *me* you should be paying attention to."

To punctuate his words, Shaitan slowly dropped his hand, knuckles brushing down her throat and between her breasts before circling back to tease one rapidly tightening nipple. His hips twitched, sending his cock slithering through her folds. Alex groaned in spite of herself. But she felt funny about being with him when Shi-Liu was right there. Again, she tried to look at the concubine. Shaitan growled and pinched the nipple he'd been teasing.

"Ow!" Alex twisted to get away, but he wasn't about to allow that.

"Am I boring you, Alexandra?" he asked with a sardonic lift to his brow. "I'll try to do better."

Shaitan rolled her onto her back and lowered his lips to the breast he'd just assaulted. Alex groaned again when he sucked the sore peak into his mouth. This time her view of Shi-Liu was unimpeded. The succubus had a lascivious smile on her face and a hand between her legs. She really did get off on this. If it was Kasdeya in another woman's arms… Alex shook her head. But who was she to judge anyone? Her fingers glided up the Prince's back into his soft blond hair. Since she was the only one holding things up, she figured she may as well get with the program.

"Groan louder," Shaitan encouraged. She could feel him grinning against her skin. "You're trying to wake the dead."

Her hands tightened in his hair and she snapped his head back hard enough to make the tendons of his neck strain. Shaitan did some groaning of his own. "You too," she said with a smirk. Then she scooted down to bite the corded flesh, inhaling deeply of his spicy, smoky scent. Why did all Fallen smell so good?

"Mmm." He cupped the back of her skull, forcing her teeth in deeper. "I think I've missed you, sweetheart."

Alex raked her nails across his back, putting all her strength into it. Shaitan yelped then laughed. "Make that I *know* I've missed you." He reached for Shi-Liu over her head, pulling the raven-haired beauty close for a hot, open-mouthed kiss.

Alex continued biting, moving down to his decorated nipples. Shaitan was purring in pleasure. "Let me man the phones for a bit, love," he said to his concubine. He rolled again so that Alex was above him and his head was on par with Kasdeya's.

Shi-Liu nodded and joined Alex at her devotions, licking and gnawing Shaitan's chest.

"Mate," Shaitan whispered to the unconscious Fallen, his lips so close they tickled Kasdeya's ear. "I have both my woman and yours working me over. Frankly, I don't care if you ever wake up. Alexandra is stunning, pale and elegant, and Shi-Liu is as wickedly beautiful as ever. They're like yin and yang, so bloody perfect it hurts." He smoothed his hands down their long hair as he spoke.

"Kasdeya," he groaned. He seemed to be struggling to keep his writhing to a minimum so that he could stay close to his brother's ear. "Their mouths. Their hands. I've *never* been this hard before. You're missing out, mate. Now, if only one of them would pay some attention to this pretty prick of mine…"

Alex and Shi-Liu exchanged an amused look. Shi-Liu slipped a finger through his left nipple ring. She motioned for Alex to do the same on his right. With a conspiratorial grin, Alex did. On a silent count of three, they violently twisted at the exact same time.

"Alexandra is—*Oy!*" Shaitan's lips peeled back from his teeth and he clutched his brother's shoulder, no doubt in an effort to keep his hands off the girls. "Oh fuck! I'm never going to survive this." Shaitan gulped a shuddering breath, his body slowly relaxing. "Do it again."

Laughing, Alex sat up. She started to say something, but then stopped. Shaitan followed her gaze, half sitting up as well to peer down into Kasdeya's sleeping face.

"Hmm," he said, using one finger to turn it more toward him. Had it been turned away before? "I think you'd better get to my cock soon, love. Time might be shorter than I'd hoped."

Kasdeya's lip was curled into a snarl, his frown deeper than ever. Alex could see a pulse beating heavy and fast in the thin skin of his temple. Her stomach fluttered. He was managing to look extremely pissed off while still being unconscious. That had to be a unique talent. "Oh jeez." She tried to smooth out the deep crease between his brows—with no success. "He's gonna kill me."

"Yeah." Shaitan looped her long hair around one fist and tugged her toward him. "But he'll be awake to do it." His lips met hers in a kiss that was sweet and sincere. "It's okay, love." He nibbled persuasively at the corner of her mouth. "He'll understand."

"Look at this little honey pot," said Shi-Liu.

Shaitan's tongue entered Alex's mouth at the same moment Shi-Liu's long, slim finger entered her body. There was no resistance; Alex was drenched. Alex stiffened and attempted to edge away, but Shaitan took hold of her shoulders, holding her there crouched in front of him, ass about a foot off the mattress. His tongue became insistent, delving deep. His concubine's finger followed suit.

Soon Shi-Liu's finger was replaced by her tongue. Two toasty little hands spread Alex's ass cheeks apart. Shaitan chuckled at Alex's squeak of shock.

"I'm surprised she's held off this long," he confided, straggling kisses from her mouth to her jaw. "She's been wanting to taste you from the first moment she saw you." Alex couldn't reply. Shi-Liu's tongue had found her clit.

"Here," Shaitan said. He wriggled back down beside Kasdeya, pulling Alex with him. This raised her ass high in the air, but Shi-Liu seemed to have no problem keeping up. "Kiss him," he continued, sweeping her hair out of the way so that he could watch. "Kiss him and call his name while you come." Shaitan ran mild fingers over his cock. "But then give this poor fella some attention, all right?"

Alex could barely nod. Shi-Liu knew exactly what she was doing. She had Alex hovering so close to orgasm that it felt like the merest breath could send her over.

Alex brought her cheek against Kasdeya's. "Dark man," she whimpered, "I want you inside me so badly. Please wake...uhh, God!"

Shi-Liu held Alex's hips still throughout the ravishment, giving her clit no reprieve from the tender lashing she was treating it to. The tiny nub started to spasm and didn't stop.

"Kiss him," Shaitan reminded her.

With lust-dazed eyes, Alex looked up to see the blond fisting his cock. She nodded and twisted her hands in Kasdeya's hair, licking at his lips and crushing her breasts into his chest.

"I love you, Kasdeya." Her voice quavered as the intense pleasure tore through her. "God, I love you so much. Come back!"

His lips moved, parted. His tongue slowly rose to meet hers. Alex began to cry, even as she deepened the kiss, sucking hard, coaxing him fully into her mouth.

He groaned. It was a tiny sound, but one she clearly heard.

"Kasdeya?" Alex reared back to see his face, unmooring Shi-Liu. She couldn't have taken any more of the woman's tongue, anyway, without passing out.

Kasdeya's cheeks were flushed and his breathing heavy. But his eyes were still closed. "Come on!" Alex hissed. "Wake up."

Shaitan flicked back one of Kasdeya's eyelids. He didn't react.

"God damn it!" Alex's fists pounded into Kasdeya's chest.

"We're close, darling." Shi-Liu wrapped an arm around Alex's waist. "Very close. Don't lose focus now."

Alicia Steele

Alex turned her face into the succubus' neck and Shi-Liu stroked her hair. "On a purely selfish note," the succubus said, laughter lurking in her words, "did you enjoy me?"

"Did I—" Alex was confused for a second, but then she realized what the other woman was asking. "Very much," she said, cheeks hot. "Thank you."

"It was my pleasure, Summoner." Shi-Liu gently took Alex's right hand and smoothed it over her own heated stomach. Then she moved it lower.

Alex felt some trepidation when her palm brushed the soft, sparse curls at the juncture of the succubus' thighs, but she didn't waver. Fair was fair, after all. Her fingers delved between Shi-Liu's plump lips. The other woman's clitoris was larger than her own—almost twice the size—but it was still familiar ground. Alex figured that what she liked, Shi-Liu would like, and she traced Shi-Liu's clit lightly.

"Mmm," Shi-Liu said with a sigh. "Hang on. Let's do it right." She placed her palm over Alex's, keeping her hand firm between her legs, then lifted a knee over Kasdeya's chest. This brought her firm golden ass directly in front of his face. If he'd been conscious, all he'd have had to do was lift his chin to have a nibble. Since he wasn't, Shaitan leaned forward to do it for him.

Shi-Liu's deep red eyes drifted shut. Her hand on Alex's pushed down, increasing the pressure on her clit. Her other hand rose to squeeze one of her small, brown-nippled breasts.

Alex smiled secretly and lowered her mouth to the woman's other breast. Shi-Liu was correct: there was no point in doing a thing if you weren't going to do it right. As her mouth drew on the rigid, peaked flesh, her fingers moved faster, briskly rasping, rubbing. Shi-Liu was gasping, groaning, her balmy body swaying in time to Alex's ministrations.

When Alex felt Shaitan's hand below her own, fingers working rough into his concubine's dripping sex, she took the bead of Shi-Liu's clit between thumb and forefinger and gave it a vicious tweak.

The succubus cried out in pleasure, bucking between them. Liquid fire splashed over Alex and Shaitan's fingers. They slowed their movements to coincide with Shi-Liu's diminishing undulations.

"Alexandra," Shi-Liu sighed, falling limp against her, "you're more than welcome in our bed any time the mood strikes." She slung her arms around Alex's neck and kissed her.

"This is all very nice and sexy as hell." Shaitan rose up to rub his cock into Shi-Liu's hip. "But I'm about to explode here."

Shi-Liu ignored him, finishing the thorough exploration to which she was treating Alex's mouth. When she was finally through, she crawled off Kasdeya's body and said, "All right, sucky Princeling, Alex can take care of you while I keep Kas up to date on the situation." She smiled at Alex. "He's going to be with us very soon, darling. All you have to do is make Shaitan come." Shi-Liu slanted Shaitan a coy look. "Loudly."

Alex glanced down at Kasdeya. His momentary color had faded but his breathing was still fast. He did seem close. Would this be enough to bring him over? Based on what she'd seen so far, yes, probably. But Lord help her when it did.

Shi-Liu curled up by Kasdeya's head. From her red lips fell the most astounding litany of erotic bullshit that Alex had ever heard. The succubus winked and Alex had to laugh; this was such a ridiculous situation she'd found herself in. "Sexy as hell," as Shaitan had already noted, but ridiculous nonetheless.

Still chuckling, Alex said, "I'll do my best for you, my Prince."

"That's all I ask, love." Shaitan wore a sly, sardonic grin. The humor hadn't escaped him either. He held out his arms to her, and when she moved into them, he easily lifted and turned her body, positioning her so that she was straddling her dark man's chest again, facing his feet. One of her legs was now caught between Shi-Liu's hot little torso and Kasdeya's rock hard one. The concubine took immediate advantage, stroking sharp nails up and down Alex's thigh.

Alex turned her upper body to see Shaitan, who still sat at Kasdeya's shoulder. "What are you doing?"

"Motivating." He grabbed her waist and tugged back, forcing her to fall forward for balance. Her hands grasped Kasdeya's knees and Alex automatically looked down.

Beneath the covers bunched around her dark man's waist, Alex could clearly see the ridge of his beautiful, beautiful cock. With a glad cry, she whipped the blanket off. Tears stung her eyes at the sight of him so hard and ready. "Well, hey, big boy," she whispered, stroking a finger down his length. "Welcome back."

Shaitan gave her another tug, encouraging her hips lower. Alex's sex came into light contact with Kasdeya's lips. "There you are, brother," he mumbled. "Shi-Liu's pussy wasn't incentive enough? How 'bout this pink beauty?"

Kasdeya's body trembled. His cock jumped right before Alex's eyes. Without even thinking about it, Alex ducked her head.

Alicia Steele

"Nope." Shaitan caught her hair to hold her back. "Motivation, m'dear, motivation. If he wants to come, he has to wake up. And anyway, it's my turn." He crawled down to Kasdeya's knees and swung a leg over them. This placed his cock about six inches in front of Alex's mouth. "Alexandra," he said, "I know damn well this is my last shot at your beautiful body, and I find myself desperate for it. So please, show the Prince a little kindness here."

Alex straightened, settling more directly over Kasdeya's lips, and almost fainted when she felt his tongue creep out to play once more. She moaned and swayed against Shaitan.

"It worked, huh? Good. Now." He wrapped her fingers around his cock. "Now it's time to thank ol' Shaitan for coming up with a *brilliant* plan."

Kasdeya was barely tickling her clit. It wasn't enough to make her come, but it was enough to keep every cell in her body jangling with arousal. "Kasdeya," she said. "He's—"

"Not awake yet." Shaitan nudged her palm in reminder. "Don't worry, Shi-Liu will tell us wh...wh... Ah, that's the stuff, sweetheart." Alex only gave him a few cursory strokes before dropping her hand lower. His balls received a quick, cruel squeeze.

"Your Summoner's hand is between the Prince's legs, Kas, on his cock," Shi-Liu said. "Shaitan looks like he's going to come at any second. His ass is tight, pushing forward..."

Shi-Liu's libidinous commentary, Shaitan's stiff pink prick in front of her and Kasdeya's gentle tongue: the combination had Alex in a surreal state of hypersexual awareness. She steadied herself on Shaitan's hip and snaked her tongue down his torso, pausing every now and again to gnaw at his creamy white skin. "Thank you for coming up with a *brilliant* plan, my Prince," she purred between bites. "I truly"—she licked down one side of his cock—"appreciate"—and back up the other side—"it." Her tongue gave a languid, lollipop swipe around the weeping crown while her hand crept even lower.

"You're wel—"

Alex stabbed a single blunt-nailed finger deep into his ass and swallowed his entire length.

"Oh fuck!" he roared, driving his hips forward. His hands clamped tight around her cheeks, keeping himself impaled. Alex sucked like a vacuum. "Fuck, Alexandra!" His seed shot down her throat. She glanced up, past his convulsing stomach. Shaitan's head was lolled back into his shoulder blades, his body bowed backward. He was panting for air at the suddenness and intensity of the orgasm she'd treated him to when another finger found its way into his body. "Bloody hell," he groaned, managing a few more spurts. "I think I love you, woman."

He hauled her up into his arms. "Be my second, Alexandra." Passionate kisses rained down on her neck and shoulders. "Screw Kasdeya, you're too good for—"

"Shaitan." Shi-Liu's voice rose in warning.

"You'd still be number one, sweetheart," he said to her, not looking back. "You know—"

"She's...no one's"—her dark man's voice was so faint Alex could hardly hear it—"second."

Alex whipped around, a joyous smile on her lips.

Kasdeya, however, looked livid. "Put your throat between my teeth, Shaitan," he wheezed, spearing his Prince with rage-filled eyes. "I can't seem to raise the energy required to...kill you"—his lids started to fall closed again—"without some...help."

Chapter 24

Kasdeya heard his Prince ordering him awake again, and he floated down deeper into his psyche. He didn't want to ever wake up. Not with Alexandra so far beyond his reach now. Because, while he may not actually be able to die of the grief eating at his soul, he'd be damned if he'd live with it. No, this Fallen had no intention of ever waking up again.

Then Shaitan started hitting him. What was his Prince's problem? Why couldn't he just leave Kasdeya in peace? He frowned in his mind. If, for some reason, he ever *did* wake up, Kasdeya vowed Shaitan would get those blows back threefold. Meanwhile, he ignored the bastard, ignored the fleeting pain, and eventually the blows stopped. Then Shi-Liu's sultry, smoky voice started whispering to him. Whispering about... Damn, not again.

The Prince's succubus was a new and twisted addition to the tortured tricks his mind kept playing on him. He kept thinking he heard Alexandra, thinking he smelled her, felt her. It was agony. Kasdeya had seen her refuse Shaitan's offer. He'd seen her die. She wasn't here. And she *certainly* wasn't doing what Shi-Liu said she was! She would never...

But wouldn't she? Did he even know what the Summoner was capable of? Had he ever really known Alexandra at all? Her cursed her, and not for the first time. What about never leaving him? What about forever? Had she even loved him? Not enough, obviously. Not enough to stay.

"Ow!" he heard her cry, clear as day. Kasdeya knew it wasn't real; it was just his broken heart recreating her voice in his subconscious. But why was it making her sound in pain? Against his better judgment, Kasdeya started to rise. It wasn't real! He knew that. But it had sounded so genuine.

Now there was whispering. Moaning. The sound of muffled laughter.

"Mate," he heard Shaitan say unbidden in his head. "I have both my woman and yours working me over. Frankly, I don't care if you ever wake up. Alexandra is stunning, pale and elegant, and Shi-Liu is as wickedly beautiful as ever. They're like yin and yang, so bloody perfect it hurts."

The full-blown image of what was being described popped into Kasdeya's head. Yes, they would be beautiful together. His heart rate quickened. His cock stirred.

No. It wasn't real. All that consciousness could offer him was pain. He fought off the temptation to wake.

"Dark man," Alexandra said, tormenting him again. Why couldn't he let her go? "I want you inside me so badly," she said. "Please wake... uhh, God!"

His breath hitched and his cock lengthened further, straining toward the beautiful dream his mind had created. The sound of Alexandra coming had always driven him wild. That sexy catch in her voice, the way she stopped breathing for a second as the first pulses of bliss racked her body.

I love you, he thought helplessly.

"I love you, Kasdeya." She seemed to answer him. "God, I love you so much."

He could almost feel her lips, her sweet, sweet mouth. Before, he'd always backed away from the impossible dream of kissing her; when he'd felt her phantom lips against his own, he'd retreated from the sensation, distancing himself as well as he could. It hurt too much. But this time, he couldn't make himself run. It may be a dream, but it felt...

"Come back!" she cried.

All right, just this once. He'd kiss her just this once. To say good-bye properly.

His mouth opened and... Ohhh, don't ever stop. He groaned at the way she latched onto his tongue.

Abruptly, she was gone.

"Kasdeya?"

No. Come back.

"Come on..." Alexandra hissed, sounding so very close.

Kasdeya ignored the sudden blinding light. The first time he allows himself to fantasize about her and she stops?

"God damn it!"

He couldn't have put it better himself. Bring that mouth back here.

But it wasn't a mouth that touched his lips next. Kasdeya inhaled deeply, enjoying the scent of a woman in heat. But the smell, delectable as it was, wasn't Alexandra's. It was the Prince's concubine. Could it be that he was finally allowing himself to think about other females? Why did that idea depress him so much?

Shi-Liu was moaning and groaning, sounding…

"…sexy as hell," said Shaitan.

Exactly.

But it was Alexandra's voice he was straining to hear—in vain. Apparently, his fantasy remained as firmly fixated as ever.

Then came an eternity of mutters and sighs. The air reeked of sex. Still no word from his Summoner. Kasdeya reluctantly started to slide back into his deeper id. The daydream seemed to be winding to a close. Pity. This was the closest he'd felt to Alexandra since she'd died. By the nine hells, he missed her so much.

A single feminine finger stroked down his cock, pulling him back to awareness with the suddenness and finality of a lightning stroke.

Alexandra…

There was the lovely scent of a woman again—a wonderfully aroused, wonderfully familiar woman. He felt a liquid slide against his lips. He could taste her on his tongue.

Yes!

Kasdeya lapped at Alexandra's delicious body, searching out the tiny bundle of nerves at her center. In his mind, he was lashing that little knot for all he was worth, but he sensed that in reality his tongue was barely moving. Still, it didn't matter; this wasn't reality. It was a mirage, his own personal dreamscape. And in this dreamscape he'd created, Kasdeya was going to make his woman scream with pleasure.

"Your Summoner's hand is between the Prince's legs, Kas," Shi-Liu whispered. "On his cock. Shaitan looks like he's going to come at any second."

She was doing what now? That wasn't right. Her hand should be on *his* cock. It was his damned fantasy.

"Oh fuck!" Shaitan roared. "Fuck, Alexandra!"

Kasdeya frowned. Although he'd heard his Prince come thousands of times, there was no way his mind could have recreated such a hoarse, raw resonance of rapture. It was too real. Too, too real.

The hurt of hearing Alexandra's name screamed in ecstasy by another male ripped through him, even if that male was his brother and friend. Hell, *especially* if it was.

Shaitan, you bastard! Kasdeya barreled toward consciousness. If his Prince had somehow saved her…

"Bloody hell. I think I love you, woman."

…but then fucked her…

"Be my second, Alexandra," he heard the prick say. His eyelids fluttered and his hands curled into fists at his side.

...Kasdeya was definitely going to kill him.

He was so damned weak. Even the effort required to open his eyes seemed beyond him. How was he supposed to tear Shaitan's head completely off his body when he was so damned weak?

"Screw Kasdeya. You're too good for—"

He finally succeeded in raising his sluggish lids. The first thing he saw was Shi-Liu. She smiled at him but the smile quickly slipped off her face. He could only imagine the expression on his own face. "Shaitan," she warned her lover.

Kasdeya's gaze turned to follow hers and his lip lifted in a carnivorous contortion of rage. His woman—*his woman*—was enfolded in Shaitan's arms, the pair of them straddling his chest like drunken bandits dancing on his grave. Sex sullied the air in warm, distracting waves.

Alexandra looked magnificent though, more magnificent than he could stomach right now with her narrow back and the swell of her hips leading flawlessly into an ass that could make any man cry. Her hair was a sheen of bronzed light rippling like water as Shaitan kissed her throat.

"You'd still be number one, sweetheart," Shaitan assured Shi-Liu, not looking back. "You know—"

"She's...no one's"—his voice was so faint Kasdeya himself could hardly hear it—"second."

Alex whipped around, a joyous smile on her lips. Kasdeya's heart hammered against his ribs at the sight of it. She'd betrayed and humiliated him, but he'd never felt more love for her than he did right at that moment. What she hadn't done, after all, was leave him.

He tore his eyes off her dangerous beauty and locked them on Shaitan. There was no doubt that *he* was the mastermind behind this debacle. Alexandra would never do something like this without having been coerced into it.

"Put your throat between my teeth, Shaitan," Kasdeya said. "I can't seem to raise the energy required to"—his lids started to fall closed again and he fought the fatigue harder than he'd ever fought against a Power— "kill you...without some...help." It was just such a relief to know that Alexandra was safe. A relief so intense his body was sagging with it.

"Right." Shaitan gave Kasdeya's leg a friendly pat and hopped off the bed. "That's our cue to leave, sweetheart." The Prince held out a courtly hand to his consort.

"Glad to have you back, Kas." Shi-Liu pecked his cheek. "I like your woman." She stood and went to Shaitan.

Shaitan laughed. "I like her too, in case you missed it." He steered Shi-Liu toward the door. "Now why don't you two have a nice long talk and get reacquainted? And, Kas, if you still want to have a go when you're up to par, I'll be glad to take you outside and tear a strip right out of your pasty white hide."

"Get out," Kasdeya hissed.

Shaitan obeyed with a smarmy salute, Shi-Liu following him.

Chapter 25

"Kasdeya…"

He kept his eyes closed against her and Alex grimaced. This was just about as bad as she'd expected it would be. Her dark man was never going to forgive her.

"I saw you die," he whispered, voice raw with pain. "I saw Shaitan offer you the contract and I saw you refuse…and then you died. I saw it."

She frowned. Okay, this wasn't *exactly* going as expected. "Yes." She lay down cautiously beside him.

Kasdeya tried to turn into her body but couldn't. When Alex realized his unobtainable intention, she moved to drape herself across his chest. "I'm sorry," she said, not sure where he was going with this. "That must have been awful for you."

He barked a humorless laugh. "You have no idea, pet." Alex felt his hand brush against her leg and she reached down to clasp it, bringing it up to her lips.

Kasdeya still wouldn't look at her. "When you died, I tried my best to follow you," he went on. "I tried…but I kept hearing your voice, kept feeling you touch me."

Alex's throat swelled with emotion. He sounded so hurt. "I *was* touching you, calling you." She laid a wet cheek on his shoulder. "You wouldn't answer me."

"I thought you were a figment of my imagination." He shook his head and opened his eyes to glare at her, his face twisted with emotions too intense to be withstood. "And when I finally realized that you aren't dead, I rush to wake only to find you making love to my brother…and his concubine…in my own damned bed." He let out another bitter snort of amusement. "Imagine my surprise."

Alex sat up, her ass snug against his still hard cock. She wasn't sure what to address first so she went with the easier issue. "I *am* dead, Kasdeya. You were right the first time."

Even though he was angry, Alex was pleased to see her dark man's gaze travel lovingly over her body as she spoke. Maybe all wasn't lost after all if he could still look at her like that.

"Then where are we?" he asked in puzzlement. "Everything's changed, granted, but I'm pretty sure this is my room. If you're dead, surely you didn't end up in Hell."

Alex stroked his chest as he talked, tracing his scars and the pucker of his nipples. She just couldn't seem to keep her hands off him now that he was awake and aware again. "I *did* sell my soul though," she said. "For—"

His mouth formed an "O" of understanding. "For the little girl."

"Nicole, yes." Alex picked up his right hand from his stomach and rubbed his palm over her thigh. "She's cured and doing great."

"But you're stuck here now, Summoner. No Egypt. No Seattle. Are you all right with that?"

She wriggled, enjoying the ridge of his cock as it snuggled into her crease. Rock hard, finally! All this talking when all she wanted to do was ride him like a rodeo bull. "I'm happy wherever you are, dark man," she said with a contented sigh.

Kasdeya took a deep breath and held it. He seemed to be trying to stay focused on the conversation. Pity. "And what about Shaitan, pet?" he asked. "Do you have an explanation for letting him talk his way into your bed…again?"

Okay, best to get this done and over with. She stopped wriggling and looked seriously into his eyes. "It was Shaitan's idea. You're right."

"I know I am," he said with a sneer.

"But he was only trying to help. I was going crazy down here. You just wouldn't respond to me, no matter what I tried." She crossed her arms over her chest. "Then Shi-Liu told me that the last time you'd been badly wounded, you slept for ten years." She tossed her head in agitation. "I didn't want to wait that long, Kasdeya! I missed you too much. I need you too much."

"How long have I been asleep this time?"

"A little more than six months."

Kasdeya was silent. His inscrutable black eyes bored into hers.

Alex's own eyes burned with unshed tears. She'd never seen him like this. So cold. "I'd tried everything else," she said, her voice tremulous. "Believe me, this was a last resort."

"But you enjoyed it, didn't you, pet?" His hips performed the tiniest of rolls and his cock slid an infinitesimal amount through her wetness. "I can feel how much you enjoyed it."

Alex gnawed on the inside of her cheek, debating what to say to such an obviously loaded question. "I'll lie, dark man, if that's what you need me to do."

Kasdeya's smile was cheerless. "No. Never that." He sighed and shook his head. "Never that, Alexandra." Under its own power, his hand crept further up her thigh until it came to press against her mons. This time his smile was more familiar: arrogant and gorgeous. "But now, pet, I need to know that you still enjoy *me* too."

Oh, thank Christ. It seemed Shaitan had been right about this as well. Kasdeya *was* going to forgive her. She leaned over to kiss him. "I enjoy you so much more."

"Yeah?" He grinned and rolled his hips again, getting a little more power into the motion. "Show me. As long as you don't mind doing all the work, that is, I—"

She didn't even let him finish the thought. Trembling with anticipation, she positioned his cockhead at her entrance and slowly eased herself down.

Kasdeya gasped at the clasp of her creamy sex. "Alexandra," he groaned, stabbing his tongue between her lips.

Kasdeya! She'd have said it aloud, but her mouth was otherwise occupied. He tasted so good. Cinnamon and spice and everything nice. Alex contracted her vaginal muscles around him, unwilling to let a single glorious inch of his length escape. It was fantastic to finally have him in her body once more.

"You've got to move, pet," Kasdeya reminded her with a soft laugh. "Unfortunately, I can't do it for you."

"I just want to enjoy the feel of you inside me for a minute."

He moaned at her words and another strong hug from her inner walls. "Please, pet."

Her sex wept at the husky desperation in his voice. "All right." Alex sat back, picking up his hands and cupping them to her breasts. She rubbed the stones of her nipples into his palms. "You asked for it."

Kasdeya groaned, and when Alex raised herself up, clenching tight around his shaft all the while, he groaned louder. His fingers clamped down on her plump flesh. Alex stayed suspended above him for a moment and then drove herself down, tilting her hips at the last second to grind against his pubic bone.

"More," Kasdeya said, his neck arching in delight.

"I love you," Alex gasped, riding him faster. A flurry of white stars flickered to life behind her tightly shut eyes. "God, I love you." Her body jolted in random patterns as the powerful climax overwhelmed her motor control. Alex threw back her head and keened in pleasure. She could feel her womb ripple, the pattern equally random.

The violent contractions seemed to push Kasdeya past his limits as well. His cock bulged against her cervix and then he came too, filling her up with the hot, milky evidence of his passion. His reply to her words was lost on his own howl of ecstasy.

* * * *

"And I love you," Kasdeya said, sometime later. "You are my first… my only…"

He had managed to get his arms around her back and cradle her close, a motion of which he was quite proud. A quick look down his body had shown Kasdeya that he still had a lot of healing ahead of him. No wonder he was weak. Six months hadn't been near enough time in the trance. But he understood that to Alexandra, so newly dead, six months would have seemed an eternity, so he'd just have to rise to the challenge and heal while awake because there was no way he was leaving her alone again.

"Your first?" She lifted her head to give him an inscrutable look.

"Mmm-hmm." He smiled contentedly at her, his beautiful angel.

Alexandra shrugged off his arms and sat up. "As in, your first concubine?"

"Yes." He cocked his head in puzzlement at the look of irritation she was starting to develop. "Don't you want to be mine, Summoner?"

She slipped off his body without answering. Kasdeya twisted his head to watch her dig through the night table drawer. He scowled when she turned back around with a pack of cigarettes in her hand.

"What?" she asked indignantly. "It's not like they'll kill me."

He had to agree. "Are you avoiding my question?" he asked, rather than get into an argument about something so trivial.

She lit the cigarette and took a drag, studying him through a cloud of dirty smoke. "I don't want to be your first, Kasdeya. Or your second. I don't want to be your concubine at all."

Now *he* was irritated. "As I said before, pet, you'll be no one's second." He struggled to sit up, frustrated anew at his body's complete lack of coordination. "I thought you loved me."

Alexandra had another damned puff on the damned cigarette. Smoking: one more thing to take up with Shaitan. His Prince had a lot to answer for.

Her belligerent expression softened. "I do love you."

"Then why don't you—"

She stubbed the still-long butt out in a gold ashtray and slipped to her knees beside the bed. "I don't want to be your concubine, dark man," she said again, catching his hand in hers. "I want to be your wife."

Kasdeya's mouth fell open. "Brethren don't..." He stopped himself, realizing that Brethren don't do a lot of things. Falling in love was at the top of the list. Yet here he was. His fingers tightened around hers.

"Brethren don't..." Alexandra mimicked, sounding sad. "Of course they don't. It was a stupid idea." She sighed and attempted to rise. "Let's just leave things the way they are then, Kasdeya. We love each other. It's enough."

"You didn't let me finish." Using the last of his strength, he rolled to face her, keeping her hand tucked inside his. Alexandra paused, looking at him with uncertain hope. "Brethren don't say 'no' when the woman they love asks them to marry them."

There came a beat of silence. "Is that so?" she whispered, a stunning smile lighting up her face.

"It is. Now get back in my bed, wench," he ordered, mock gruff. When she obeyed, he said, "I can do a dress and flowers, but if you want a minister, we may have a problem."

"I want everything. Dress, cake, flowers...church and minister... friends and family. The princess wedding every little girl dreams of." She nipped at his chin. "But I'm not an idiot. I know I can't have everything." Her eyes shone with love. "And as long as I have you, I have everything I *really* need."

Kasdeya's heart ached at her words and he vowed, then and there, to get her exactly the wedding she wanted. How? He had no idea. But she *was* going to have her fairy-tale wedding. He'd make sure of it.

Chapter 26

One year later

There was a discreet knock on the door, and then Shaitan stepped in the room. "Ready, love?"

He looked wonderful in a tuxedo so darkly crimson it looked black. An inverted gold cross rested proudly in the gap of his mostly undone dress shirt.

Alex skimmed her hands down the fitted waist of her floor-length, antique-lace wedding dress and took a deep breath. This was it: she was marrying the man of her dreams. "As I'll ever be."

She cast one more glance in the mirror before gathering up the gown's six-foot train. She looked beautiful, just the way she'd always imagined she would. Her hair was caught up in a loose confection of curls, tendrils of which escaped to frame her carefully made-up face. Pearls and tiny white roses decorated the updo. A matching pearl choker graced her throat. That was the only ornamentation she needed; the gown was a work of art all on its own. The fitted, corset-style top left her arms and her back entirely bare while lifting up her breasts until her décolletage was not only visible, it was admirable. Seed pearls and diamonds, in intricate whorls, crusted the entire piece, glittering in even the dimmest light. The slim lace and silk skirt in the same elaborate whorled pattern fell past her toes to puddle on the floor.

Alex had cried when Kasdeya had laid it in her arms earlier that day. He'd just smiled and kissed her cheek, saying, "It's not nearly as beautiful as you are, pet," which just proved that he was perfect. Who else but the perfect man could come up with such a perfect thing to say when giving her the perfect wedding dress? She had to dab at her eyes again as she thought of it.

"Come on." Shaitan took her hand and tucked it formally through his elbow. "No crying. There's no time." Alex grabbed her bouquet off the bed as he whisked her out the door. "Your *guests* are waiting, after all," he said, all studied nonchalance."

"My guests?"

Shaitan grinned. "Yeah, them."

Alex's hand flew to her mouth. He'd done it. He'd somehow managed to bring her friends and family down to share this special day with her. "Oh, Shaitan!" She threw herself into his arms and kissed him soundly. Her flowers got a little crushed, but she was too happy to care. "Thank you!"

She'd thought that, perhaps, her relationship with the Prince and his consort would be strained after they'd all shared a bed—and their bodies. But no such thing had occurred. If a hand sometimes lingered on her ass, or a kiss "hello" lasted a tad longer than propriety might dictate, what of it? The dynamic worked for the four of them.

Yes, four. Once Kasdeya had been well enough, he and Shaitan had settled their differences quietly—and violently—somewhere deep in the forest. Alex had taken her cue from Shi-Liu and had held her tongue when they'd wandered in bloody and torn the next day, arms around each other's waists, big stupid grins on their faces. Males were crazy, no matter what species they were.

Shaitan laughed and whirled her around in a wide circle, kissing her back with quick ardor. "Glad you're pleased, sweetheart." He set her back on her feet and made a big production of smoothing nonexistent wrinkles out of her dress. "But to paraphrase a ridiculous white bunny, 'We're late, we're late.'"

"Well, then by all means." Alex lifted her skirt high and sprinted down the hall. "Let's not keep my guests waiting!"

He took off after her, still laughing. "You don't even know where you're going, dummy!"

* * * *

"Wait here," Shaitan said, leading her to stand in front of a pair of massive wooden doors. "I'll go get your wedding party."

Shaitan had led her up into reaches of the castle that Alex hadn't even realized existed to end the journey here. She looked at the doors in surprise. A huge cross was carved into the dark wood of each, highlighted by gold and gems. The cross was the right way up.

"What—"

"My private chapel." The Prince chuckled at the gape of astonishment she was too slow to hide. "Kasdeya had the same look on his face when I brought him here yesterday." He shrugged. "I don't know why everyone's so surprised. My father and I need to communicate from time to time—coordinate events and the like—and I find it easier to reach him in a space dedicated to doing just that, that's all. Plus he *is* the Creator, even of me."

"Oh, right," Alex said doubtfully. She'd had no idea that Shaitan was still in touch with God. But then, the Shaitan that she got to see on a regular basis was just a nice, sexy, normal-seeming guy. He was a little silly, a lot flirty, but always very sweet. He liked to drink tea and rich red wine, had a taste for B-grade horror movies and never wore his wings or sported horns and cloven hoofs. So, for long stretches of time, Alex would simply forget that one of her best friends was "the Devil." Somehow, this brought it home again.

Coordinate events? Like what? Visions of Armageddon danced in her head and Alex shut her mouth on the question, deciding she didn't need to know.

Shaitan's hand was on the gold door handle. "You look nervous." He reached into his chest pocket and produced a pack of cigarettes. "Want a quick puff before the festivities begin?"

Alex was tempted. Oh, she was tempted. But she'd promised Kasdeya. He hated the way it smelled and the way it looked, and quitting was the only thing her dark man had ever asked of her. "No, I'm good. Thanks."

"Okay." He pecked her cheek. "Be right back." He opened the door a crack and slid inside so that Alex had no chance to see the room's interior.

As the seconds ticked away, the butterflies in her stomach got more and more restless. What could the holdup be? Alex was wishing she hadn't been quite so hasty in refusing that nicotine injection.

The door opened again and Rose walked out, looking fabulous in a poppy-red, high-collared sheath gown, Shi-Liu on her heels. Both were dressed identically, but on Rose the dress looked elegant and almost regal, while on the succubus the same outfit was pure sin.

Both bridesmaids exclaimed over how beautiful Alex was and tearful hugs were exchanged. There wasn't much time for Alex to get reacquainted with her friend, however, as the door opened again at once and her brother Josh came out with little Nicole in tow. Shaitan was last. "Okay, people line up like proper sheep," he ordered.

"We'll have time to talk later." Rose squeezed Alex's hand. "I took the week off work and our room's only a floor above yours and Kas'."

Tears threatened again at that welcome information, but Alex willed them away, not wanting to waste the half hour she'd spent making up her face. Hold on though… "'Our' room?" she echoed.

Rose grinned, blushing prettily. "Mine and Sam's."

"Oh, Rose, I'm so—"

"Happy wedding day, Alex!" said someone with a high little voice from the vicinity of Alex's waist.

"Hey, honey." She knelt down in front of Nicole. "How are you?"

The little girl grinned, showing a gaping hole where her front tooth used to be. "I'm the flower girl!" She swung her basket of red rose petals up in the air, spilling half of them. "And I got a new dress!" She pirouetted with charming enthusiasm to show off her pink taffeta outfit. More rose petals fluttered into the air.

"Yes." Alex smiled, fingering Nicole's pink, puffed princess sleeve. "You look just lovely. And I hear you're feeling better now, is that right?"

The little girl nodded, suddenly solemn, making her blond curls bounce against her cheeks. "My head doesn't hurt *at all* anymore," she confided in a loud whisper.

One tear escaped to slip down Alex's cheek. "I'm so glad, sweetie." She stood back up and motioned Nicole forward. "You're the most important, Nicky, so you go first, okay?"

"Okay!"

"Hey, sis." Josh stepped up to give her a hug. He was looking admirably pulled together in dark gray slacks and an Armani jacket. "I'm still in shock here," he admitted with a self-deprecating laugh. "I mean, this is just so fucked up. Satan himself showed up at my door yesterday and told me my presence was required in Hell, because my sister—who's dead, by the way—was getting married to a demon."

Alex grimaced. Put that way, it did sound a little fucked up.

"I thought *I* was the black sheep," Josh concluded with a wry twist to his lips.

She patted his cheek. "Oh, you still are, baby brother. Don't worry."

His gaze searched her face. "You're happy?"

"I'm very happy," Alex replied. "Happier than I've ever been."

Josh nodded and seemed to relax. "Then I'm happy *for* you, Lexie." He held out his arm. "I'm supposed to give you away now. Weird, huh? You've always been the parental figure in this relationship, and I guess I never realized that it would be me walking you down the aisle." He shrugged. "Seems like it should be the other way around, doesn't it?"

Yeah, it kind of did. She loved Josh so much, but when she'd pictured this day in her mind, even after Dad had died, it wasn't her brother beside her on the processional walk. That person had always just been "someone to be determined at a later date."

Alex looked past him to where Shaitan was on his knees, picking up rose petals with one hand and holding Nicky's ankle with the other. The little girl kept trying to dance her way out of line, talking a mile a minute all the while. The High Prince of Hell was looking comically perturbed by the whole situation.

"Speaking of *my* wedding," Josh yammered on happily, "after the ceremony, I want to introduce you to Curtis. I think he's really the one this time."

"Great," Alex said. "I'd love to meet him." She leaned up to whisper in his ear. "Honey, would you mind terribly if..."

* * * *

The great doors swung slowly inward as the opening strains of Wagner's *Bridal Chorus* swelled. Alex saw a number of Brethren on Kasdeya's side. And on hers...

She shed some more stupid tears as she realized that the list of guests must have been Kasdeya's responsibility. Only the people he'd come to know were present. Still, it was enough, and so much more than she'd expected. Sam, Josh—he'd hurried to slip back to his seat—and a handsome blond man whom Alex assumed was Curtis took up the front pew. The second held just Sandy, Melynda and Dovescot's housekeeper, Mrs. Kirpatrick. And in the third, Jen sat alone waiting for her daughter.

Melynda waggled her fingers, looking thrilled as hell to be here, and Alex winked back. Before she'd had to leave so abruptly, Alex and Mel had been heading toward a solid friendship. It would be nice to continue it. Plus, she couldn't wait to introduce the witch to the succubus. Alex knew they'd get on famously.

Nicole hardly waited for the doors to open before she raced down the red carpet, dodging playfully in and out of the crimson tinted rainbows thrown by a huge stained-glass window over the alter. She tossed down all her petals in the last two feet of aisle and then threw herself into her mother's lap. Everyone, human and Fallen alike, laughed at her antics. Rose and Shi-Liu followed at a much more sedate pace.

Shaitan, looking as proud as any daddy, led Alex toward her dark man. "Something I should probably mention," he whispered, out of the side of his mouth.

Alex hardly heard him. She was staring at Kasdeya. He was simply majestic, utter perfection clad all in black, with his wings flared out behind him. Her dark man's expression was tender as he looked down the length of the chapel at her. His smile was love itself.

But his brows were also drawn down and his stance was rigid, almost confrontational. Was he having second thoughts? Had Alex pushed him into doing something he really didn't want to do?

"Father," Shaitan was saying, "insisted on it. I couldn't get your friends down here without agreeing."

Alex had no idea what he was talking about, and she realized that she hadn't heard a word he'd said for the last fifteen seconds. Her heart was a panicked bird in her chest. "What?" she asked, louder than she should have. "What are you saying?"

Every step took her nearer to the man she loved. The man she may have foolishly and selfishly forced into a marriage ceremony he didn't even believe in. They were only a few feet away now.

"The minister," he hissed. "I had no choice. He was handpicked by God."

They'd reached the end of the red carpet and Shaitan handed her over to his waiting brother. The minister? Who cared about the damned minister? "Do you still want to do this?" she whispered to Kasdeya, clutching his hand in anxiety. "We don't have to. I—"

Kasdeya, ignoring protocol, swept her up in his arms and kissed her, easing her doubts with his talented, insatiable tongue. "Pet," he said, breathing heavy and pausing between words to continue ravaging her mouth. "In front of God, the Devil and anyone else who cares to take note, I *am* going to marry you today. So if you've changed your mind, I suggest you bloody well change it back. Is that understood?"

Alex smiled. "Perfectly," she said, treating him to some pretty spectacular kisses of her own.

"I'd like to start now," Alex heard someone say sarcastically. "If you're quite done with the theatrics, that is."

Alex felt Kasdeya's body stiffen into the same confrontational tension that had seeded such silly doubts in her head in the first place. He lifted his head to glare at the speaker and she slowly turned her head to see whom God had chosen to join together a Fallen angel and a dead mortal soul.

The minister had tawny wings, mahogany skin and cold green eyes. He crooked a brow at her, raising his chin in derision. His braided hair clinked softly, looking like hundreds of tiny black snakes against the glowing white of his robe. "If you don't mind, Summoner," Uriel sneered. "I have demons to hunt yet today. Can we get on with it?"

Who says God doesn't have a sense of humor?

Meet the Author

The Summoner started its life as a simple writing project—plot and character development—for a creative writing course I'd impulsively signed up for one dreary January afternoon in '05. After reviewing the first three chapters round-robin style, everyone in the class had pretty much the same things to say: solid writing, interesting characters, much too sex-heavy (and I hadn't really gotten to the sex yet) and perhaps a tad too free with the sarcasm. "Edgy," the prof said. "Sex and profanity," said the older gentleman in the pale gray cardigan. "I couldn't even finish the pages." Well, Jeez, and here I'd been holding myself back, trying to stay tame for the nice folks. So anyway, as soon as that class was over, I signed up for a new course—this one on erotic writing specifically. And then I finished "The Summoner" the way I wanted to: sex-heavy, chockfull of sarcastic characters saying real things in a real way, and hot as hell.

Since writing "The Summoner," I've had many other stories published. You can check out my website, www.alishasteele.com, for my latest release information. Still, Kasdeya and Alex will always be my first—my favorite—couple, and I hope you've enjoyed reading about them just as much as I enjoyed writing about them.

Alisha's Website:
http://www.alishasteele.com/
Reader eMail:
Alisha@alishasteele.com